MW00579764

THE SILENT HEN

THE SILENT HEN

HELEN MONTAGUE FOSTER

atmosphere press

© 2023 Helen Montague Foster

Published by Atmosphere Press

Cover design by Ronaldo Alves

No part of this book may be reproduced without permission from the author except in brief quotations and in reviews. This is a work of fiction, and any resemblance to real places, persons, or events is entirely coincidental.

Atmospherepress.com

For my family

In memory of the courageous women and men
who served with the OSS during World War II

CHAPTER ONE

Hart
September 11, 2001

He awoke to a murmuring of Arabic voices and an unfocused sense of vulnerability, which he related more to his confinement in a hospital bed than to his dream of chasing a gharry through a crowded street in Cairo. He was eighty-one-years old, days post-operative from a second knee replacement, and Margie had been dead for more months than he cared to count. Without her, all he could do was hobble forward. Then what? Then nothing. He neither feared nor wished to hasten death. Since his home on the Northern Neck of Virginia was a long drive from the hospital, a foreign service friend had arranged for his transfer to Alspy House, where, if the name meant something, old spies reunited before they sank to oblivion.

Hart groped for a call button, which he found clipped to the sheet. When he pressed it, a bell chimed somewhere beyond his privacy curtain. He set his jaw and struggled to a sitting position that allowed him to register a dim presence. "Who's there?" he called.

"Lucy." The curtain billowed as she stepped between beds into view, that elegant face, wrinkled and haloed by white hair, unmistakably belonging to one of his few surviving friends from the OSS and its successor, the CIA. Hart's pulse accelerated, increasing the throbbing of his knee and the sound of cicadas. Both of them had lost spouses, and soon all they remembered would be gone.

"I'm looking for Gordon."

Had she forgotten he'd died? Hart hoisted his leg over the side of the bed with another jab of ear-ringing pain, his mind weighing possibilities. He had missed the funeral, but it didn't seem likely Gordon's death had been faked.

"I want Gordon to call Bella." She looked at him with an unguarded and trusting expression that made his heart strain toward her, her irises still walnut brown but now ringed with opaque blue, some change to do with age. "Hart, is that you? Can you help me find my husband?" A nurse rushed past. Several phones rang at once. Fatima, his nurse, appeared in the hall gesturing urgently to a dark-skinned man, whatever he was, mop-pusher, orderly, his face contorted with distress as if he wished to run or sob.

"A war is starting," Lucy said. "I need to find Bella."

CHAPTER TWO

Lucy
1943

The shadows and new barbed wire at the edge of the Willard-Roosevelts' woods made her feel like a character in a book, endangered yet excited, nothing like the comfort she usually felt striding past familiar homes where others were beginning to rouse. Until her first interview, the combat had been too distant for action beyond writing letters and hanging blackout shades that made her imagine she was inviting death for a visit. Lately, she'd imagined what she would do if someone tried to force secrets out of her.

When she was small, the fact that her street ran south, uphill toward the center of Fairfax, had forced her to rotate maps in her mind's eye. Uphill should have been north but was south. Right, where large homes overlooked the street, was not east but west, where the sun set. A ditch, yards deep for a stretch, ran between the brick sidewalk and road. In her dreams, it might plummet to a depth of forty feet—though she hadn't fallen or even stumbled there since the day she ran to tell her great-aunts of her father's death—and its earthen bottom was never more than six feet down.

When she'd walked far enough to see the cannons and brick arches at the courthouse, she picked up her pace. Everyone in town knew everyone else, but her early trip into the city should arouse no suspicion. Anyone seeing her board the trolley would assume she was heading to her job at the Smithsonian. She'd packed what she needed in her largest handbag and prepared to answer with a raised eyebrow if anyone asked if she were carrying the kitchen sink.

She'd already spent days in Washington, scoring well enough to be invited back for more training and interviews for a job she'd been informed was not for the faint of heart. Only after her acceptance would she hear what it entailed. The recruiter had been the uncle of a former Sweet Briar roommate, but his niece and Lucy hadn't encountered one another in the five or so years since graduation. Lucy chalked up their failure to stay in touch to Margie's reserve and to not being as important to Margie as the other way around, but she tried not to let that hurt her feelings. All kinds of circumstances could interfere with friendships.

Her fantasy was that she would be asked to go behind enemy lines. *Oh, Lucy*, her mother would say. *Do you lack all instinct for self-preservation? Whatever would make you want that?* But why else would she have been approached about her availability to travel and willingness to do "something secret?" Why had he asked which languages she spoke?

She did not lack instinct for self-preservation—real danger made her quite cautious—but her conscience had never allowed her to sit idly in a crisis. It was as if her childhood daydreams of traveling into peril as a missionary or a teacher were coming true. If she had lived during the Civil War, she would have risked her life to help slaves escape north. Or so she hoped. There was always the possibility of joining the Biblical Peter in some cowardly denial before the crow of the cock.

Just as she arrived at the tavern by the trolley stop, a cardinal began to sing: *Cheer, cheer, cheer* or *fear, fear, fear*—it sounded like both. As she boarded, a few passengers tipped down their newspapers but gave her no more than nods. The press tried to put a good face on the war, but a childhood friend had been shot down over France and was presumed dead.

When the electrified car jolted into action and clattered north, she turned her face to the window. The narrow-gauge tracks ran along a ridge with views of cows and an occasional horse grazing; sky lit like a painting by Turner; fields, hills, and streams radiant in the morning light. They passed frame houses, many with barns. Villages with brick homes and church spires. Her father had been the lawyer for the Southern Railroad. After his death, she'd been provided with a pass to ride anywhere on the line, and her great-uncle, surviving patriarch of her extended family, had insisted she remain in Virginia for college out of respect for her mother.

"I understand you like to travel," her friend's uncle had said when he proposed an interview. Perhaps he'd seen the Sweet Briar yearbook, *The Briar Patch,* that listed Lucy's ambition to work abroad. Or perhaps he'd spoken to his niece or to Lucy's boss at the Smithsonian, who knew of her broken engagement and wish to serve.

When Lucy stepped off the trolley, she proceeded casually, feigning calm, though unable to stop her imagination. Was she reading too much into the allusion to travel? Would she have the courage to go behind enemy lines?

She walked briskly through an open gate, her heels tap-scraping like the amplified ticking of a grandfather clock. The building where she'd been instructed to report was brick with white columns and long windows. She stood straight, climbed the steps, and hesitated at the double doors of the entrance. Of course, she had a sense of the need for safety. She was twenty-six and knew well that the future held unknowns for which one could not fully prepare. Pearl Harbors of one size or another could burst upon the world without notice.

The inside was like a college administration building with a high ceiling, polished floors, and a girl behind a desk, who directed her around a corner where an MP asked to search her bag. She cringed as the MP checked her belongings, pushing aside her spare undies to probe deeper. He removed her wallet and inspected her driver's license. "Down this hall, miss. Third office on the left."

When she reached it, she knocked lightly, and a male voice directed her to enter. "Hello," she said with a determined smile. "I'm Lucy Walton Moore, here for my interview."

She suppressed any outward sign that the man greeting her resembled her father but fleetingly imagined kissing his cheek and saying she missed him—meaning her father, whom she'd lost to blood cancer—not the stranger assessing her with eerily familiar eyes. "Have a seat, Miss Moore." She judged him to be in his early fifties, Father's age at the time of his death.

She accepted the chair he indicated, one close enough to his desk that she didn't need to decide between crossing her legs for show or pressing her knees together for modesty.

"What do you think about our operation, Miss Moore?"

"I haven't been told enough to know anything."

He looked at a folder on his desk. "You've been fingerprinted?"

"No, I haven't." She glanced at her hands, manicured with no polish. She'd returned her engagement ring.

"We'll get your prints taken shortly. Tell me about your background." From his accent, she guessed he was from Boston. He closed his mouth, lit a pipe, and waited.

"I work for Dr. Charles Abbott of the Smithsonian Institution."

"And your duties, Miss Moore?"

"Statistics for his astrophysical projects monitoring sunspot activity. I majored in mathematics at Sweet Briar."

"Have you traveled?"

"A semester in France and a tour of Europe with my two brothers. My minor was in French. I studied Latin, French, and Spanish in high school. I had a semester of German in college."

"Are you Jewish?"

She felt herself blushing but feigned calm. "Episcopalian." Her Jewish classmate, Margie, had been the object of unkind whispers from two classmates who should have known better. The interview question seemed to pose a moral dilemma. "I would be proud if I were," she added.

He looked straight into her eyes, almost accusing. "What were you told about our mission?"

"I was offered an opportunity to help with the war effort. He said there was a need for math majors." She meant Margie's uncle, who'd recruited her.

"You did well on your aptitude tests." His pipe wisped aroma, his expression somehow coolly insincere, more like Ray Milland, the actor, than her father, who'd been blessed with what her mother called that "awful Moore conscience" and would have been torn between protecting her and inspiring her to live her obligation to her country.

"Today, we're sending you to Station S. From here on, you will need to assume another identity. The staff will know who you are, but your fellow students will not, and you are not to refer to your actual circumstances, even with staff."

"Literally starting now?"

"Yes. You'll have to come up with a name and details about yourself. Be consistent. Start thinking up details. Under no circumstances should you reveal your actual identity to your fellow students. Tell me your name, please?"

Who would she be? She focused inward. "*Patricia.*"

"*Patricia* who?"

"*Ford?*"

He shook his head as if to criticize her hesitancy. "Now tell me, *Miss Ford*, would you be willing to give your life for your country?"

"Beg pardon?" Her heart thudded rapidly enough to distract her, but she kept her surface calm. "If you've just asked if I'm willing to give my life for my country, the answer is yes. Though I have no death wish, you understand."

"Would you be willing to work overseas?"

"Yes, I would."

"Have you heard of the Espionage Act?"

She had, though he held her with a stern look and reminded her that traitors would be executed. The penalty for any breach of secrecy was twenty years in prison.

"Information in the wrong hands puts our country in grave danger. Anything you have seen or heard thus far is considered classified information. You're an attractive young woman, Miss Moore, but there is no exception under the Espionage Act for young women. What happens here is secret and must remain secret. Do you understand?"

She pressed her lips together and nodded. "*Ford*," she said.

"What did you say?"

"My name is *Ford. Patricia Ford*."

The fingerprinting room struck her as the most ordinary-looking place she could imagine. Two chairs, an oak desk into which someone had carved marks, a basket of worn hand towels, a file cabinet, and a dark green metal trashcan. No window, only the transom, which was closed.

"Wait here, miss." The MP touched the back of a chair, which she supposed meant she should sit, so she did for a count of ten. He shut the door after him, but she had the odd feeling someone might be observing her and found herself recalling a motion picture in which peepholes had been concealed behind the eyes of a painting. But there were no pictures on the plaster walls, not even a calendar or bulletin board. She stood up and stretched. Someone had inked inside dot-and-dash cuts on the desk, the Morse Code, from dot-dash A all the way to Z, dash-dash-dot-dot.

When the MP returned, he pressed her fingertips onto an ink pad and rolled each onto a card typed with her true name. When he was done, he handed her a towel and took her handbag. "I'll keep your identification."

She tried to look unruffled as she wiped her hands.

"It'll be safer here than where you're going. You'll get a duffel bag with what you need. When you get to Station S, you'll be expected to ferret out what you can about your fellow students. All of you will be free to jimmy locks, listen at keyholes, whatever it takes. You can leave your street clothes here after you've changed."

The trousers were too large, and while she was readjusting the web belt, a man and woman in similar Army-style clothes emerged from the fingerprint room. The woman was her former classmate, Margie, with her raven hair redone in away-from-the-face curls, but Lucy kept her mouth shut so as not to reveal they knew one another. At Sweet Briar, Margie had worn bangs to her eyebrows and a ponytail that showed off her graceful neck.

Margie raised her eyebrows and tapped her lips. Meaning what? Stay mum? Don't mention her uncle?

Except for his height, which exceeded six feet, the man had such a regular and ordinary appearance that, if not for his furtive glances at Margie's figure, Lucy would have been hard-pressed to describe him. He stood straight, slightly wincing as he gestured for her and Margie to precede him into the empty hallway.

"You two could pass for sisters." His accent was not local. Not East coast. A bit country. His brown eyes betrayed amusement as if he were play-acting suave.

In any other setting, Lucy would have smiled and asked his name, but the intrigue so far stalled her at a smile.

Margie intervened. "Maybe we are."

"Then we shouldn't admit to being sisters?" Lucy asked, though she and Margie weren't even sorority sisters. They'd been roommates one semester and doubles partners in tennis. Twice when Lucy invited her home for a visit, Margie declined without an excuse, and Lucy had felt rebuffed.

They lined up in a corridor with two other women and ten men, all of them outfitted in nondescript government-issue clothing, and faced the man who'd reminded her of her father. He told them not to be concerned, that they would be safe, which made her wonder if he were trying to worry them.

They were to take their duffel bags, board an Army truck outside the building, and remain hidden for a drive of less than an hour. Under no circumstances were they to peek out from under the canvas. They were not to mention the trip to anyone. "Ladies and gentlemen, you have been selected with the idea some of you will be sent behind enemy lines. How you perform today and tomorrow will contribute to our assessment."

He opened a door to a parking lot, leading them in a brisk walk into sunlit mid-morning, where an Army truck with a canvas cover awaited. When they were all in place, sitting against the metal truck sides, the driver raised the tailgate and lowered a tarp over the back opening, throwing them into semi-darkness.

"Naptime," a man whispered, his breath betraying drink and cigars. He raised his knees, rested his elbows on his thighs, and laid his head in his hands as if to sleep, but the truck jolted and shook them so thoroughly that he moaned off and on through the trip, making it difficult for Lucy to picture their route. After too many turns, she supposed they'd left the city and entered Virginia. She mistrusted her perception. South was not always downhill. At one point, she heard a train whistle and imagined herself near Fairfax Station.

She and the others whispered among themselves, and some shared smokes, but they'd been instructed not to tell their real identities, so they mostly commented on the ride. When one of the fellows addressed Lucy as "Beautiful," she didn't respond until he introduced himself with what she presumed was a false nickname. She told him she was *Patricia Ford*, and he lifted his head, exhaling the odor of beer and tobacco. "I'm

Patrick Packard," he said, making the truckload of them burst into laughter.

Eventually, the truck rumbled up a dusty road. Soon they stopped, but—per orders—stayed put until someone outside bellowed for them to exit. *Patrick Packard* shouldered his duffel and jumped off the truck bed before Lucy. When he offered his hand, she instinctively accepted, though she could just as well have jumped down on her own. They gathered under a large tree with leaf buds arrayed like Christmas tree lights. She thought she knew that tree. A ginkgo she'd once climbed with her neighbor, Kim Roosevelt. Could it be that she was back in Fairfax where she'd started her day?

CHAPTER THREE

Lucy
Station S, 1943

Margie's face telegraphed concern, which apparently only Lucy recognized. She was tempted to confide that they were only a mile from her home, but before she could decide, a grizzled man with a pipe stem protruding from the pocket of his tweed jacket led the group to a barn, beyond which loomed the grand but recently emptied Layton Hall, where Belle Willard, wife of Kermit Roosevelt, had grown up. Earlier that winter, Lucy's Aunt Edith had overheard from a clerk at the Piggly Wiggly that enough groceries for an Army had been delivered to the Willard house. Despite Aunt Edith's advanced age, she'd walked through the pasture and woods to call on the Willard-Roosevelts and ask for a donation for the Community Chest. The sight of young men climbing hand-over-hand on ropes had turned her around. Lucy could picture Edith in her dark ankle-length dress and brass-tipped cane sneaking away through the woods. If the men were alert, they would have seen her. Perhaps they had.

Their host in tweed spoke like a college president used to being recognized. He did not give his name. "You've been invited to Station S," he said in a nasal, but otherwise posh, voice, "for testing to determine how you can serve the war effort. Unfortunately, most of you won't be up to what we ask." Margie's eyes cut to Patrick Packard, who grinned with Jimmy Stewart sincerity and shrugged. Lucy focused on what they were being told: to keep their true identities secret and remain convincingly in their invented personae. In thirty minutes, they would muster for training. Meanwhile, they lugged government-issue duffel bags to the large house with its turret, gables, and third-floor dormers. Patrick Packard whistled through his teeth at the sight.

Without the comfortable porch furniture where the Willards had previously enjoyed mint juleps, the house seemed less inviting. If Aunt Edith had ventured this far, she would have known, even without spotting men in trees, that the Piggly Wiggly order was not for the Willard-Roosevelts.

Throughout Lucy's childhood, the Willards and Roosevelts had been frequent topics of conversation. Her Great-Uncle Walton confessed to heartbreak when Belle Willard married Kermit Roosevelt, son of Teddy. Uncle Walton never married, and Lucy's family had persisted in using the Willard name for Belle. When they referred to the Roosevelts, they meant the current president and his wife, Eleanor, whom they admired greatly and had entertained at a large garden party shortly before Uncle Walton's death.

The man in the tweed jacket, who still had not given his name, inspected the group one by one as they entered through the front door. The luxurious antiques, Persian rugs, and family portraits Lucy remembered had been replaced by office furnishings, though she recognized a watercolor of foxhounds. She knew that a closet in the kitchen led to back stairs and that, if need be, she could sneak home on a path through the woods. Her advantage made her feel both smug and ashamed. She did not like thinking of herself as someone who would cheat.

A young man led the women to bedrooms on the second

floor. Crystal doorknobs still adorned the walnut doors, but the room she was to share with Margie was modestly furnished with two Army cots, one chair, a small nightstand, and a desk with a single drawer. The moment their escort left them, Margie searched the desk, mumbling to herself, as she'd done when they'd shared a room in college. "Notebooks. Pencils. Some kind of handbook."

"If we're going to be spies, you'll have to give that up," Lucy said.

"Give up what?"

"Saying aloud what you're thinking."

"I'm not saying what I'm thinking. I was saying what I was doing in order to cover up what I was thinking."

"What were you thinking?"

Margie waved Lucy closer, drew the hair away from Lucy's ear, and whispered with more breath than sound that her uncle thought they didn't have it in them.

"Have what?"

"The courage to kill."

Lucy wasn't sure what to say back. She and her fiancé had broken off their engagement, partly because he declined to accept that she was competent to go to war, but it was true that she did not like the idea of killing. She believed in strategy, and her immediate task was to pass the training and evaluation. "Do you suppose they put us together because we know one another?" she asked.

"Hush," Margie answered in a bothered tone that kept Lucy from finishing her question: Would the two of them report on one another using what they already knew? Or should they concentrate on the strangers? Margie crooked her finger, beckoning. "Our neighbors could be listening in," she whispered.

"I was just going to say: we know one another already," Lucy whispered back. "We'll be at a disadvantage in finding out about the others."

"How so?"

"Because we aren't rooming with them," Lucy said. "But we could pretend to feud and ask to swap roommates. or—"

Margie's face fell, surprising Lucy and making her next breath ache. She hadn't meant to hurt Margie's feelings, if that's what it was.

"Or what?" Margie answered in a tight voice.

"Of course, I'd rather room with you," Lucy said. "I meant we'd have a better opportunity to spy on the others if we split up and pool our observations."

Margie looked so sad that Lucy's eyes began to well up in sympathy. In college, Margie had seemed more guarded than sensitive, sometimes so reserved that Lucy had wondered if she lacked emotions.

"We can pool our observations either way," Lucy added.

Margie turned away, still emitting sadness. "Let's stay together."

"Of course."

Margie handed over the booklet *Simple Sabotage Field Manual,* and Lucy, hoping to help them past the moment, asked Margie's *nom de guerre.*

"*Ava Ennis* from Philadelphia, Pennsylvania."

"Pleased to meet you, *Ava Ennis.*" She held out her hand. "*Patricia Ford* from Arlington, Virginia.

Ava squeezed Lucy's hand and gave her an intense look, close to tears again. "If we get through this, I'll tell you some things."

"Tell me now."

"No," Margie said. "Too much is happening. Just stick to your cover story. And I'll take your advice to heart. I'll stop talking to myself."

Their lectures on evading and detecting pursuers lasted until after midnight. The next morning at breakfast, a GI dropped a stack of trays behind Lucy, making half her classmates jump and her own heart race, though a household with brothers had taught her to suppress visible reactions. At least it woke her up, as did the lukewarm coffee and buttered toast with marmalade.

As she left the dining room, the man in tweed escorted her into an office and handed her specifications for constructing a wooden frame. She was to go to the barn, locate a pile of materials, and instruct two men, Kippy and Buster, in assembling the project.

"The clock starts ticking when you arrive on-site," he said. "You'll have ten minutes to complete the structure."

"Yes, sir," she replied, though she'd been taught that ladies did not say sir or ma'am. "Excuse me," she asked. "What would you prefer I call you?"

"*Dr. Mack* will do," he answered in such a gruff tone that she supposed it was not his real name. "This is a leadership test."

Although she suspected rushing might trip her up, she looked over her instructions and hightailed it to the barn, where she found the promised two men, one with a dimple in his chin and one with red hair, loitering beside an assortment of wooden poles the diameter of broom handles, some as long as six feet, which leaned against a wheelbarrow. Both men avoided looking at her directly. The dark-haired one with the chin dimple was film-star handsome.

"Hi, fellas," she said, pushing herself to sound strong. "I'm your project leader. We've been asked to put this together in ten minutes."

"Ten seconds? Who'd'ya think I am?"

Dark, handsome, and rude, she thought. "Either Kippy or Buster," she said aloud. "And—lucky us—it's minutes. Let's do this together."

The freckled redhead identified himself as Kippy and stumbled into the poles. The dark-haired one was Buster. Whether intended or not, the looks he gave her made her feel him through her skin. He argued with her instructions at each step, claiming the poles wouldn't fit into the connector blocks. All it would have taken to correct a bad fit was a bit of drilling or sanding, but it turned out the poles fit perfectly. She could have assembled the project on her own, which would not have shown leadership, so she demonstrated by putting together a square, which Buster pulled apart with a self-satisfied smirk. She gave him her kindest smile, imagining herself as a neighbor's maid who'd always managed to seem cheerful despite the neighbor's many unreasonable expectations. "We can do this," she said, smiling at Buster's complaints but finally frowning when Kippy let the project slam to the ground. Eight minutes had passed.

"Don't you dames know how to build anything?" Buster complained, though it was Kippy who kept sabotaging her project. Finally, with only the poles on top left to connect, she asked Buster to place the last diagonal. He shook his head, tapping his wristwatch to indicate she'd failed. Thus, with time up, her composure intact, but her armpits trickling sweat, she walked away with Buster's eyes burning her back. Perhaps it was her own frustration, but she had reminded her of the time she beat her younger brother at tennis, and her mother suggested she let him win.

"Please come in, *Miss Ford.*" *Dr. Mack* held the door open to a small parlor with a view of lawn and trees. He showed her to a suede chair, settled into a similar but larger seat next to hers, and lit a pipe. "Have you enjoyed your assignment here?"

Lucy noted his use of the past tense and felt her forehead tighten. "It was interesting."

"I'm afraid you didn't pass your construction test this morning."

She inhaled her disappointment, keeping her voice calm. "I suspected."

"I want you to be entirely frank. Was it difficult for you?"

She kept her face neutral, though she felt like huffing. His pipe filled the room with an aroma that reminded her of her Uncle Walton, who had nixed her plans to study in Montreal after her father died.

"Try not to worry," *Dr. Mack* added.

She released a breath, still not sure what to say but reacting to his small prompts for her to explain why she'd fallen behind. "I could have done it on my own if they'd let me." It seemed likely she would go back to the Smithsonian, spend the war running numbers to find patterns in sunspot activity, and die a childless spinster like her Aunt Edith. "I think my error was in leaving just because the time ran out. I should've kept at it."

"Has anything like this happened to you before?"

Better not to mention her ex-fiancé, whose mother disliked Eleanor Roosevelt and had wanted him to marry someone who would stay home, his unkind excuse for calling off their engagement. "I used to play with boys," she said, sparking a flash of interest in *Dr. Mack's* eyes. The look might have meant nothing, but they'd been warned not to abandon cover.

"One friend didn't like being told what to do. If I'd had to tell him how to build something, he would push me out of the way and do it himself."

"What do you think went wrong today?" *Dr. Mack* asked.

"They may not have liked taking orders from a woman. Or they might have been sabotaging me on purpose. Not that those are mutually exclusive."

Dr. Mack sat silently, fingers laced across his middle.

"They could have had any number of motives, from personal resentment to some covert purpose. In most cases," she ventured, "people have their own concerns that outweigh—" She didn't know how to put it.

"Outweigh?"

"I mean they may not have been trying to sabotage the

project. They could have just been feeling—" She thought of *Patrick Packard*, who'd obviously tied one on before they left for Station S. "Hungover or grouchy. But this isn't an ordinary situation. You're testing us. I think Kippy and Buster were supposed to make the project hard."

Lucy fell back on her cot, boots and all. "Dr. Mack said both of us are still in."

Margie beamed. Her sad and "not-pretty" agenda for later discussion seemed safely parked out of sight, and Lucy decided not to press it.

"Could I see that handbook you showed me before?"

"You bet." Margie pulled the *Simple Sabotage Field Manual* out of the desk drawer. "Have you read it yet?"

"Skimmed." She flipped pages trying to find the part that had caught her eye. "Here," she said. "If you have to work for the enemy, they suggest loading or unloading cargo carelessly."

"Did you have Kippy and Buster for your helpers?" Margie asked.

"I did."

"What did they look like?"

"Kippy had red hair and freckles. Buster was dark and almost looked like a movie actor, handsome but smug."

"I suspected," Margie whispered.

"Suspected what?"

"My *Kippy* had dark brown hair," Margie said. "My *Buster* was a blond."

"Now that's transparent: playing parts and using the same names with different actors? What do you think was the point?"

Margie shook her head. "I don't know, except men like making games of war."

CHAPTER FOUR

Hart
Station S, 1943

Hart planted himself near the back of the classroom to watch the others enter. Nine men and four women. Each member of the fairer sex was a looker; shapely, lithe, and slender, all with pretty faces, though not a one of them blonde. Each of them radiated a kind of poise and wholesome beauty, especially long-necked Margie, going by *Ava*, who resembled the actress Ava Gardner but with a dimple on her left cheek and emitted something that made him want to gather her in his arms. It was irrational—a movie cliché—to equate dark hair with competence, but he'd recently been dumped by a blonde who couldn't balance a checkbook. Someday he would find a wife who was smart as well as beautiful, and they would travel, live in Paris, and write books, but first, the war needed to be won.

His task of the moment was to size up recruits while adhering to his covert identity as Dartmouth graduate *Ed Wheeler*. Actually, he'd attended the University of Tulsa and enlisted a semester short of graduation. All he knew about Dartmouth was a drinking song about Eleazar Wheelock and a Latin motto, *Vox clemantis in deserto*. Fitting, as he'd felt like a voice crying in the desert on his previous assignment in Africa, where he and four other OSS men had roamed about undercover as Pan Am Airline employees, never encountering the enemy.

Several promising recruits had been nixed, some for fear they sympathized with Stalin and others for responses on inkblot tests or for letting slip their real names to psychologists who were in on the whole charade anyway. Hart felt as much under the microscope at Station S as those he'd been assigned to assess, though, unlike this class of doomed souls, he probably wouldn't get locked in a dark basement overnight.

Meanwhile, to maintain cover, he would have to keep his shirt on. The parachute harness on his last practice jump had bruised his chest in stripes that were yellowing across his side. Unsettling as a metaphor, he thought, yellow stripes. His distance from action was making him hesitate. Not that he considered himself yellow. He'd just noticed that courage came easier when he didn't have to wait too long at the gaping door of a plane in flight.

He kept his eyes on the dames, all college grads with a reputation for being smart with numbers and cultured enough to mingle with diplomats. Outsiders claimed OSS stood for *Oh So Social* or *Oh So Special*, names that didn't fit him, though he was getting better at play-acting the part. Two of the Mata Hari applicants finding their seats for the next lesson were from Wellesley, and two, including Margie, from Sweet Briar. He doubted they could survive interrogation by the enemy, but he would know soon enough how they would cope with handcuffs.

"Hello, Ed." Margie-*Ava*'s voice, behind Hart, conveyed enough moxie to rev his ticker. She tilted a chair and slid into his row. This was the second time she'd come up behind him. The first was back in Washington after he hummed a few bars of the Eddie Cantor song "Margie" to see if she reacted to her real name. She'd taken the bait that time, followed him down a corridor, and said, "*Ava Ennis* to you. And you're off-key."

Yeah, he couldn't carry a tune, but her ability to get under his skin had to be a good sign. A spy had to have spunk. Her friend, *Patricia Ford*, on the other hand, looked the part of an

Egyptian but struck him as too polite to be tough. Her stress interview and eight hours in lockup would tell.

Lucy made a point of taking a corner chair in the back row behind the Dartmouth man, so she could observe the entire class. He seemed to be assessing everyone, but especially Margie. He hadn't ridden in the back of the truck with them, and if not for his Midwestern accent, she might not have been sure he was the six-footer she'd seen before they left Washington. He'd aced the cipher test they took that morning—as had she—after a wrong turn. The most common letters in the English language were E, T, O, N, A, I, R, S, and W, which she'd memorized by picturing English schoolboys at Eton, all of them heirs. The idea was to count letters in a coded message and substitute them using trial and error. She'd looked for common one-letter words and common two-letter words, but the sentence they'd been given to decipher was thirty-five letters long and contained twenty-six different letters, not exactly ripe for parsing with the most-common-letter tactic. Not impossible, but unlikely, for coincidence. She'd quickly spotted two identical three-letter words, plugged in the common word "the," and was satisfied to guess that her group had been given a simple cipher of the "quick brown fox" sentence of typewriting fame.

They'd spent the rest of the afternoon learning a method called *Playfair*. Except for the Dartmouth man, who barely took his eyes off Margie, everyone in front of Lucy seemed to be straining to memorize the steps. They were supposed to fill in a five-by-five grid with all but one of the letters of the alphabet, regroup words into two-letter pairs, and substitute with letters in the grid by rules involving shifting their positions one way or another. Interesting and a bit more challenging than the giveaway "quick brown fox."

After lectures, the group was to sup together and report

for evening assignments. Most would memorize what they saw in rooms in the carriage house, wait a few minutes, and reenter to identify changes. A lampshade rotated. An absent pen. Dust wiped off a wood surface. A few in her group would be summoned to the porch to await a rigorous one-on-one interview, possibly about what they'd observed about one another. "I *regret* that some of you won't be involved in the memory exercise," were the exact words their instructor used. Regret.

At dinner—stewed tomatoes and chipped beef on toast—Lucy learned that most of the others had been given instructions on lock-picking, a process that the conversation left to her imagination. Paperclip or bobby pins in keyholes? The man with a Slavic accent, who knew the most, gave no hint of where he'd acquired his skills.

As they were finishing, Dr. Mack appeared with a list and sent all but the man from Dartmouth, herself, and two others to their rooms for a break, after which they were to report to the carriage house. He gave an apologetic look to Lucy as if to say, you poor child, and told her to proceed to the porch, where she should wait until summoned.

CHAPTER FIVE

Lucy
Station S, 1943

Moonlight. Southern breeze. Those were comforting despite the disturbingly shadowed porch where Lucy waited, trying to prepare herself. There were only four women to the ten men in her group. Failure on her part would reflect poorly on her sex. She'd been born during the last world war, when women didn't have the right to vote. Now that they did, they should rise to serve their country, and she had no intention of shirking.

"Why were we singled out?" she asked Ed Wheeler, the Dartmouth man, when he joined her.

"I'm supposed to brief you for a timed exercise with an interview."

"Will you be there?"

"I can't tell you yet."

"Are the others meeting us here?"

"I'll tell you what I know, if you tell me about Margie."

"Is this part of the exercise?"

He shook his head. "No."

"What do you want to hear about?"

"Why is she following me?" he asked.

"I don't know that she is. Besides, you met her before I did." False, but Lucy was working back into her cover story.

"Was she following you?"

"You aren't sisters?"

"Not unless Father had something going on I didn't know about." *Forgive me,* she thought. He would turn over in his grave hearing her even joke about his morals. "So, what about this exercise?"

Ed glanced at his wristwatch, a glow-in-the-dark with a radium dial, not the one they'd been issued. "I've been assigned to prepare you for an interview. Here's your situation. You were snooping in a government building, and the night watchman caught you."

Lucy listened closely, glad to be back at spy practice.

"You shouldn't reveal actual details about yourself. If you're captured, the enemy could use it to impersonate you in a message. Don't even say what you eat for breakfast. Make up a credible cover story and stick to it. Deviate one bit, and they've got you." He gave her a hard look, eyes narrowing.

"You aren't an employee of the agency in the building where you were caught, and you have no identification with you. A guard will take you to the security office for questioning."

"Where's the building supposed to be?"

"Washington, D.C. You have ten minutes to come up with an innocent explanation for being in the office. I'll signal you when the time is up and escort you to the basement."

She would start by feigning embarrassment. Maybe the person who used the office had stolen her wallet. Or taken it by mistake. But why in the world would she be snooping in a government office in the USA?

She heard the creak of hinges and footsteps but didn't turn around despite caution vibrating down her back. Would it help to plan a false confession in case her first story was inadequate? On second thought, better to keep repeating her original excuse for being in the office. Looking for her wallet.

If she needed a backup story, what would it be?

"Time's up," *Ed* said. "Here's the guard."

Despite the shadows, she recognized *Buster* from the construction project. How odd that she could feel attracted, yet already disliked him. At least now she knew he was playing a role and might not actually find her repulsive. That had been the hardest part of her engagement, realizing her fiancé had gone along with his mother when she promoted their relationship and then when she went sour on it. "Miss," he said, "you'll need to show me your identification."

Lucy patted her pockets. "But that's why I'm here. I can't find my wallet. Unless it slipped into the lining, I don't have it. My friend's jacket was like mine."

"I'll have to take you to my office." Was that a flash of pity she read on *Buster's* face? If so, it was gone in an instant, replaced by the same hard look *Ed* had given her.

"Oh, is that necessary? If my wallet is still ... well, I don't know. It could be at the restaurant, and someone might steal it."

"Come this way. We can discuss it in the office."

Lucy nodded. "It was blue. If you let me use your phone, I could call the restaurant." They entered the Willard house, where *Ed* waited at the door to the cellar. He opened it for her, and *Buster* led her past a dangling lit bulb, down plank stairs into more shadows, where she smelled sawdust and burnt rubber. Streaks of light extended from a partially closed door. He guided her through it into a room with a cement floor, brick walls, a desk, and two chairs. "Please have a seat." He gestured toward a straight chair and sat on the desk. There was a small window above his head.

"Thank you," she said reflexively, and followed his order to sit still until he aimed a large photographer's lamp directly into her eyes. She turned her head.

"Look directly into the light."

"Is that required?"

"It is," *Buster* answered gently. He switched off the overhead light, casting all of the room except the blazing light into shadow. "Keep your eyes open, please."

All she could see was a giant disc of glare, duplicated in dizzying afterimages. At least he seemed apologetic.

"The office is closed. Please tell me what you're doing here." His voice was protective almost, though it would be unwise to trust him.

"My friend and I met at the place across the street for supper. When I got home, I realized I didn't have my wallet, so I went back. It wasn't at the restaurant. She said she works here. The door was unlocked, so I came in looking for her." Lucy was pleased with herself for leaving open the possibility that her friend had lied, though, of course, *Buster* would try to trip her up.

"Which door did you come in?"

"Front."

"Well, the office closed an hour ago. The door was locked."

"A man left by the front door," she said, noticing activity beyond the light. "He must have forgotten to lock it."

"How many offices did you go in?"

"Just one. The door was ajar, so I thought someone would be inside, but there wasn't anyone there."

"What's your friend's name?"

"Jean."

"Jean who?"

Time for her meaningless confession. "This is so embarrassing. I don't know her last name." If they were in an embassy, Jean's last name might be foreign, thus easy to forget. So not bad for a cover story. She wasn't contradicting herself.

"How long have you known each other?"

"We go to church together. She sits in the pew ahead of me, and we chat after the service."

"What church?"

"St. Patrick's Catholic."

He frowned. "What's your *real* name?"

The lamp had forced her into a painful squint that made her head throb. She briefly glimpsed his teeth while his silhouette multiplied in glowing negatives. "Patricia Ford."

He repeated the name with a German accent, and her head hurt more. "Show to me your driver's license."

"I can't. I don't have it."

"Your friend's license, then."

"I don't have it."

"You're lying. There's no Jean."

She wasn't in real danger, but despite herself, her muscles contracted. "Why would I lie?"

Buster clamped his hand on her shoulder and dug in his fingers. "But. You. Are. Lying."

"She took my jacket, and I got hers."

"Then you would have *her* wallet, wouldn't you?"

He released his grip on her shoulder—a relief—but lit a cigarette and breathed smoke into her face until she coughed and her eyes watered. "Nobody named Jean works here, *Patricia Ford*, if that's your real name. The door to the office where I found you was locked. You. Lie." He drew back his hand and smacked her cheek hard enough to make her cry out and miss something happening behind her. "Maybe they forgot to re-lock the door," she said, raising her palm to her cheek.

"Liar!" He pulled her hand away from her face.

"I did not."

"That was not smart, *Fraulein*. The others will not be so gentle."

"Let me go. That hurts!"

"Keep your hands out!" The German accent was gone. *Buster* clamped one of her wrists, then the other, in handcuffs, clicking the latches shut. "You may think this is a game, but we execute spies. You broke into a restricted area and lied. Now you must answer every question." He gentled his voice again. "Do you like cute little children?"

"That has nothing to do with your office."

"But you are a Jewess, aren't you?"

"I have something in my eye," she said. "I can't answer questions like these."

"Another chance?" a voice whispered from the shadows. "The bucket?"

"Jean told me she sometimes sleeps in the office. I was looking for my wallet."

Buster took hold of her chin and turned her head. "Look at the light. How did you get in?"

"I walked right in. The door was unlocked."

"Both doors?" he sneered. "I don't think so. You met Jean at church? What do you say at confession?"

"Father, forgive me, for I have sinned."

"Say a rosary."

She was Episcopalian and had no idea how to say a rosary. Why had she picked Catholic? "Mary, mother of God," she mumble-whispered, "daughter of holy Ann"—that part she'd overheard once—"in the name of the Father, Son, and Holy Ghost." She shut her eyes.

"All right, miss? We're done. Tell us your real name, so we can send out your file."

She didn't answer.

"You'll stay here until you're ready to tell us. One hour. Four hours. We have all the time in the world." Her shoulder was still sore from his squeezing, her cheek hurt, and she wanted to slap him. "Next time, we'll have the bucket with water in it," he said. "It's not for drinking."

Footsteps converged on the door. "I'll be taking the lamp with me," Buster said and switched it off. The door latch clicked, and she heard a groan. When she stood, the dark was too dense to see more than after-images, her handcuffs invisible in front of her face. For a while, she worked on extracting her hands, but succeeded only in causing them to hurt and swell. She could walk, but that was small consolation, and the complete dark made her jittery, though what was she afraid of? More pain?

Nobody had said a thing about escaping, but it would have been as uncomfortable to wait passively as to look for a way out. There wasn't a sliver of light under the door or the slightest glow from the basement window. She found the knob and tested it quietly. Locked. Probably that awful Buster was waiting outside to catch her, and if she kicked him, he might really hurt her.

Occasionally she heard small sounds and possibly a man retching, which she hoped had nothing to do with the bucket. Her eyes adjusted enough to see a faint rectangle of window over the desk, but she had to grope through the dark to reach her chair. She pushed it flush against the wall behind the desk, steady enough for her to step onto the seat and stand with her cuffed hands on the brick wall. She felt for the window and fumbled to open it, but it was too high, and the handcuffs were an obstruction. The whole thing was unreal. Maybe *Buster* and his helpers weren't bright enough to realize Jean in her story could have been the spy.

She climbed down and shoved the desk until it touched the wall, this time hefting the chair until she could lever it onto the desktop. For a while, she listened and heard her own breathing and someone moaning. Footsteps crossed the ceiling. Was the hallway above her? The side parlor? When the walking stopped, she crawled onto the desk and set the chair upright on the bare top. She stepped onto the seat, held onto the back, and straightened until her head touched the ceiling.

It took everything she had to tilt open the window and crawl through the small opening. In the process, her cheekbone collided with an edge so hard she had to pant to keep from yelling. She dug her chin into the dirt and pressed her lips together. *Ouch, ouch, ouch, ouch, ouch*. By elbowing the ground, she got enough purchase to worm her way out and kick the window shut behind her. As a child, she'd played under porches, but never at night. She rolled on her back and scooted away from the window. *I'm doing this for my country,* she told herself as she turned again and belly-crawled in the dirt.

With the moonlit yard in view, her fears seemed ridiculous. But she was handcuffed, filthy, and unsure what to do next. Run home through the woods? That would be a breach of security.

She knew her way to the Willard kitchen. If no one stopped her, she should be able to reach her room. What she wanted most was a bath. Not a shower, but a long soak in Belle Willard's tub. Or anyone's tub. She slunk between the shrubbery and foundation, rustling, stopping, watching for guards, but seeing no one. In the distance, she heard a shot. They should be careful; the neighbors would hear. In fact, the people in Fairfax had been hearing gunshots all month, chalking them up to hunters.

The kitchen porch was separated from the main veranda by a space of thirty feet, part of which was shielded by an entirely dark, stone springhouse. She was glad they hadn't locked her there. She would have had to batter down the door or dig her way out. The pantry and kitchen lights were on, and from the motion of shadows, she could tell someone was working in the kitchen. She would have to bluff.

"Hey!" yelled a soldier, peeling potatoes, one of the guys who'd served dinner. He didn't see her until she rushed past him with her hands under her shirt to hide the cuffs. She kept running. "Sorry, part of training. Don't tell anyone you saw me." When she got to the back stairs, she fumbled with the knob, made it in, and kicked shut the door after her. If he said anything, she didn't hear it while she was double-timing up the stairs.

As she expected, she reached a windowless pantry like the

place at Aunt Edith's where cured hams hung from the ceiling. A ladder on the wall led to an overhead panel, which she was sure was a door to the attic, not an easy climb with her hands chained. She balanced by pressing her knees against the side rails, thought about each new hand position, and managed step by step. At the top, she pushed up the door with her head and scrambled into a dim attic. If only she could ditch the handcuffs. She found a nail on the floor. Too big to fit the lock. Better to ask for Margie's help.

The door to the Willards' side parlor stood ajar, though not enough for Lucy to see if Dr. Mack was inside. When she tapped lightly, his footsteps crossed the floor. He looked out with a concerned expression, inviting her in. "You've had a hard night, haven't you?"

Lucy remained composed but nodded her agreement.

"How'd you get the cuffs off?"

"The lock-picking expert from dinner. Margie got him for me."

"*Who* got him for you?" Dr. Mack gave her a disappointed look.

Her cheeks warmed, though she counted on what her family had always said: She might feel she was blushing, but nothing showed.

He shook his head. "I'm sorry, Miss Moore. You identified your roommate as Margie."

"Oh no. It's Miss *Ford*. Ava is my roommate."

"You called her Margie. You broke her cover."

"No, sir," she said. "I wasn't referring to my roommate."

"To whom were you referring?"

"The nurse. I don't know her last name," she said. "Did you think I meant Ava?"

He burst out laughing. "You can't succeed at everything.

Some people just aren't cut out for this work. I'm sure Dr. Abbott will be happy to have his assistant back. Personally, I prefer not to send as lovely a young woman as you into danger."

"What did I do wrong?"

"You seem defensive. Perhaps I remind you of your father? Was he harsh when you failed?"

Was he harsh when she failed? He'd been dead since she was fifteen. Maybe he wouldn't have wanted her to go overseas. "I'm not sure."

"Tell me about him."

Perhaps she'd failed, but just as likely, Dr. Mack was still testing her, so she made up something about her father being in the Army until their family moved to Arlington. She would have preferred to tell him about her real father, a lawyer, for whom truth and duty were all important. Her eyes welled up, thinking about him. "Both my parents would want me to do what was right." She thought of the story of Abraham willing to sacrifice Isaac, which, until then, had made no sense to her. Why would a parent offer up his own child? Why would God, the Father, ask for that? But there she was, with her country at war. Many more lives than just hers or those of her brothers were at stake. She felt phantom pressure on her shoulder, as if her father were trying to heal the place Buster had squeezed too hard. That sadist. If the stress interview had been a sorority initiation, she would have quit. But then she'd decided against sororities. This was quite another matter.

Dr. Mack rose from his chair beside hers, retrieved a folder from his desk, and stood, indicating she should also. He tapped the folder. "You've done well, Miss Moore."

Done well? She lifted her chin, showing her bruised face. "I hope I'll be able to contribute in some way."

"I've no doubt of that. In the meantime, your stress interview is our little secret."

She raised her brows, eyes aching, and nodded. "Certainly," she managed. "I won't tell a soul."

"That includes your roommate. You passed, by the way. Another day here, a week of training, a week off, and you'll be on your way overseas."

CHAPTER SIX

Lucy
Washington, DC, 1943

Lucy ran a comb through her hair, watching Margie powder her nose. During their truck ride back to Washington, Margie looked like her old emotionless self and said nothing. When they finished in the locker room, all four women looked like career girls again. Lucy leaned close to Margie. "We didn't do so badly for a couple of Sweet Briar alums."

"We went to Wellesley," one of the others said, but Margie barely nodded.

"Rooty, toot, toot. What's next?" Lucy said when she and Margie were alone. "You said you would tell me about something." She straightened her skirt and inspected the seams of her stockings.

Margie shook her head sadly. "I shouldn't say anything."

"Whatever you want, but I can listen."

Margie shook her head.

"Will I see you again?"

"In North Africa."

Africa? Lucy frowned. North Africa? She'd hoped for France. "Wait a minute. Is that what you were going to tell me? I thought it was something personal."

"It is. My uncle was hearing from family. Then nothing." Margie's eyes overflowed, but she didn't speak.

"Can you tell me?"

Margie shook her head.

"Is it secret?"

"You don't want to know," Margie said. "That's all."

"Of course I want to know, but if you aren't allowed to tell, I understand. If you want to tell, I want to listen."

"You know my uncle and I are Jews."

"Yes." Of course she knew. A few of their classmates had been snide about it, though those were girls she'd tended to avoid. She nodded. Margie looked very uncomfortable.

"My mother's family is Sephardic. Do you know what that is?"

She felt as if she should, but didn't. "I'm sorry. No."

"From Spain. But not since 1492, when they got kicked out and settled in Yugoslavia. My maternal grandmother spoke Spanish. She called it Ladino, but it was Spanish."

Lucy nodded.

"My grandparents came to America after the Great War, but all my grandmother's family stayed in Yugoslavia. She had four sisters and two brothers. They lived in a village near Belgrade where there were lots of Jews and Christians and Muslims. Before the War, they got along nicely. The Jews there spoke Ladino at home. They called it the language of God and the angels.

The weight of Margie's distress and the force of whatever she was straining to say made Lucy forget they were due for a meeting. Soon after, she would have a trolley to catch.

"Do you know what *Judenfrei* means?"

From Margie's anguished expression, Lucy knew it couldn't mean Jews had been given their freedom.

"My uncle found out the Nazis have declared Yugoslavia *Judenfrei*. They're claiming all the Jews have been removed."

"Expelled?"

"Murdered."

Nothing Lucy could have said would have been enough.

Don't give up hope? "What can we do?" she asked, expecting no answer. Yugoslavia, free of Jews? She opened her arms, but Margie shook her head.

"*All*," she said. She shook her head again. "But my uncle heard about an escape. That's all I can tell you. But yes, I must have hope."

Margie might have told her more, but footsteps approached. A man knocked and called out their names. They were to have one last interview. *Last* interview. It sounded odd to Lucy.

The soldier led them to the fingerprint room. Margie was taken for her interview first, so Lucy was left waiting, this time preoccupied with what Margie had said. How could *all* of the Jews in Yugoslavia have been wiped out? Who had escaped? Someone had gotten the word out.

It would have been awful enough for any Jews to have been singled out and killed. But all? How would that even have been accomplished? Why hadn't such atrocities appeared in banner headlines? She saw why Germans would keep mass murders a secret, but wouldn't America want the truth in the open? She wondered if she should keep Margie's confidence but decided, of course she should, though she would ask more when they were together again.

Her last time in the fingerprint room, she'd felt observed but hadn't searched. Now with Station S under her belt, she gave the room the once-over but found no holes or listening devices under the bulletin board. She inched open each file drawer and felt for microphones, examined the underside of the desk. The carved Morse code was the same, though this time, the inked-in dots reminded her that entire pages could be miniaturized to the size of punctuation marks for sneaking out information.

"Miss Moore." The man who tapped on the door was the officer who'd reminded her of her father. She'd often felt critical of the stoicism of her older family members with their rigid posture and emphasis on correctness, but now she tucked in her own feelings and relied on her manners. He ushered her back into his office. He was taller than her father, nice-looking, and this time friendlier. He shook her hand firmly. "Are you certain that you want to undertake this mission?"

They seemed to ask that same thing each time they revealed something to her. When she agreed that, yes, she was certain, he opened a drawer and presented her with three small tins.

"What are these?" she asked, well in control of herself as he explained once again that capture was possible, and she could be tortured into revealing secrets. He explained that the pills in one were sedatives and, if necessary, could be put into someone's drink. The second tin contained an emetic in case she needed to feign illness. "And this one?"

"I hope you'll never have to use this one." He opened the smallest tin and showed her a cream-colored capsule the size of a pea. He explained that it could be temporarily concealed in the mouth.

She felt removed as he explained. It was as if she were asleep and gradually awakening to an awareness that a Nazi stood hidden behind the thinnest of curtains, raising a weapon, and the curtain would be drawn open. Her breath quickened, which she tried to conceal by holding her chin up.

"This is your L-pill. It contains cyanide, but it's coated with rubber. If you swallow it by accident, it will pass harmlessly through your body. If you bite down, the poison will be released, and you will die quickly."

CHAPTER SEVEN

Lucy
Fairfax, Virginia, 1943

Aunt Edith often wore her deceased mother's black ankle-length dresses, brooch at her throat and long sleeves buttoned at the wrists. Her other dresses were similar, and Lucy had been surprised to meet the grandparents of school friends and discover that not all elderly women dressed in black or gray and wore lace-up old-lady shoes. Some even wore lipstick, rouge, and mascara.

Fortunately, Lucy's mother hadn't insisted on ramrod posture enforced by hour-long sessions in straight-backed chairs, but Edith and her sisters had endured corsets, posture training, and other discomforts of their era, which Lucy supposed had left Edith with an unyielding sense of duty, which she was exercising by summoning her great-niece for an audience.

"Lucy," she said. "I've invited you for tea, because I have something to ask of you." She sat straight on the horsehair chair that Lucy had avoided, finding it too prickly on the backs of her knees. "Would you pour, please?"

Lucy, erect on the unyielding brocade sofa, which dated to the Civil War, obliged, filling two china cups from the sterling silver tea pitcher that Simon had placed on a tray on the coffee table between them. "Cream?" she asked, though it was milk. Edith would and did decline but asked for two sugar cubes which Lucy tonged from the Revere bowl.

Aunt Edith sipped her tea and set her cup and saucer beside the autographed photograph of King George of England presented to Uncle Walton on a diplomatic trip. She cleared her throat. “I understand you’ve told your mother you may go overseas.”

“Yes, I’ll get to travel.” Though Lucy hoped Aunt Edith wouldn’t ask for details, she would’ve loved to mention the closeness she felt to her father’s spirit.

“Your mother suspects you may go someplace dangerous.”

“She shouldn’t worry,” Lucy lied, thinking of the L-pill she’d been doled. “I’ll just be doing secretarial work. You know, typing and filing.”

“Lucy, I know you’d hoped to go to college somewhere out of the States, but this isn’t the time to make up for it.” Edith spoke in her stern voice, entirely serious. “There’s a war on.”

Lucy suppressed her wish to explain and sipped her milk-thinned tea. She placed her cup carefully on the silver tray. Edith would go on, she knew. “Of course,” she answered. This part, deliberately misleading her family, was hard but necessary.

“The reason my brother Walton forbade you to leave Virginia for college was that your mother was a new widow. She needed you. We didn’t expect you to fully understand that when you were a schoolgirl, but you are an adult.” Edith’s piercing blue eyes and wrinkled face showed disappointment and, at the same time, authority. “Your mother has had many losses.”

“I know that, Aunt Edith.”

“People have their limits.”

Lucy stayed silent but thought of saying her mother handled losses extremely well. She’d reacted to her husband’s death with grief and occasional belly laughs and had taken charge of her life while seeming as agreeable as ever.

“Hear me out, Lucy. Do you know why we don’t celebrate

your mother's birthday?"

Lucy nodded, holding her palm to her breast. Her mother's mother had died in childbirth, and her mother's father had held it against her.

Aunt Edith sat up straighter, if that were possible. "That isn't all you need to know, Lucy. Your brother Thomas was not your mother's first child. She had a little girl who died of diphtheria when she was six months old."

Lucy inhaled sharply. Had she been shielded all her life? She was suddenly dizzy, thinking of Margie's relatives, L-pills, and of her mother losing a child.

"With Tom in the Marine Corps and Bobby in the Army, she can't help but worry. If you leave, she'll be beside herself."

Lucy took a painful breath, wheels turning. Perhaps it was Aunt Edith who would be beside herself. "This is important to me."

"Where is your conscience? Your brothers are fighting for our country, and you want to travel? I'm sure you could do something useful without leaving home."

Lucy couldn't even say she would be in North Africa working on codes. What came to mind was her father trying to explain to her why Abraham had been willing to sacrifice Isaac. He'd spoken of the Great War and an older cousin's injury. "I think Mother approves."

"Your mother is willing to sacrifice herself for others."

At that moment, Lucy felt outside herself and realized that was what "beside herself" meant. She imagined her father looking down through the ceiling from some spot in heaven, holding a tiny girl. A sister she hadn't known about.

Aunt Edith didn't need to know about the OSS, but she needed consolation. "If things go well, I may eventually have an opportunity to visit the Holy Land," Lucy offered. "Remember how much Father wanted to visit there?"

Edith looked stern. "After the war, you mean?"

"Of course."

"Women should vote, but—"

"I know, Aunt Edith. You were a suffragette."

"I was speaking, Lucy. I did not go through all that so you could put yourself in danger."

"If women have the privilege of voting, shouldn't they have the responsibility to serve their country?"

"You haven't joined the WACs, have you?"

"No, no, no."

"Are you going behind enemy lines?"

"I'll be safe doing secretarial work."

"Your mother said you won't say where."

"I'll write to you."

If Lucy were still in the company of Margie or the other new OSS girls, she might have made a goofy face, compared family pressures to stress interviews, and dissolved in hysterical laughter. But she was expected to have more self-control than Aunt Edith. She couldn't call Margie because Ruby, the town telephone operator, would overhear. Maybe she and Margie should develop their own code because they would be traveling together. At least she'd been allowed to tell her mother that much. The work would begin out of harm's way in Cairo, Egypt, and would involve decoding messages. Perhaps that was all it would be. Lucy had avoided out-and-out lying to her mother by stressing the safety and routine nature of the work.

What she hadn't told anyone outside the OSS was that she would be working overseas on messages for operations running out of North Africa to Eastern Europe. Hints had reached her that her work might involve more. Was she willing to die for her country? Yes. Would she be parachuting behind enemy lines into Yugoslavia? Probably not, but why had she been issued a suicide pill?

CHAPTER EIGHT

Lucy
USA, 1943

She'd been warned to keep her suitcase packed but hadn't imagined she would have barely an hour to dress, gather sundries, and meet the morning trolley. Her orders were to report to an Army base in California three days hence for transport to North Africa.

There was something about morning, a kind of echoing, as if waking moments were interspaced with distance. Sounds, ordinarily buffered by the day's activity, stood out, calling for her attention. The latch of her suitcase. The clink of her spoon. Coffee filling her cup. Footsteps on the stairs.

In the shadows on the porch, her dear, comforting mother asked her not to worry about the people at home. They would all be fine. "I'll keep the home fires burning, Lucy Goosey, and try not to set the house afire. Aunt Edith has seen a lot, you know. She was alive in the Civil War. But she'll be fine too."

And so, Lucy, with arms full of the memory of an embrace from her mother, rode the trolley to meet Margie at Union Station, where they carried, bumped, and dragged their luggage through throngs to purchase tickets to Chicago and San Francisco. Neither knew how they would get the rest of the way to Camp Stoneman, only that they would board a ship and that their final destination was Cairo, Egypt. Lucy hoped to meet some of their Station S compatriots on the journey, but neither she nor Margie spotted familiar faces in the rush to the train.

When the locomotive came to life and clattered away from the station, it was afternoon. They were both famished, so they made their way to the dining car, where they managed to find a seat despite the crowd. A hand-lettered sign gave them the choice of bacon and tomato on toast or meatloaf and potatoes. Lucy chose the latter, which came with several lima beans and a puddle of cold gravy, which they gobbled to make way for the many waiting passengers, most of whom wore uniforms: sailors, soldiers, several nurses, and two WACs from the newly active Women's Army Corps. One of the latter complained in loud whispers about women too privileged to help with the war effort. Lucy guessed it was natural to size one another up and would have said so to Margie if they were somewhere they wouldn't be overheard.

It was only after they climbed together into Lucy's berth with the metal-on-metal groaning of the train masking their own whispers that they felt confident to speak their minds. Margie was full of the story of the Biblical Esther and began questioning aloud whether she would be willing to yield her body to save others.

"That's not what they asked us to do," Lucy said. She'd read the entire Bible, but all she recalled about Esther was that she married a king with many wives whose advisor wanted him to slaughter Jews. Somehow Esther prevented this, though it hadn't previously occurred to Lucy that this had to do with the sexual act. Margie's debate with herself challenged Lucy to rethink. How would a member of a royal harem please her king enough to rise to Queen status?

The idea of a virgin—both she and Margie were—using sexual wiles for their country reminded Lucy of boarding school; freshman girls asking one another if they would run outside in the nude if the dorm caught fire while they were showering.

The issue was less an unyielding prohibition against sleeping with someone before marriage—she'd likely have given way if her former fiancé had so wished—than general insecurity about her looks. Margie had never been engaged, and Lucy's fiancé had displayed an aversion to touch that, along with his determination to please his mother, split them up. It seemed to her that the question of the morality of using sex for a higher purpose was parallel to the other question that troubled her. How was one to keep the Commandment *Thou shalt not kill* while defending one's country?

"Don't you think it's something we should decide in advance rather than waiting until the possibility of it being forced on us?" Margie asked.

They were still crammed into one lower berth. Lucy went hot, and she peered outside the curtain as if she expected to see her mother sitting there. "But it may never come to that," she said. "Somehow, it seems more ... ethical to wait and decide in the moment. Isn't that the difference between a soldier and a murderer? One prepares to kill if need be, and the other plans to kill?"

"That's like saying a spy who saves her people by cozying up to the enemy is a prostitute," Margie said. "When there's a higher purpose, training for extremes is vital. Armies plan to kill."

"You're not suggesting we practice."

"Oh, hush," Margie said. "I didn't mean that at all."

Lucy wasn't sure if she was more shocked by women spies using sex or by the fact Margie had brought it up—shy, introverted Margie.

"We have to get over the idea there's some clear line we should never cross," Margie said. "If we're faced with extreme circumstances, we should be ready when the situation arises. How can you make such important decisions on the fly?"

"I don't think I would kill," Lucy said. "But I see what you mean. If someone assaulted you, I would try to stop them, and if I killed them in the process, well, so be it."

"Well, thank goodness. I'd do the same for you."

Camp Stoneman reminded her of Girl Scout camp, which she had disliked because of a bossy, but not very bright, troop leader. The buildings sat in rows as though plotted on a grid, rectangle after rectangle. Some were barracks. Some were for dining. Some were for medical care. Some were for laundry, and some for ping-pong and pocket billiards. In another, they showed movies. She bristled when she caught a glimpse of a man resembling Buster, but he disappeared around a corner. Probably not really Buster. With so many troops, sooner or later, she had to glimpse people familiar enough to trigger recognition. On second take, she would realize she'd been wrong. Not her neighbor's husband. He was MIA. Not either of her brothers.

At times people seemed to make the same error with her, their faces lighting up with recognition and then closing in disappointment. She and Margie were among the few not in uniform, to which the military men and women reacted either with curiosity or total lack of interest, more the latter than the former.

They were assigned a room in an Army barracks for women awaiting passage on the *Nieuw Amsterdam* and warned not to reveal their destination. Lately, when people quizzed her about things she wasn't supposed to reveal, her cheek smarted. "Does my face look red?" she asked Margie outside the PX.

"Not a bit."

"Why did the clerk tell you your husband was a lucky stiff?"

"They think we're officers' wives," Margie said. "Good cover. We just have to keep our bare ring fingers out of sight."

At breakfast on their third day at Camp Stoneman, passengers for the *Nieuw Amsterdam* were ordered to report to the ferry with their duffel bags. Troops in uniform gathered in squads to march to the dock, but individual travelers like Margie and Lucy straggled behind with suitcases, alternately rushing and stopping to get their bearings.

"Was that *Buster*?" she asked when she spotted a man in uniform speeding on foot around the massing troops.

"I didn't see him," Margie told her.

He didn't seem to be at the pier, thank goodness. They were bottlenecked in one of those wartime hurry-up-and-wait situations, the entrance to the pier blocked by a checkpoint where a soldier at a folding table demanded name, rank, and serial number. Eventually, he found them on a list of civilian employees and filled out a shipping tag for each with a room and bunk number. "Wear this on your right pocket flap," he said without looking up and went on to the next in line. As she and Margie weren't in actual uniform, that was impossible, so they looped their tags on a jacket button. Another soldier handed Margie, then Lucy, a life preserver, and they struggled up the gangplank, each with one suitcase, onto the crowded ferry, where she feared they might encounter either disapproval or catcalls. A tall soldier winked, though, and made a spot for them near the rail. He told them he had sisters and a brother in Hoboken, and his brother had worked refitting the *Nieuw Amsterdam* for the Brits after the Netherlands fell to Hitler. Soon, troops jammed the ferry stem to stern, bantering, yelling, and singing bawdy ditties. With the escalating din and added throb of engines and waves against the hull as they entered San Francisco Bay, communication beyond smiles and shrugs became impossible. Then almost at once, the voices stopped, and all heads turned to stare at the *Nieuw Amsterdam*.

She remembered standing at the base of the Coliseum in Rome and looking up at the stone walls, unable to take it in from so close. This was the largest vessel she'd seen in her life, and it filled her with emotion. These people around her were going together to risk their lives. In that moment, every one of them knew the risk, but their vulnerable looks faded as the ferry pulled smartly behind the ship and the gangplank met the pier. Military Police were everywhere, herding troops.

The crowd swept Lucy and Margie off the ferry, and MPs guided them onto a steep gangplank with rope side rails for which they had no free hands as they struggled along with their suitcases and life jackets. Near the top, the line jammed. MPs were reading luggage tags and telling them where to bunk. As Lucy hoped, she and Margie were to stay together, this time in a former second-class room refitted with two three-level bunks. Two of their roommates were nurses, and two were WACs. To their delight, their room had its own bathroom.

Due to crowding on the ship, the only meals would be breakfast and dinner served on four schedules, A, B, C, and D. The two nurses got mess card A, the WACs mess card B, and Lucy and Margie mess card C, which meant they were to eat at nine AM and six PM, while the others ate earlier.

"You'd better stick together," said the nurse named Flo, who'd taken the top bunk in the three-level stack with them. "You're fair game."

"What do you mean?" Lucy asked.

"I mean, be careful. This ship has more than 7,000 men and less than twenty women."

Fewer than, Lucy thought, but this wasn't school. They were heading overseas where there would be all sorts of risks. Once again, her heart filled with the idea of all these young men offering their lives for their country. "We're all on the same side," she said.

"Well, some Romeo groped me in the dining hall," Flo said. "If you know any other passengers, I'd suggest you look out for each other. At least travel in pairs. They hushed it up, but a woman on the last trip was raped."

CHAPTER NINE

Hart
The Nieuw Amsterdam, 1943

Hart found his hammock at the end of a row, second layer from the bottom, in a throng of bunks five-high, crowded into what used to be a full-sized auditorium. Each man was assigned a bare canvas sling lined with grommets and laced to a bunk frame of metal pipe. They each got an Army blanket and pillow. His bunk was at a reasonable sleeping height, though so close to the one below that he was kicked, off and on, throughout the night. He'd hoped the motion of the ship would lull him to sleep like the swaying of the sleeper car on the train he took to San Francisco, but no such luck. He tossed and worried, berating himself for failing to catch the train with Margie and Lucy. He hadn't yet seen a single woman on board.

Unlike shipmates complaining about a meal of room-temperature Spam, he'd missed supper altogether. His stomach growled all night. Spam and cold mashed potatoes would've been a feast. Eventually, the holders of Mess Card A rose and left for early breakfast, but he'd drawn Mess Card B. Breakfast wouldn't be served until 7:00 AM. He dressed anyway, took his mess kit, and headed out to explore the ship, which was already out of sight of shore. The ocean and vast sky, streaked pink and vermillion with dawn, should have moved him, but he was too hungry. He scanned faces and saw a few men he'd glimpsed in the bunkroom. They all seemed to travel in groups, but as he strode around the deck, stomach growling, he thought he saw a familiar profile. Gordon Aldrich? The man was looking out over the rail and, as Hart approached, spun around as if ready to fight. They met eyes, both relieved, and Gordon pumped Hart's hand.

"You heard they nearly gave me the boot, right?" Gordon said.

"Why?"

"The slap."

"You mean the stress interview? I was there."

"They said I hit her too hard."

"What?"

From what Hart had heard, none of the later girls had been hit. Just Lucy, who'd had a bruise and goose egg on her cheekbone. The rest stayed locked overnight in the basement and had their heads dunked. He decided not to press for an explanation, but thought it most likely the psychologists had been messing with Gordon. "You're here," he said.

"She might be too. I thought I saw her on the ferry."

"And?"

"I can't very well call out a superior officer, but he gave the order and changed his mind when he saw her. I'm mighty sorry she got hurt, but I don't think I gave her that bruise."

Hart clapped Gordon on the back again. "Which meal card have you got?"

They both had B and soon were in line with their mess kits for scalding coffee, reconstituted eggs, and boiled bacon. Each man was served a pat of butter with a small loaf of freshly baked bread, still doughy inside but delicious to Hart, for whom any kind of food would have tasted good.

"Did she pass?" Gordon asked.

Hart's mouth was full. "Damn right."

"I was hoping she'd wash out."

"Why?"

"She and her friend want to serve behind enemy lines in France. You know how the Krauts treat the enemy. If hitting her harder than I meant kept her safe, it would have been worth it."

Lucy

"Did you hear that?" Margie asked when she and Lucy were threading the crowd of men on deck after breakfast.

"On the PA? Sorry, I missed it." Lucy ducked away from a leering private.

"Somebody paged Hart McCann to the Orderly Room."

"Who's Hart McCann?" she asked.

Margie grinned like a teenager asked to a dance. "Dartmouth from Station S."

"How did you find out his real name?"

"From my uncle."

"Your uncle isn't on ship, is he?"

"No."

"What's the Orderly Room?"

"I have no idea."

"Finding out should be right up our alley," Lucy said. She'd already overheard enough to know that the ship captain was Dutch and the troop commander was British. The crewmen were mostly Hollanders who came with the ship and Brits who oversaw the conversion for troop transport. There were also numerous US officers and a smattering of civilians. Most of the soldiers seemed to think they were heading for Alaska.

Margie winked and kept walking. They passed the lifeboats and rounded a corner where a knot of soldiers impeded traffic. "See that man with the beard? He must see everything."

Someone on the crowded deck above whistled and leaned toward them. "Hey, babes, come up here with us!" Lucy ignored catcalls and whistles while Margie pushed her way around to a bearded man bent over a chess board, his back still to Lucy. He looked up at Margie, her face sunlit with relief as if he were a refuge from the thronging male energy around them.

"Sir, do you know where I might find the Orderly Room?" Margie shouted.

"Next to the theater. It used to be the purser's office." His accent was Slavic and hard to hear above the din, but Lucy, unable to see his face, thought she caught his name: Benzimra. Margie thanked the chess player, and they set out in search of the theater, which had been converted to a dormitory, part of the refitting that allowed the ship to transport 7,000 troops. Fortunately, signs had been posted for both the theater and Orderly Room—theater with the British spelling: theatre. When they were almost to the Orderly Room, they spotted Dartmouth in front of them, talking with someone else, and, for a moment, all Lucy saw of his companion was the top of his head and the angle of his shoulder. Her heart nearly stopped when she realized it was *Buster*. She tapped Margie with her elbow, unable to speak and suddenly hot, as the men disappeared into the Orderly Room.

Hart

After Hart identified himself, the staff sergeant rose from behind a desk, handed him a mimeographed list, and told him he would be first sergeant of the casual EMs, in charge of thirty-one men traveling under individual orders. Casual enlisted meant OSS. Hart was to hand in a report by 10 AM each day. He scanned the list of names and bunk locations. No women. "Who would be in charge of casual women?" he asked.

"I don't know what you're talking about." The staff sergeant turned to Gordon. "And you are?"

"On his list," Gordon answered. "Sergeant Gordon Aldrich."

Hart cleared his throat. "There were two women we're

supposed to look out for."

"I'm sure that's been taken care of." The staff sergeant returned to his desk, but at that moment, the door opened behind them, and in walked Margie and Lucy.

"We meet again," Hart said.

The staff sergeant stood again. "Miss Moore and Miss Aarons, I presume."

Lucy

She turned sideways to step by *Buster* and Hart McCann but, at the last moment, looked and saw *Buster's* face. Eyes apologetic and vulnerable as she left him behind.

"Do you know Sergeant Aldrich?" The staff sergeant asked after he'd led Margie and her down an inner hall into an office with another raised sill to step over.

The name meant nothing to Lucy, so she only raised her eyebrows. She'd been thinking *Buster* might turn out to be a nice person after all. Was his name Aldrich?

"You looked as if he'd startled you. In the meantime, someone you know wants to speak to you. If you'll take a seat, I'll get him."

She and Margie exchanged looks. Someone she knew? She hoped it would be one of her brothers, though that was unlikely. She was even less prepared when Kim Roosevelt peered in at them, wearing glasses and a rumpled suit. She started to speak but stopped herself. The Roosevelts liked their privacy. She looked from him to Margie to him, but Margie showed no sign of recognition. "Margie, this is—"

He raised his hand to interrupt: "*Tom Murray*, Lucy's friend from the Smithsonian." His stare was intense enough to remove doubt, if she'd had any, that Kim Roosevelt, the Willard-Roosevelt's eldest, who'd played tennis with her brothers, was asking her to go along with his civilian cover.

"This is my friend, Margie Aarons. We went to Sweet Briar together."

"Both OSS," he declared rather than asked.

Neither of them answered, though Lucy's cheek ached from the temptation to break cover.

"What are you implying?" Margie finally responded.

Kim smiled, his eyes still serious. "I'm with OSS too. If you'll have a seat, we'll discuss it. I'd like your assistance." He explained that a rumor had started on the ship that a Roosevelt was on board, and he was trying to track down the source. He addressed Lucy: "Hopefully, you don't take after your Aunt Edith."

Shame on him for suspecting her. Under other circumstances, she would have asked about his wife, Polly, his children, and his parents, but she narrowed her eyes and kept quiet.

"I saw her poking around a restricted area," he said as if Aunt Edith had stowed away. "Do you know the men who just left?"

"Yes," she and Margie answered together.

"Hart McCann is keeping a roster of OSS people on the ship," *Tom* said. "You can ask him for help if you need it, but unless you object, I'll ask you to check in with me daily. I need you to keep your ears open for shipboard rumors about the president or anything that rouses suspicion." He went on to brief them about foreign nationals onboard, many Jewish. Lucy wondered if he knew that Margie was Jewish and had lost her parent early on, something she'd refused to speak of in college. Her uncle had been her guardian.

"Some of our agents have Communist leanings, but Germans are our biggest worry. Keep an ear out for anything suspicious, anyone speaking German. Anything about dignitaries, no matter how ludicrous. Please report directly to me. When we reach Cairo, we'll be running operations in Yugoslavia." This time *Tom* addressed Margie. "I understand you have relatives there, Miss Aarons. I know your uncle."

CHAPTER TEN

Hart
The Nieuw Amsterdam, 1943

A bearded old fellow playing solitaire chess looked up as Hart completed a counterclockwise circuit around the deck. They nodded at one another. The fellow's mustache looked twisted rather than trimmed. On his second circuit, Hart said "hullo," trying to sound British, and the man introduced himself as Wally. Perhaps he'd been recruited by OSS, but he wasn't on Hart's list. Why was he on a ship of American troops?

His last name was Benzimra, which he told Hart was a Jewish name. He'd fled Austria in 1938 but had not come from there originally. When Hart asked more, he clammed up, though he cleared his board and invited Hart to play.

Hart's recent poses as a Dartmouth man made him feel ignorant, though he knew he was smarter than lots of the men on the ship. He'd been valedictorian of his tiny high school in Montana on the Fort Peck Indian reservation. Because he'd enlisted in the Army, he hadn't finished college, and although he had been picked for OSS based on intelligence tests, he knew little more than the basic rules of chess and the names of the pieces. Apparently, Wally divined his lack of expertise from watching him set up the board. Or perhaps from watching his face as he laboriously calculated each potential move. While Hart could see two moves ahead, Wally seemed to have the consequences of every move well plotted and, in no time, had Hart checkmated. "Next time I teach you, no? We play one game a day?" Wally smiled widely, showing a missing front tooth. On some unfathomable impulse, Hart thanked him in Spanish.

To his surprise, Wally answered in Spanish that they should meet before lunch the following day and that he looked forward to getting to know Hart better.

Hart would have been less surprised had Wally lapsed into German or French. "*Yo no supe que se hablan español en Austria*," Hart answered.

Wally replied in Spanish that his ancestors had migrated from Spain and settled in Yugoslavia. He'd left his village to study first in Belgrade and later in Austria. When Hart asked—also in Spanish—about his family, Wally stiffened, his face broadcasting an instant of guilt.

Or was Hart misreading? It was like a complicated chess game, fishing for information, falling into traps. This one, the trap of unfounded suspicions.

That night, with the ship rocking and several bunkmates retching, Hart lay awake and brooded. Would a Nazi spy disguise himself as a Jew among Americans? In his heart, he knew Wally was the real deal, likely working for the alliance called ABC for American, British, and Canadian or for OSS and just not on his list. But, still, his formerly trusting nature had become a casualty of the war.

Lucy

The communal dishwashing tubs on board started out boiling but invariably cooled to greasy room-temperature scum, perfect for breeding germs. Lucy had escaped the resulting intestinal epidemic, but the smell and motion of the ship left her and Margie gagging. They were under blackout conditions each night, so the only light on deck was from the stars or an occasional smoker who failed to cover his cigarette glow. A woman wouldn't survive going near the saltwater showers in the former swimming pool. Not if the crude language and catcalls she and Margie got anywhere on deck were an indication. Lucy whispered what she'd overheard: even a nun would get a short-leg salute out there.

"What's that?"

"Don't you have a male cousin?"

Yes, Margie did, but not one prone to explaining male humor, and she'd never been engaged, so Lucy whispered an explanation. Their first day aboard, when the shipload of males—in order of mess hall assignment—had been ordered on deck in uniforms of birthday suits, raincoats, and shoes, the nurses warned them to stay below. The short-legged salute euphemism buzzed among the nurses afterward, but Margie—bless her heart—had supposed the short leg was some sort of test of reflexes. Rubber hammer tap to the knee or elbow. Lucy had figured it out right away and begun plotting ways to disguise her sex.

"I knew they were being called in for a physical exam, but venereal disease?" Margie made a face.

"At least penicillin cures it," Lucy said.

When it was finally morning, she led the way into fresh air, both of them in trousers, their mission to listen for spies. Fog would have been the appropriate atmosphere, but nature did not cooperate. The sky shone a brilliant, dangerous blue, which meant any passing Japanese planes would see them. There were not enough lifeboats for even half of the troops, and a prime rule on ship was for each passenger to carry a lifejacket at all times.

The down-stuffed ones they'd been issued came with orders prohibiting use as a cushion or pillow. Since there were no chairs on deck, most troops ignored the warnings. She and Margie stepped over extended legs as they made their way around the ship, listening in on conversations, concealing their hair under caps to look as male as possible. If they stopped for long, they would be noticed.

The majority of troops either came from the school of hard knocks or had lied about their ages to enlist, or both. One skinny boy bragging about marksmanship looked barely into his teens. Her thoughts tracked of their own accord to her Station S training and then to that irritating *Buster*, Gordon Aldrich, and her irrational wish to pay him back with a smack across the cheek, something not at all in her nature.

On their second circuit, Margie elbowed her in the ribs and pointedly glanced at the bearded man who'd given them directions to the Orderly Room. He was setting up a hinged chessboard, and this time, as Lucy turned toward him, he looked up, astonished. Tears flowed onto his old-world mustache. Though she didn't recognize him, his tears made her weep too, and they stood face to face, wordless, her throat in spasm as if she'd encountered her father or Uncle Walton.

Margie nudged past her and spoke to him gently in English, but he stayed fixed on Lucy, gradually furrowing his brow in disappointment. She was not who he thought. Margie spoke softly to him. He murmured something in Spanish and then bowed to Lucy.

His homespun tweed, mustache, beard, and unkempt hair made him seem impoverished, yet he carried himself with Old World dignity. "You resemble," he said, pronouncing the *s* like *s* instead of *z*, "the wife of my brother."

They accompanied him to the rail, Margie on one side, Lucy on the other, pushing through GIs. If the Japs raided, they would be sitting ducks, but the sea was beaten with a vast sheen of reflection and a kind of living translucence superimposed on the opacity of depth. It was as if the presence of the ocean and this bereft man from Yugoslavia, the land of Margie's relatives, had stripped away her emotional skin. His name was Wally Benzimra. He was Ladino Jewish, like Margie's family, and his brother's wife, brother, and their young daughter had not been heard from since the Nazis forced them and the rest of the Jews in Štip onto trains. He did not use his sister-in-law's name, as if to do so would be more than he could bear, but Lucy resembled her. He told Lucy and Margie that Germans were both organized and brutal. They had begun with the larger cities like Belgrade, where he'd once lived, and then smaller cities, then villages, herding people onto vans and trains and shooting any who resisted. He'd received letters describing the labeling of Jewish businesses and the requirement to wear stars of David, but his family had not believed the horrors to come could be true. He had wished—still wished—that the bigger horror of *Judenfrei* was false, but his contacts in the resistance could not refute it.

Margie's face paled, and Lucy's throat constricted, more in sympathy than in full belief. Ghettos and labor camps were believable, but what monsters could kill tens of thousands of people? Who would care for the children? She'd heard of the *Kindertransport* to England, children flown out of Germany and Austria, but their numbers would be only a tiny fraction of the orphans created from killing so many. "Hundreds of thousands?" she repeated.

"More," Wally had whispered, and Lucy focused on the sea and inhaled salt air. Why had she not known this when she was still in the United States?

CHAPTER ELEVEN

Bella
Near Štip, Yugoslavia, 1943

Of her last week at home, Bella recalled only flashes of kindness from her mother, a jar of beans, and the smell of face powder and lavender soap. Sometimes the comfort of her mother's lap and arms was with her, but as time passed, a terrible fear grew inside Bella that she would not know her mamika when she came. What was the shape of her nose or of her lips? Were her eyes the same brown as Nura's?

When Señora Nura allowed her out of hiding, Bella chopped cabbage, sorted wild greens, boiled eggs, peeled potatoes, and swept the floor with bunched straw lashed to the stub of a tree limb. She tried hard to be a good worker, but when Nura whispered to Abdullah in a foreign language or when he jumped at the sound of wind or a wooden spoon falling to the floor, it was as if locomotives had roared upon them from someplace she could not see. Then she dropped to the floor and shut her eyes.

The stone house in which the Behnams lived squatted on a hillside of fields and meadow surrounded by forest. Though Abdullah scraped his boots before he came inside, he tracked in clods of dirt that made Nura shake her head and mutter, "*Muškarci.*" Men. In those moments, Nura shooed Bella away or sent her back to practice hiding, too far away to understand what they said, though she heard his growls and hard breathing.

One day Abdullah brought his tools into the kitchen and gave Bella the job of watching for visitors. She looked out the window at the green field and the forest in the valley, veiled in mist that she could not see through, and waited so she could tell her mother and father that she was trying very hard to be good. But they did not come. When Abdullah hefted the cupboard away from the stone wall—raising one side and then another, step by step—the plank shelves made sounds that scared her. She watched him and not the window. If they find you, they might kill you, he growled under his breath. She thought he meant fairy-tale wolves who gobbled bad children, but the idea gave her a hollow feeling inside, and she said nothing.

Although Abdullah looked fierce, he was her grandfather's friend and was building her a new hiding place in the wall. When he said there were dragons in the forest, Bella asked Nura if that was true.

"No, little mouse. Men like to tease. There are no dragons in the forest, but he is not teasing about the Nazis."

"Where is my mother?"

"Shh. Someone might hear you. I am your mother. Your name is Esma."

Another day Bella sat on the floor in a square of warm magic made by the sun shining through the window. She stood up and spread her arms to see the light on them, but Nura trembled and said no and draped a dark shawl over Bella's head. Someone might see you. Keep this on your head, so when you look out, your face will be in shadow.

Abdullah chiseled, chip-banging at stones, muttering that the house would fall, but each time he removed a stone, he wedged wood into the opening, and no walls fell. In the evening before dark, Abdullah walked the cupboard back against the wall, because, after nightfall, they could be surprised by thieves or Nazis or Chetniks or Russians. Or wolves, she thought, but they could not get into Abdullah's hiding places.

Every day, she practiced being quiet. Sometimes she carried her hen, Tišina, down a ladder into the secret cellar in the barn, and Abdullah shoved the square door into place. Then she would hear the scritch-scratch of the rake above her, and it would be like the darkest night, and they would sit in the straw. Tišina's name meant *silence*, and she did not cluck; she sat warm and still with her soft feathers in Bella's lap.

"You must be even quieter than Tišina," Nura said. "If anyone finds you, you must remember your name is Esma, and you are playing a game of hiding."

If it was very cold, Nura and Abdullah Behnam brought Bella into their bed to huddle behind Nura while the wind moaned outdoors and dreams took Bella into dark places and shadowy forests with wild beasts. But she tried to be like Tišina and did not cry out in her sleep. Every morning Señora Nura reminded her that she should be quiet as a little mouse. Sometimes, while Abdullah was working on her closet, he would invite her inside to test the size. "You will grow, little mouse, but for now, this will do."

He built a false back to the cupboard where they stored wooden bowls, little bowls inside of big bowls that she could stack into towers while he worked. When the shelves and the back of the cupboard were moved out of the way, Bella could crawl through into her closet, where she could stand, sit, or lie on her side. If she slid away a piece of floor, Bella could drop down into Abdullah or Nura's arms in the root cellar and climb with them back up the ladder and help them spread a rug over the trapdoor and move the table over it.

Sometimes when Bella was hungry, she pretended to be a tiny mouse for whom a crumb of bread would be like an enormous loaf. She imagined being so tiny she could sneak into the sunshine and run as much as she wished. She liked it when

Nura kept watch from the kitchen and let her help Abdullah plant potatoes. He dug a pit and hammered together a frame to make an underground hut, a place where their son Adem could hide if he came with his Partisan friends. Or where they could hide Tišina and the other hens. Rooster had escaped into the woods and no longer crowed, but from the time she was a chick, Tišina could not peep or cluck. The two other laying hens proved to be too noisy to take into hiding.

Once, as Abdullah leaned against his spade, a small mouse ran across his boot, and he tried to stomp it. Bella was glad it escaped.

"We have to keep vermin out," he said. "They will eat our food."

Bella did not say a word, but she thought and thought. She was like the mouse that Abdullah almost stomped. She was like Tišina, who did not speak. She knew he had been friends with her grandfather in the war, but it was cruel to stomp a mouse that was only trying to stay alive.

The following day while Abdullah was digging, Nura told Bella to go outside and tell him his porridge was almost ready. "We don't have much," Nura said, "So let him eat first."

Bella found him standing near the woodpile. "Vermin," he said.

"Look at this," Abdullah growled as his spade cut into the ground. He shoveled earth off the roof of a burrow, opening a badger tunnel that led beneath the wood pile, near the patch of sprouting potatoes. "Get me the axe," he ordered, and Bella froze. He looked so fierce, she didn't know what to do, but she brought the axe, and he raised it in the air like he'd done over Tišina's sister when he chopped off her head. Bella crouched and shut her eyes. She wondered if a person with her head chopped off would feel like a body running blind or like a head blinking in the dust.

Standing trembling, waiting for him to push her to the ground, she heard thuds and frantic squeaks. Abdullah called for Nura to bring a knife. Bella shuddered and tried to send herself into the past where sunshine glinted off the surface of the river. If only she could be a fish and hold her breath forever. She saw stars and shut her eyes tighter. If she were a fish, she would die because there was no water, but if she were really a little mouse, she could hide in the smallest of places. She hoped Nura had not attacked Abdullah with the knife. And she hoped Abdullah had not chopped up his wife. She did not want any of those ideas to be true. When she opened her eyes, Nura was dangling a glistening badger carcass by its back legs.

"Meat for goulash," Nura said and nodded at the pelt on the wood pile. "Fur for a hat. Pick wild greens and onions, my Esma."

Bella was not Esma, but she did as she was told and kept her distance as Abdullah split firewood. Her heart thudded with each whack of steel into wood. Nura called her inside and gave her a knife to cut up the onions, greens, and potatoes. Soon the house was filled with the aroma of spices, simmering meat, and vegetables.

"If only Adem were here," Nura said softly.

If only my mother would come, Bella thought, her tongue pressed hard into the roof of her mouth wishing for Mamika.

Adem had joined the Partisan, and had met a hero called Tito, who rode a beautiful white horse. Once Bella had tried to ask if her mother and father had joined the Partisans, but Nura had hushed her, and Abdullah stomped away. Day after day, Bella listened when Abdullah and Nura talked. Sometimes they forgot she was hiding near them. Even girls could be in secret armies fighting the Nazis, she learned. Very bad things were happening in Štip, they said.

When she was allowed outside, a kind of rush and fear came from them. "We are mice, too," Nura said once and pressed her pale lips tight together. "Do you know the story of Thomas of Torquemada?"

"Did he make my people leave the country of Spain?"

"Yes," Nura said. "He was a cruel man. He made our Muslim people leave Spain, too."

At other times village people stopped by to speak to Abdullah, and he sent Bella into hiding where she could listen in on them as they spoke in the language she knew. More often, Nura and Abdullah whispered in another language. Bella had the feeling they were speaking of her or of her family. At those times, a stone formed in her chest, and she expected to faint and die.

When she was six years old, her grandfather had taken her in a carriage to carry a basket of sweets to the Behnam family for the holiday of Purim. Her mother had told her to be very nice because Nura had lost a daughter who liked to sing and dance and make them laugh. The idea of parents allowing a child to become lost in the woods frightened Bella. She had not understood until much later that "lost" meant that Esma had died of fever. Nura had fussed over Bella and told her that if she ever needed a new family, she could stay with her, Abdullah, and their son, Adem. It had made Bella afraid, and she'd stiffened and run with her empty basket back to her grandfather's horse-drawn wagon.

She remembered her grandfather comforting her and saying that he had fought with Abdullah in the World War and that Muslims and Jews were descended from Abraham. Abdullah's ancestors were from Persia, where they had a tradition of *zakat*, a kind of giving, and would help her. And Bella's beautiful mother, with her kind face and beautiful brown eyes, told Bella over and over that if anything happened to them, she should trust the Behnams.

CHAPTER TWELVE

Lucy
The Nieuw Amsterdam to Cairo, Egypt, 1943

For an instant, Lucy forgot Kim Roosevelt's assumed name, but it came to her as she and Margie reached the Orderly Room. They joined a queue at the sergeant's desk, expecting to wait to be summoned, but there he was, *Tom Murray*, beckoning them after him.

"I should have counted on you finding one another," he said, confusing her. She and Margie hadn't been apart. What he meant became apparent when he opened the door to his office and she saw the others: Wally Benzimra, Hart McCann, and Gordon Aldrich, whom she'd known as *Buster*.

"Spies tend to sniff one another out," he said.

She cocked her head, wondering. Did he mean spies on the same side, birds of a feather drawn to one another? Or that a collaborator would be caught?

"Lucy and Margie, I understand from Wally here that we have an interesting development. Show her," he said to Wally, who carefully extracted a worn leather wallet from which he removed a tiny photograph. He handed it to Lucy as if it were a holy relic, his distress making Lucy say a silent prayer for him. She bent her head to examine the little photo and extended her palms so the others could see. The picture was of a face close enough to her own to startle her.

"Lucy's resemblance to Wally's sister-in-law may be useful," *Tom* said. "You'll be working together in Cairo; I thought you should know. It's given me an idea."

It would have been cruel for her to ask if it were possible any of Wally's Yugoslavian relatives were still alive. He hadn't mentioned a fiancé or wife. She'd assumed he had no children, but grief could be encased like a mummy, the most important losses wrapped tightest. At that moment, what she most wanted was to help him find the family he had likely lost.

"We can't let the Germans know that we read their messages," Kim said. "If we leak the contents to the press, the Nazis will realize we've cracked their newest Enigma, and they'll change to something we can't decode. If we point to credible sources, we can reveal what we need without betraying allies." Each threatened country had shown at least some support for a policy of appeasement, he explained. "Before they're snookered into helping him, we need them to realize Hitler will as soon betray friends as enemies."

"Lucy," he said with uncharacteristic intensity. "You will be our credible source. I want you to pose as Wally's sister-in-law and accept an award for bringing us information on the mass killings in Belgrade."

If she posed publicly as the woman on the identification card, she thought, Wally's sister-in-law or anyone left in his family could be put in danger. Her own scruples against taking false credit added to her opposition. She focused on *Tom Murray's* face and tried to make her own face show that she was thinking it over as he explained she was to have escaped a mass burial that they could only have learned about from a spy with a radio or German transmissions. Did he mean that he knew Wally's actual sister-in-law had been killed?

"Double duty," Kim said. "Less evidence of our activity on both scores." For an instant, Wally looked stricken, but Kim had moved on. "Besides the bit of disinformation," he said, "my cover role is encouraging economic development, but I'll be looking for places to slip in some of our people. The villa we rented for OSS headquarters in Heliopolis is bursting at the seams. We'll need space for more Americans to live. I'm hopeful we can get a larger estate in Cairo without bringing undue attention. We, by which I mean OSS."

"What sort of attention are you trying to avoid?" Gordon Aldrich asked.

Something about his question, his voice, or perhaps his too-handsome face was getting under Lucy's skin. She inched away.

"If the embassy does all the renting," he said, "we might as well send out a public announcement: here are all the Americans."

It was all messy, Lucy thought. Nowhere near as neatly planned as she had hoped. If there was one advantage, it was that all of them had been chosen as operatives who could think on their feet. It made her think of the leadership test with giant Tinker Toys.

CHAPTER THIRTEEN

Bella
Yugoslavia, 1943

When Nura and Abdullah argued in their other language, Bella learned to close her eyes and cover them with her hands, so she would not see. Nura liked King Peter, a boy younger than their son, Adem, but Abdullah did not, and Bella was afraid to ask why.

One day, as she left the outhouse, a man with a long and ragged beard appeared from behind the Behnams' barn and caught her by surprise. He grabbed her hand, and she went limp, and he lifted her around the waist and carried her under his arm to the house as if she were a sack of potatoes. If she hadn't just done her *kermah* into the hole, she might have dirtied herself.

Nura rushed out in her apron, trembling, and listened to what the man said. After he lowered Bella to her shaking legs, Nura called her Esma and gave Bella a stern look that meant to pretend Nura was her real mother.

He was not a Partisan like Tito, who rode a beautiful white horse, or like their son, Adem. The man had rotten breath and broken teeth, and when he ate the egg and potatoes Nura cooked for him, bits dropped on his long beard. He was a Chetnik serving under Mihailović in the Army of the Fatherland. He would not shave until the Nazis were defeated, he said.

When the Chetnik was gone, Abdullah spat on the ground.

If not for Chetniks, the *Italianos* would not have arrested his cousin, Mehmed, he said.

"If that man had helped the Italians and Germans, he wouldn't be sneaking half-starved through the forest," Nura said. That night Bella dreamt she was such a bad girl that her parents packed suitcases and rode away on a train without stopping to see her.

Another day, two men with long beards and one man with no beard came limping out of the woods, and Nura sent Bella to hide in the place behind the kitchen cupboard.

The men demanded food. They told Nura that the Nazis would kill anyone who helped a Jew. They were Partisans like Adem, but they did not know him. They wanted money, and Nura gave them what she had.

While Bella was hiding, the men stomped away, and the Behnams argued in their other language until Nura cried. Bella needed to use the outhouse or the little pot in the hiding place. If the men were still there, they would have heard the noise of her tinkle into the tin pot, so she tried to wait. She heard heavy footsteps but kept quiet. She heard the beating of her own heart. She heard whispers but stayed still as she could possibly stay, though her feet felt like pincushions, so numb and pricked that they ached. She wiggled her toes and held back her pee.

"My Esma," Nura moaned between but did not open the hiding place.

Por fabor, Mama, Bella prayed. *Please let me out. Come for me.* She needed the outhouse. She reached for the pot and heard the rustling of her arm against the wall. If Nazis were in the house, they would hear her, but her pee came of its own in a gush, silenced by the cloth of her skirt and apron. She heard heavy footsteps and finally, with relief, Abdullah's voice, gruff and panting. "They're gone, but they took all but the hidden potatoes and all the chickens except Tišina and Cluck."

"Did they find any of the hiding places?"

Bella listened but did not hear Mr. Behnam's answer. Her legs were stinging wet. She tapped the wall quietly, and soon the cabinet pulled away from the wall. She was afraid they would be angry, but Mrs. Behnam held her tight in her arms, squeezing out her breath and another gush of stinging pee.

Mr. Behnam clapped his callused hand on the tabletop, making it shake. "Tito must be hard up to take them."

"He *is* hard up." Mrs. Behnam held Bella so tight she couldn't fill her lungs. She wiggled away to step out of her wet underwear.

"They're thieves posing as Partisans," Abdullah said and switched to his other language. Soon Nura was weeping again, and he slapped her cheek and stormed away to look for Cluck, who had run into the forest.

Bella found a bucket and ran to the well so she could wash her clothes. All the while, she imagined Abdullah stomping back in with a switch to punish her. Her mother never hit her. Never. But sometimes Nura gave her a slap on the backside, and now Mr. Behnam had hit his wife in the face. When Bella returned with the water, Nura turned her back and rummaged in a cabinet for a bar of lye soap.

"Heat the water first, Esma." Mrs. Behnam's voice was dry and tired. She kept her eyes averted, as if she were angry that Bella was not Esma. But Bella couldn't make herself into someone she was not. She couldn't even make herself into a little mouse.

"Why were you fighting?" she asked in a whisper.

"The neighbors know that Esma is gone. If the Nazis question them, they may tell. Abdullah thinks those Partisans, if that's what they are, will not keep our secret. He wants to send you away."

"Where would I go?"

"They would take you."

"Who would take me?"

"The Partisans."

"Would they give me to the Nazis?"

"I don't know what they would do. You saw; their clothes are rags."

But Bella had only heard their gruff voices and footsteps. When the teapot came to a boil, she added hot water to the cold in the wash basin and scrubbed herself and washed her underclothes, skirt, and apron. What did their clothes have to do with what they would do with a little girl? Did they need her to sew for them? She imagined sitting around a campfire with them and mending torn clothing. As she scrubbed her skirt with lye soap in the heated water, she imagined washing their clothes in a stream.

"Nura!" Abdullah bellowed, and his wife rushed outside, leaving Bella in the kitchen wearing nothing but an apron. Fortunately, the day was sunny, not hot, and not too cold. She overheard him whisper in the Serbo-Croatian language she understood, but the only word she made out was "poison."

"You would knock down a wall to drive a nail," Nura told him. "If anyone tries those mushrooms, it will be me."

"No," he said. "It will be the mouse."

"Are you stupid as a rooster?" she shrieked. "I will never agree to that."

"We have no more potatoes," he said. "If she eats them and dies, her final rest will be with a full stomach. If she eats them and lives, we can fill our stomachs too."

CHAPTER FOURTEEN

Hart
The Nieuw Amsterdam, 1943

So far, so good. Hart hadn't heard a whisper that President Roosevelt was onboard or that the ship was on its way to Cairo, but other rumors abounded: a submarine had fired torpedoes at the ship and missed; three nurses onboard were raped by a German spy with a fencing scar; the crew had spotted three surfacing Jap submarines; an enemy plane had flown nearby in the night. Though these were all false, troops were ordered to stay below deck after sunset and continue blackout conditions. To confound any spies among the ranks, snips of false news were announced with the regular war updates: after Alaska, the ship would refuel in Hawaii; a Radio Detection and Ranging system had been devised to track the movement of submarines; the German Army had issued white flags to their top officers. The latter was meant to reduce Nazi morale. Before their first stopover, Hart and Gordon sent out a lie of their own as a test to see how long it took a story to travel around the ship: Hitler had contracted syphilis from his mistress and developed a gaping chancre on his tongue that made him lisp. Hart told a GI on the port side near the stern. Gordon told the same story on the same side near the bow. Less than thirty minutes later, Hart and Gordon heard their story from three separate GIs on the starboard deck, but there were still no leaks about their destination. A spy among the ranks might have been confounded, though the brass and most intelligence officers on board knew where they were going. The absence of actual leaks did little to relieve Hart of the sitting-duck tension of cruising with so many men on such a huge ship with so few lifeboats.

Their first stop, New Zealand, was announced only hours before arrival. All members of the armed services—Hart and most of his crew among the thousands—were ordered off the ship to parade in dress uniform through the streets of Wellington. Preoccupied with keeping his men in step, Hart didn't see what happened to the OSS civilians, Lucy, Margie, Wally, and *Tom Murray*. Gordon and Hart's twenty or so in uniform marched smartly down a street lined with old people, women, and small children, who waved at the miles of troops as if cheering their own sons, husbands, or fathers.

"Have you spotted Lucy?" Gordon asked as they lined up to get back onboard, but Hart hadn't, and Gordon cussed under his breath. Hart could have done the same, but self-control was the name of the game. It took effort to keep a poker face or a chess face when Margie spurned him. She scooted away when he approached, leaving him to slink around corners and blow into his palm to test his breath. He even wondered if the lust he felt for her had its own odor. Though that wasn't all he felt. He'd never met anyone who so matched the image of the woman he wanted. Day after day, he made his one contact with her to vouch for her presence on board. Then she would eye him like a wild filly and disappear only to show up later in serious conversation with Wally, Frank, or Lucy, invariably hushing as Hart approached. Even if the smarter strategy would have been to leave her alone, he tried to run into her as often as possible and to read her delicately sculpted lips from a distance. Her masculine disguise utterly failed to conceal what he knew was beneath it, and he'd have given anything just to plant a kiss on her Shirley Temple dimple.

After they rushed off and on the ship at Wellington, they cruised into cooler climes where clouds like smoke blew over cannon-barrel waves. Hart was reminded of jumping from a blimp in a parachute drill. Unlike the mindlessness of lining up for a shove out the door of a noisy plane into the wind, he'd had to make a conscious decision to step into a silent, windless void. This felt like that. Too much time to think. A Brit told him the story about the torpedoes had been true. They rounded Australia and turned north, disembarking at Fremantle for another parade, but soon were underway.

His last glimpse of the sky that night was an over-the-shoulder look toward starless darkness. The ship cruised without running lights under cloud cover too dense for even a hint of moon. In the bunk room, the motion reminded him of the back of a buggy where he'd napped on the way back from delivering laundry after his pa deserted his family. It made Hart miss his ma and sister. He drowsed and awoke in the middle of dreams, brooding about the war and secrecy and danger.

Days passed, and his chess game improved. Margie kept her distance. Wally, who expressed a variety of opinions about the war and the psychology of collaborators, did not mention her or comment when Hart inserted her name in conversation, hoping for information.

In Ceylon, where the streets were so jammed that it was impossible to even walk two abreast, they were granted three hours of shore leave with no required marching. Their orders were to avoid eating or drinking anything while ashore, but Hart and Gordon were tempted by mouth-watering smells and sights. Barefoot locals hunched over small burners cooking curry and rice dishes that they served on newspaper or in tin cans. Hart's eye was caught by a shirtless, bronze-skinned man in a turban squatting on his haunches, eating some kind of meat with sauce. He reminded Hart of newspaper photographs of Gandhi, as did many of the others he passed, some bareheaded and others in turbans.

Soon Hart and Gordon spotted Pete, the OSS man from a Greek family, who was part of their group of "irregulars." He joined them as they browsed carts of ornate fabrics and clothing cut like long nightshirts for men and women. Other vendors sold spices that smelled like curry, cloves, and mint. Pete sniffed and rattled off names like cumin, coriander, and cardamom while Hart cringed at his own ignorance. They browsed souvenirs and tempting fruit, much of which was unfamiliar but smelled deliciously ripe. Military men from the ship swigged beer or vividly colored soft drinks, packing the streets and swarming the forbidden pushcarts. On his last African tour, Hart had been told to avoid raw fruit and vegetables, but that fruit with peels could be considered safe. When he, Gordon, and Pete could resist no longer, they bought a half dozen perfectly ripe bananas, which they peeled and savored, one luscious bite after another.

Their brief shore leave put them all in good spirits, but when they returned, they discovered that, in their absence, many British troops had departed, replaced by a battalion from India, clad in British khakis and felt campaign hats. Word spread that the Germans were retreating in Russia, and the *Nieuw Amsterdam* was headed for Cairo. Meanwhile, the ship was packed to overcrowding and buzzed with talk about pyramids, the sphinx, and the Nile. Hart learned that the Eighth Air Force would be headquartered in Cairo and other troops were bound for the Persian Gulf.

As the bunks were already filled to capacity, the infantrymen from India camped in the open on the rear of the main deck. They carried British Enfield rifles but no bedding and were under orders not to leave their area of the deck. Hart found out as much as he could from the new men, though many spoke only rudimentary English. Under such crowding, his usual exercise pattern of walking fast around the upper deck and down and around the main deck was impossible, and he couldn't find Margie or any of the women. Even Wally, usually so close-mouthed about the women, admitted he hadn't seen Lucy or Margie. Hart worried they'd left with the British troops in Ceylon.

In the several days it took to reach the Persian Gulf, neither Lucy nor Margie appeared. The staff sergeant in the orderly room finally snapped at Hart to quit asking. Nobody was missing. No one had jumped ship.

When they reached the Straits of Hormuz, Hart composed a note to Margie in his mind while he stood on the top deck, where land was visible in the hazy far distance on either side. He wished she were with him to see it, but since the Indian troops had boarded, none of the women came out on deck. He hadn't seen Margie in the dining hall or the orderly room, though nurses had eaten at his breakfast shift. He hoped she and Lucy weren't ill.

Meanwhile, they cruised forward toward a span of open horizon. *Where sky meets sea*, he thought and planned to write Margie a poem describing the vessels in the far distance rounding the curvature of the earth, setting like the sails that had taught Aristotle the earth was a sphere.

CHAPTER FIFTEEN

Lucy
Cairo, Egypt, 1943

Tom Murray walked around Lucy and Margie to lock the door and close them in his little office. "Have you told Margie who I am?" he asked when the three of them were alone.

Lucy hadn't, which seemed to surprise him.

"Polly is good at secrets, too, but I can't tell her everything."

"Who's Polly?" Margie asked.

Lucy waited as Tom explained that Polly was his wife. He looked expectantly back at Lucy, making her suppose he was uncomfortable saying he was a grandson of Teddy Roosevelt and thus a cousin of the current president and first lady. As Eleanor had no living parents at the time she married Franklin, Teddy had walked her down the aisle. But Lucy refrained from sharing this or anything at all until Kim gave her the go-ahead in plain American English.

"Margie," she said. "I would like to introduce Kermit Roosevelt. He goes by Kim since his father is also Kermit. Their family has property in Fairfax." She looked to Kim for direction, but he was wearing his innocent and sincere expression. She watched his face as she added that his maternal great-grandmother had been a spy.

Kim still gave no reaction, making Lucy wonder if she'd misread his intent, but when Margie looked away, he winked approval without moving another muscle. Lucy found it confusing that he was breaking cover. The answer arrived posthaste after he swore Margie and her to secrecy. His cousin, the president, might be traveling in secret to Cairo to confer with other world leaders. Kim, undercover as *Tom Murray* and with her assistance and Margie's, would be assessing the area to prepare for the president's visit. They would leave the ship in the morning.

"Tomorrow?" Margie asked, her wheels of thought obviously spinning. It was those hazel eyes reacting to everything that made Lucy glad for her own brown eyes, dark enough to conceal the widening or shrinking of pupils.

"We'll be taking an early train into Egypt," Tom said. "I expect we'll dock in the wee hours. You should have your luggage ready."

The sun was not yet up when Kim Roosevelt led Lucy and Margie down the gangplank of the *Nieuw Amsterdam*. Though the horizon glowed and they could see the train platform, stars still shone overhead. After weeks of shipboard din, the silence through which their footsteps sounded struck her as eerie. Lucy heard her own breathing. None of them spoke. Kim's plan was to lead them onto the Egyptian State Railway unnoticed before the troops were up.

They boarded a coach with a wood floor and upholstered seats beside open windows. Margie sat beside Lucy, and Kim shared the facing seat with their luggage. Most of the other passengers were men in robes to their ankles, some with red felt tarbushes atop their heads. Others with skull caps. A few European men in linen suits boarded and lit cigars while Kim bought orange drinks from a vendor carrying bottled drinks in a tin bucket of crushed ice. Soon the car filled, the vendors left, and as the sun rose, they chugged slowly away from the dock area. Kim passed out the drinks and reminded Lucy one of her duties would be to pose as Wally's sister from Yugoslavia and pose for a photo while accepting an award.

"I'll try," she answered. "Do you speak Serbo-Croatian? Isn't that the language of Yugoslavia?"

"No, I don't, but we'll be in Cairo."

The car bumped along slowly while the engine chuffed and groaned. "Do you speak Arabic?" she asked.

"A few words."

"How does one say, 'thank you?'"

"*Shukran.*"

She noticed a man across the aisle sit straighter, as if listening in. She didn't think she'd given anything away, but they were in a carful of people, any of whom might speak English. Two women in black huddled in scarves and robes across from the man, and one glanced at her with fear. Why? Lucy wondered if Americans were the source of fear or something else. Germans? British rule. Men in charge? Maybe the fear was of white women. Or of the man with them. When she turned around to face the window, she felt eyes on her back.

"Kim," she whispered. "Have you acquired radar for what's behind you?"

"What?"

"Hair-on-end when we're being watched?"

"Why?"

"I feel it now. I think the women over there have their eyes on us."

"Never thought to worry about women watching me."

Typical for a man to underestimate women, she thought. "So, you feel nothing?"

"Nope." He craned his neck to survey the back of the car, then gave her that infuriating look that meant he was teasing.

"Let's work on Arabic," he said. "*Ana* means *I*. If you give something to a beggar child, others will rush up calling, '*Ana kaman*,' which means, 'me too.' That will bring attention to your being American. So, chin up and walk on."

Oh dear, she thought. Children begging. Of course, she'd known there would be beggars. But how could she help them? To think that winning the war was all that mattered was naïve, though, of course, lives were at stake, and she did see that a crowd of children could draw attention.

CHAPTER SIXTEEN

Hart
1943

Hart hadn't seen Margie or Lucy in days. While he slept, the *Nieuw Amsterdam* docked at Suez. Soon he was blinking at the brilliant sky, hoping to spot them from the top deck. Endless dunes flanked the ship. He saw no females onboard but then spied a nurse. And then another. But not Margie or Lucy.

The public-address system blasted static and, finally, an announcement that had troops straining to listen. They would be debarking after breakfast to catch a train to Cairo. A private lobbed his flattened lifejacket over the side and shouted an obscenity as it sank into the dirty harbor. Two other soldiers tossed theirs: one bobbed on the surface, and the other plunged into the depths. Hart had known all along there weren't enough lifeboats.

Soon most of the troops appeared on deck lugging duffel bags, but there was no sign of Margie or Lucy. Looking out at the shore, he saw no American or European women, just natives wearing red fezzes and Brits in uniform. A steam locomotive appeared in the distance trailing a long plume of smoke and steam. While they watched, the engine approached and backed onto a side track parallel to the ship.

At eleven, British sailors began herding troops down the gangplank. Hart and four of his already overheated OSS companions threaded through the crowd into a dirty wooden coach, where they squeezed together on a wooden bench. Soon soldiers and Egyptians were cramming into the aisle with their luggage. The car was stifling, passengers swatting at flies and conversing in a mix of languages: French, Arabic, something that sounded like Portuguese, and American, British, and pidgin English.

When the car was packed, the engine hooted and chugged slowly west into the surrounding desert. The cars creaked and swayed, wheels rattling over the tracks, while Hart studied dunes through the open window, expecting the train to pick up speed enough to generate breeze.

"Did you spot Lucy?" Gordon, pressed shoulder to shoulder with him, asked.

"Nope," Hart answered. "You see any officers?" It felt as though insects were creeping down his shirt and up his trousers.

"Not on this car," Frank Braverman answered. Flies buzzed about them as they stared out at a distant caravan of camels like a scene on a Christmas card.

"When are we getting this show on the road?" Hart was drenched with sweat, and the train was still crawling along at less than twenty miles an hour. An insect bit his ankle, and he slapped it through his trousers. "These sand fleas are the devil."

Behind them, someone laughed and jabbered in Arabic.

"I thought they were bedbugs." Frank Braverman scratched through his shirt as the locomotive reached an area shimmering with rock outcroppings and on through endless sand and heat, never fast enough to make a breeze.

"Those come out at night," someone said behind them.

Hart dozed upright and jerked awake, his throat parched, his stomach aching for food. What he wouldn't give for a swallow of cool water. Next to him, Gordon and Frank were dozing, breathing loudly, while outside, the sun blazed onto sand and more sand. The car jolted along, shaking unpredictably.

Passengers fanned themselves with hats and newspapers. His thirst was intense. “I’m getting up to search for water,” he said aloud, intending to visit the lavatory as well, though his thirst was primary. Perhaps one of the better-prepared travelers would sell him water. It was desert. Certainly, regular passengers would have brought along something to drink. The train lurched and made him wonder what would happen if it broke down and stranded them. It was beginning to get dark, the sky pinking at the horizon and shadows of the train cars stretching into the desert. He wove his way through other passengers, hanging onto seat backs for balance and asking other troops if they knew where to get safe water. When he’d reached the lavatory, he was not surprised to find a line, some troops waiting turns to piss off the side between cars, others holding out for the official water closet. Each time the door opened, a stomach-turning stink arose from the latter. A corporal ahead of him muttered. “I’m not filling my canteen in there.”

Hart hadn’t even dug his mess kit out of his duffel bag. He felt stupid. But they’d been warned about drinking local water. The corporal extended his hand, his face distinctive: alert brown eyes, bushy brows that met in the middle, and a short nose with large upturned nostrils. “Bernie Ingram.”

“Hart McCann.”

“Beg pardon?” the corporal said.

“My first name’s Hart. H. A. R. T.”

“Like the stag. Hart laughed and agreed. “Where’re you headed?”

“Camp Huckstep.”

Outside Cairo. Hart knew that much. “Do you know how far we are from Cairo?”

“Nope.”

He found out Bernie was with a company of MPs and had gone to college on the Eastern Shore of Maryland and that they belonged to the same fraternity. While they talked, the sun set, and stars appeared over the desert. The train rattled to a stop with much screeching and lurching. To their surprise the engine uncoupled and pulled away, streaming smoke, leaving the cars behind, surrounded by desert, and them without water. The moonless sky grew dark. He and Bernie squeezed back through their car, and Hart traded seats with an MP so they could finish their conversation. "What do you think is happening?" he asked, his throat dry as cotton. He'd seen no cacti for squeezing out liquid, no shimmering oasis, no glow of distant city lights.

"Beats me," Bernie answered, nodding toward the passengers in the ankle-length garment worn by Egyptian men. "Those guys don't seem rattled."

To their relief, a troop of barefoot Egyptian vendors materialized with buckets chocked with crushed ice and bottled soft drinks. Hart offered an American dollar bill for a red drink and was handed back Egyptian coins. His first swig was cherry-flavored, cool, and barely carbonated. He glugged the rest, hoping food vendors would appear as miraculously, but instead, the vendors sold their drinks and moved on. The lights went off in the car.

Nearby Americans called out conjectures about what would happen next. They'd seen enough movies to imagine a raid by armed bandits, but Hart, remembering delays he'd encountered his last time in Africa, wondered if the locomotive repairmen were simply taking their time. His stomach growled with hunger, but at least the car was no longer stifling. The night brought pleasant cool air and then a chill. He and Bernie got up and shut windows.

"I don't smell anything cooking, do you?" Bernie asked.

Hart didn't and endured Bernie's ensuing monologue about his favorite foods. Anything would have tasted good, but he'd lived through hard times and knew not to dwell on hunger. Soon most of the passengers were grabbing their twenty winks, many snoring softly, all of them probably dreaming about what would come next. In his own dream, he was in the dustbowl in a *Grapes of Wrath* landscape, searching for his father, who in real life had left him, his mother, and his sister in Montana to fend for themselves. Several times he awoke wondering if the locomotive would return. His father hadn't.

CHAPTER SEVENTEEN

Lucy
Cairo, Egypt, 1943

In the midst of dreaming—something about a hayride—Lucy heard her mother call for Aunt Edith and jolted awake. She was seated on a train facing Margie and Kim Roosevelt, her foot pins and needles, her neck bent uncomfortably forward. The sun had crested the horizon, still low in the sky, casting dramatic shadows across cultivated fields with palm trees, and ahead, emerging through clouds of dust or smoke, a city with domes and hundreds of minarets wavered above the horizon. The tracks followed a canal of reflective brown water, beyond which trudged a steady procession of white-robed men, women in long black dresses, heavily laden donkeys and camels, and wooden carts piled with bundles. Most of the people were barefoot, and as the heat increased, she wondered if they carried sandals for walking in the desert or on hot pavement. She wondered if they were happy or if they were sick at heart from their various burdens. She thought about her own privileged life and the fact that she was riding in the train and that the flies were no longer biting.

"Those are date palms," Kim said.

She was more interested in the women in their black cloaks. "What do you call their robes?" she asked. She wished she'd been given at least a phonetic phrase book to study, though she'd been cramming from a German grammar text to prepare for decoding and might have to learn Serbo-Croatian. Whatever the garments were called, they were voluminous enough to hide in. She could imagine donning one and moving unnoticed through the streets of Cairo.

Margie merely opened her eyes, but Kim bent his head to answer that the white garments worn by the men were *galibayas* and the black garments the women wore were called something similar. In the city, a woman might wear a wide dress called a *tob sebleh* and a wrap called a *malaya luf* in which she could carry things.

Some of the women carried small children in their *malayas,* but there was little chance of seeing the babies' faces as the train chugged on ahead. Lucy watched intently as the numbers of people and animals and buildings increased. The height of some buildings surprised her, eight or ten stories and European in style, constructed with columns and pedestals. The horse-drawn cabs were called *gharries*. Some were brightly painted coaches, others not much more than small wagons draped with fabric. Occasionally they passed automobiles, but the train slowed to a crawl and eventually pulled into a station at *Midan Ramses*. "*Midan* means square," Kim said.

Several Army officers awaited them on the platform. One came forward to greet Kim as they exited. He led them to a dark-colored sedan, held the door for her and Margie, and they piled in the back. Meanwhile, Kim approached a group of ebony-skinned boys in white *galibayas*. They were all quite handsome and graceful. Even Aunt Edith would have approved of their straight posture and dignity. As she watched, Kim reached for his wallet and peeled off some sort of paper money for one of the boys, who smiled broadly and bowed in appreciation. They seemed to be having an animated conversation.

When Kim was back, he introduced himself to the driver as *Tom* and addressed the others. "I hired a houseboy. His name is Mahmoud, but his brothers call him Meer. He's Nubian." After the briefest pause, he announced that the Nubians drove out Alexander the Great, reminding Lucy of her brothers showing off knowledge, jousting for position. Her mother had taught her to sit out their disputes, but Aunt Edith had usually weighed in. "They went after Alexander's army on their elephants," he added, and Lucy decided that whatever the reason for his tutorials, they were enlightening. "Nubians are reputed to be scrupulously honest. Anyway, tonight we spend the night at Heliopolis Palace Hotel. Our boy Meer will meet us there in the morning tomorrow before we check in at headquarters."

Where was headquarters, they all wanted to know?

"14 *Sharia Ibn Zanki*," *Tom* answered. "*Sharia* means street. *Ibn*—some just say *bin*—means *son of*, but I have no idea who *Zanki* is or was. In the meantime, we're going to have to get some local clothing for you two ladies in case we have to deliver messages on the sly."

When they set out the next morning, Lucy intended to learn their route through Heliopolis, but incessant horn-blaring, rising dust in the street, and the fact she was seated in the middle between Margie and *Tom* kept her from registering their turns. The sergeant driving needed a haircut. The Nubian boy, Meer, seated directly ahead of her, had a slender neck, smooth skin, and wore a red felt hat. He'd arrived at the hotel before breakfast, reminding her of her younger brother in the way he'd eyed her pastry. She'd slipped him one wrapped in a napkin, and he ducked behind a column to gobble it.

The lieutenant who'd greeted them at the train station sat in front on the passenger side, occasionally turning to comment on buildings blocked from her view along the palm-lined main street. The car stopped at a small villa with a masonry garden wall, and Kim exited with Meer, apparently to give instructions. The top of the boy's head, fez included, came to

Kim's shoulder. Lucy guessed he was about twelve.

They were greeted by a man dressed similarly to the boy, in a white robe and red fez. After an extended conversation, Kim stood straighter—he'd been standing the whole time—but this was a substitute for a goodbye handshake, she supposed, a formal parting. Meer's face, in response, looked both pleased and serious, as if he had been paid a compliment. He accompanied Kim back to the car and removed two suitcases, hers and Margie's, from the trunk and lugged them back through the gate, where the man, who resembled Meer, took one, and they disappeared into the house. Kim climbed back in the car carrying a large paper-wrapped package. "You girls will be living here, but we'll return to the hotel first." He explained that the man who'd greeted them was Mustafa, a cousin of the boy they'd hired, Mahmoud Meer.

When they were underway, Kim gave them a quick lesson on Egyptian money and told the cautionary tale of a spy named John Eppler, a German by birth, who'd been raised by an Egyptian stepfather and had been caught spying for the Germans. Counterfeit currency with repeating serial numbers had led the Allies to him.

Once again, they were let out in front of the hotel with its palm trees and series of arches facing the street. "We'll be available if you need us," the lieutenant said in parting, and they returned to Kim's room, where he opened his package, which contained Yugoslavian costumes. The immediate plan being for Lucy and Margie to meet the American Ambassador, Alexander Kirk, who would present Lucy—in the guise of Wally's sister-in-law—with some sort of award. Her Uncle Walton had often remarked that the field of foreign relations was a bit like a battlefield in that everything was experienced piecemeal. She saw what he meant. The big picture was for historians. Or perhaps the president, who, Kim confided, would be coming to Cairo for a secret meeting.

Although she had met the president twice and experienced his skill in making it seem that whomever he was talking with was a treasured friend, she doubted he would recognize her. But Kim, from the Teddy Roosevelt branch, apparently thought otherwise. He was the most approving of the current president of his group of first cousins, and had always struck her as sober and responsible. She supposed her growing affection for him was partly an artifact of their situation, a familiar and handsome face in a foreign land coupled with his guidance in a time of peril. She could not permit herself even a daydream of a closer relationship. At their meetings on the ship, he'd often been midway through a letter to his wife Polly and their sons.

CHAPTER EIGHTEEN

Hart
Lancaster, VA, October 2001

Hart reached his kitchen door before his foreign-service friend, Jim, and pocketed the envelope taped inside the storm door. "I owe you," he said, unlocked the door, and backed against it so Jim could pass with the suitcase.

"Don't mention it." Jim squinted at the too-bright sky and river and set Hart's luggage inside near the kitchen table piled with unread mail. "Like me to carry this upstairs?"

"That's not necessary."

Everyone entering the house was drawn to the bay window view of sky and river. The latter was blue and rolling gently with near-white patches from small reflected clouds. In places, waves gleamed and sparked like gold and diamonds and made him imagine Margie sitting on the patio, reminiscing about the day he surprised her with an engagement ring.

If Jim weren't with him, Hart would be talking aloud to her. She'd been the one who talked to herself, though she never spoke of secrets. It was more her way of organizing her thoughts. He didn't believe in ghosts, but since her death, he talked to her often and imagined her answers. When he was first in love, trying to get her attention, he had felt the same way. She'd been fixated on saving the world and her people. Anyone with a lick more sense would have known that a gentile had no chance with her.

He thanked Jim sincerely for the ride back from Alspy House, joked about his bionic knee, and when he was finally alone, tapped his breast pocket, addressing Margie: "What do you think this is?"

She would have made a guess, though he saw no need for conjecture. The envelope was sealed and taped shut, but blank. He slit it open with a paring knife and unfolded the contents: two block-printed sentences. No phone number or return address. 9/11 might have made an old Company colleague or asset like Meer or his son Muhammadu too cautious to leave a number that an intruder could collect. Bella worked for Mossad, or so he suspected, because she worked at the Israeli embassy. Anyone in Israeli intelligence would be on high alert.

I stopped by, hoping to connect. Give me a call when you have a chance.

He removed the shade from a lamp in the living room and scorched first the note and then the envelope over the bulb, but no message emerged. He felt like an idiot. Old man in his dotage. The scribble could very well have come from someone other than Bella or Meer. Someone from his church?

For a while, he'd hidden a spare house key inside the plastic handle of a broom on the screened porch off his and Margie's bedroom. If the note had been from Bella, she would have looked there and might have jimmied the lock or hidden a second note on the porch. If not for the attacks, Hart wouldn't have been up for a thorough search. *Margie,* he thought to himself. *Where did you put Bella's number?*

Margie had a holiday greeting card list, which she'd updated each year on index cards, though they hadn't sent out cards that last December. *Thank you,* he thought, but didn't know where she kept it. Her desk? The bookcase in their bedroom? A box in the attic? Her leather book of telephone numbers was somewhere. He hadn't thrown it away. For a while, he'd memorized Bella's number, but, of course, that kept changing, and his memory was as fading as the cushions on the porch furniture.

His knee was much improved, but using the walker and transferring from wheelchair to bed, et cetera, had done something to his left shoulder, which ached from his shoulder blade to his elbow. He had been prescribed anti-inflammatory capsules before the surgery. They were in his bathroom, and that was where he found the second note, though it wasn't from Bella. It was from Meer, hand printed with instructions to call him from a burner phone, which fortunately was provided. Hart had never seen one before, though he'd read a novel in which the hero (unfailingly correct in distinguishing villains from innocents) bought such phones at convenience stores.

He swallowed a capsule for his shoulder pain and examined the phone. If it blew up, so be it. He dialed and walked to the window to look at the water, which changed as he waited. A blanket of gray clouds spread across the river, casting shade the color of slate onto the water. The color of grief, he thought. This 9/11 Pearl Harbor would shake the earth. The phone rang in some far place, and he thought of Muhammadu Meer, who resembled his father and had been twelve or so when he was stolen in Somalia and made to fight. Gone almost a year while Meer searched. In Hart's old age, he'd realized that the world of humans was as changeable as the sky and sea. As he watched, breeze stirred the slate. He heard but could not see a helicopter.

He waited through three more rings and was about to hang up when Meer answered, his greeting voice aged but firm and recognizable as the Meer whom Hart knew. The British and Egyptian and American English. The dignity. In a way, it was as if Meer, who was young, was much older than his years, and that was reflected in his voice. *Not "as if,"* Margie would say, *actually. He has aged. We all have.*

"Hart here."

"Where have you been? I am in your country."

Hart cleared his throat. "Needed some carpentry. I was in Arlington. Where are you?"

"I come tonight."

CHAPTER NINETEEN

Lucy
Cairo, Egypt, 1943

Ambassador Kirk, in his summer suit, with his aging square face, mustache groomed into separate right and left feathers, and eyebrows so elegant they must have been trimmed as well, posed like an actor. John Barrymore in *Grand Hotel*, she thought. He seemed particularly glad to see Kim and greeted Lucy and Margie kindly, if with slightly exaggerated graces. He showed them around his residence, a palace he'd rented, pointing out architectural features. Occasionally he made subtle quips about their "sheep's clothing," meaning the wool outfits they were wearing for the sake of the upcoming photo. He'd grown up in Wisconsin, she learned, had once met her mother at an event at the White House, and was acquainted with Margie's uncle. The ambassador's grandfather made the family fortune in the soap business, Kim confided later.

Ambassador Kirk inquired, with an excessively solicitous expression, about Kim's father, Kermit, as if he knew something they didn't. Kim, where the ambassador was showy, was quiet and serious, though he knew his way around Ivy League wordplay. Lucy, preoccupied with her upcoming pose as a refugee, heard him demur when the ambassador quipped that she and Margie would be more useful as blondes. She tried not to take it as an insult and kept her lips placid, though the photo seemed like a bad idea to her.

According to Ambassador Kirk, Cairo was securely in Allied hands, but the enemy still controlled Albania, Yugoslavia, and Crete. As Cairo was within easy reach of German planes taking off from Crete, anti-aircraft batteries remained on Gezira Island, relatively close to OSS headquarters in the *Ibn Zanki* building, which locals knew was occupied by Americans. No one was so naïve as to believe the Germans had no undercover ears left in the city.

The photo was to be outdoors beyond the colonnade in the garden near palm trees, under a trellis, and in the presence of workers who were suspected of passing on information. To Lucy's relief, there would be no speaking during the "ceremony," just the handing over of a certificate. There were no reporters, only some Egyptian servants and the photographer, an Englishman with a missing front tooth and tobacco-stained fingers. Lucy expected to see Wally, but at the last minute, he had been called to Camp Huckstep for preliminary parachute training. Still, they maintained the pretense, and she tried to convey courage. Any servant spying for the Germans was to get the impression she had escaped from Yugoslavia with reports on Nazi troop movements.

It must've seemed odd to the observers that neither she nor Margie spoke. The photographer assessed Lucy and her worn clothing with some sympathy as she pretended not to understand the English directions he gave. Kim took her by the shoulder and moved her and then Margie into place, meaning facing the sun in squints. In that moment, posing as someone else, she found herself wondering whether Wally's intense reaction to first seeing her was more than surprise that anyone in his family had survived. Had he been in love with his sister-in-law? If so, how potentially tormenting to encounter someone resembling her. What would it mean for the other person, in this case, herself? She briefly imagined herself spending her life with a man with such heavy losses.

CHAPTER TWENTY

Bella
Yugoslavia, 1943

Bella did not like to hear Abdullah and Nura quarrel, but from inside the kitchen wall, it was impossible to ignore them. Their voices were like the banging of nails and the tromping of soldiers. They were like the axe on the chopping block. She was hungry, and they were arguing about mushroom goulash. Nura wanted it for herself, and Abdullah wanted her to give it to Bella. It was not Bella's birthday. She did not think it was a Muslim holiday. The Behnams did not often speak of their religion, though she knew Abdullah had memorized parts of the Qur'an. They did not eat pork, and they did not gamble with dice, which Nura often said was forbidden in the Qur'an. Much of what they said, Bella could not hear or understand, for Nura lowered her voice to a murmur like a river over stones.

Bella pretended she was Tišina in the sunny yard with her sister Cluck pecking the ground for grubs and seeds or chasing a cricket through the grass. If the Partisans came, Nura would bring Tišina to hide in the wall, and Bella would hold the warm hen against her beating heart.

Abdullah called to Bella in his stern voice, and instead of coming for her through the basement, he removed shelves and bowls from the cupboard, slid away the wooden back, and told her to squeeze out. This she was able to do because of her small size. Nura was not in the kitchen, but steam rose from a wooden bowl filled with goulash.

"These mushrooms came from the woods," Abdullah told her, his eyes like gleaming black stones, his brows thick with black and white hairs, most laid flat like the hair on his temples. "You are the grandchild of my dear friend. Before you came to live with us, he told me that you, as a girl less than three years old, said that you wished to save others. Is that true?"

"Yes," she said. He waited as if he wanted to hear more. "I want to save others," she said. "But I do not know how except to be quiet so the Nazis do not find me."

"Little mouse," Abdulla said, "to save others is not so easy. The path is filled with many choices. Here is one for you. This bowl may be filled with nourishing delicious mushrooms, or it may be filled with poison."

"Which?" she asked.

"I do not know, but we are hungry. Your tradition tells that your people were delivered by God from starvation. Did you remember that?"

She'd sat through the whole megillah of Queen Esther's story, and she remembered the story of Passover and the story of David and Goliath, but she had been hiding a long time and did not know what Abdullah meant until he began to explain about the Israelites in the desert. God sent the Israelites manna from heaven, and they did not starve. Her mother had told her the same story, so Bella knew it was true.

As Abdullah spoke in his low rumbling voice with his eyes making her look at him, Bella felt her forehead tighten. She knew Nura had not wanted Abdullah to give her the mushrooms to eat because she feared they were poison.

"Do you want Nura to die?" he asked.

Bella shook her head no. She did not want anyone but the Nazis to die.

When she took her place at the table, her mouth watered

at the sight and aroma of the full bowl. She was used to going without food, but to have such a feast in front of her made her open her mouth and imagine spooning bite after bite. Her mother had said God would be with her. She filled the wooden spoon, tipped the contents to her lips, closed her eyes, and let her tongue explore the tastes. The broth was flavored with wild onions, greens, paprika, salt, and mushrooms as soft as chicken simmered all day. The spoonful entered her mouth with a gentle sip, soft as the finest noodles. Certainly, they were sent by God.

Abdullah's low voice came from behind her, his chant reminding her of her father and grandfather. She had heard him praying before but had never seen him on the floor, facing Mecca. She took another spoonful. The taste and warmth reached her stomach. It was better than an egg or a pastry, and for the first time since Abdullah had come for her, she felt safe and strong. This was manna from heaven, and God was with her. Abdullah prayed, and she ate, and when the golden light of the evening sun shone through the window, Bella rose from her seat. Abdullah paused and looked up.

"This is not poison," she said.

CHAPTER TWENTY-ONE

Lucy
Cairo, Egypt, 1943

Lucy didn't see a thing wrong with their quarters, but Margie had been shaking her head and mumbling to herself since they returned to the villa: modest in comparison to the ambassador's palace but more than adequate. White plaster walls. Four cots in the bedroom they would share. For the time being, they could each use a bed for sleeping and another for laying out clothes. An ornate chest of drawers stood against a wall. The bathroom had a claw-footed tub.

"For crying out loud," Margie muttered as she unpacked.

"Shh," Lucy whispered. "Meer or Mahmoud might hear you."

Margie gave her a sharp look. "Do you think they listen in?"

"Human nature is to listen in," Lucy answered, lips close to Margie's ear. On their way back from the photography session, Kim had told them they would be accompanying him to meet King Farouk and that neither of them would be going to Yugoslavia. "Are you unhappy our friend doesn't want you to go to"—she lowered her voice even further—"Yugoslavia?"

"I'm pouting because I have the curse, but the answer to your question is *yes*. If he's concerned about our safety, why did they give us L-pills?"

That didn't require an answer. The ceiling fan hummed

above them, stirring the hot air. Something long and thin disappeared behind the bureau. Lucy peered into the narrow space and was relieved to see a green lizard rather than a snake or large insect. "I'll ask about supper," she said.

A married couple already lived in the house. Counting Margie and Lucy, that made six for the time being. The two of them, plus the Nubians acting as servants, and the couple, Jill and Henry, whom they'd met on the way in. Jill's hair was the color of ripe wheat and shone with a platinum halo. According to Kim, King Farouk had the hots for her and hadn't seemed to get the message that she was married. She, with her pale freckles and unmade-up face, was relieved that other American women would be joining them. This, Lucy discovered, was the origin of the ambassador's quip that she and Margie would be more useful as blondes. Thankfully, more women would be coming later.

The adult Nubian, Mahmoud, was the cook. His English was quite good. Young Mahmoud Meer was chopping vegetables for a stew of lentils, spices, and vegetables, the older Mahmoud explained in English. Meer looked up, clearly understanding, and gave her a shy smile, possibly remembering the pastry she'd given him at the hotel. He became almost chatty when she accompanied him outside where he went to gather mint leaves and okra for cooking. Though he appeared no older than twelve, he told her that he was, in fact, fourteen years old, and this was his first job.

Since arriving, he had found out from his cousin that American men were living in a house nearby. Two of his brothers, who used to work for an Egyptian, had been hired by Americans after the Egyptian went away. Meer thought that his brothers might be working in the nearby house, and that made him happy.

When she asked him about the story of his ancestors riding elephants and driving away Alexander the Great, he lit up and retold the story with many gestures and allusions to place names she did not know. Cairo had always been invaded by Europeans, he said.

The windows to the kitchen were open, and while they were outside, the elder Mahmoud called out to let Meer know he was going to the market to get mutton for dinner.

"Does your mother live nearby?" Lucy asked.

Meer gave the tiniest head shake in the negative, and his large eyes welled up. He was a handsome boy with a graceful, long neck, and a small straight body, clothed in a white garment that made her think of a crucifer. "I have no mother," he said, "but I had the same father as my brothers."

She told him that her parents had both lost their mothers when they were small. "Do you have a stepmother?" she asked.

He held up two fingers.

She wanted to ask if he remembered his mother, but instead asked if he thought much about the time when he was small.

When he hesitated, she asked if the boys in Egypt played games with balls, and he told her that he and his brothers had played soccer among themselves and that he could play table tennis, though, as the youngest, he did not often win.

CHAPTER TWENTY-TWO

Hart
Egypt, 1943

Stars shone outside their immobile railroad coach, but passengers were beginning to stir, and faint light glowed above the horizon. The train had been at a standstill in the desert for the whole night. Although they'd shut the windows when it cooled, enough sand had blown in to sift inside their clothing and dust them with grit. Hart shut his eyes again and reentered a technicolor dream in which his father, who'd never served in the armed forces, was dressed as an Army Captain in charge of some military strategy involving risking soldiers on the train, either a sign of his Pa's courage or his downright selfishness. Someone near him was speaking: "What happened to the dang engine? That's what I want to know."

"They ran out of fuel," someone else answered.

Hart opened his eyes again. The sky was cloudless, star-studded, and ranged from midnight blue to violet and plum over the dunes where the coming sunrise glowed brighter moment by moment. He stood up, brushed himself off, and wiped his palms across his sandpapery stubble. Tim, next to him, did the same. Bernie, the MP he'd met waiting at the lavatory, yawned. "They had fuel enough to get out of here. They just aren't ready for us at Camp Huckstep."

"Either we get there, or we don't," Gordon said.

"They won't leave us here," Tim said. "I'm not setting out in this desert without water."

Hart tried to wet his finger in his mouth, so he could wipe the grit off his eyelids and lashes, but his tongue was parched. Even his teeth were coated with sand. He raised the window to look down the track where the locomotive had steamed away in the night. Blue shadows stretched across the desert, reminding him of something, a feeling of longing, something about his childhood and a tent revival. Odd. He wasn't all the way awake, but he shut his eyes and prayed.

The next time he looked out the window, the sun was glaring as a red half-disc above the hills. Something far away, no more than a dot on the tracks, caught his eye, and as he watched, a locomotive appeared with a straight line of smoke rising over the desert. He heard a low babble of Arabic, and a man called out in English. After a moment, the entire car cheered. People started moving about, brushing off sand. He walked to the front of the car and remained there until the engine coupled with the lead car.

Before long, they were bumping along slowly, and after several hours, they began to see palm trees and a canal and a stream of barefoot people and burdened donkeys, donkey carts, and camels. The men were dressed in white ankle-length *galibayas*, and all the women seemed to be wearing long black garments. Leaning out the window again, Hart caught his first distant view of Cairo through a haze of dust: a city of domes and minarets. As they traveled on, they came to modern buildings. Soon the train chuffed into the city, and the sand gave way to paved but dusty streets with automobiles. The clothing became more varied: uniforms, Western suits, and long patterned garments. Horse-drawn gharries clopped along, passing heavily burdened donkeys and occasional camels. He was reminded of the feeling from the tent revival again. It was as if some Biblical world had opened in his heart. Lessons from that firebrand preacher of his childhood were searing through his skin, but he couldn't remember any of what the man had said, just that the feeling from the crowd and the singing had seemed to lift all of them off their hard benches and folding chairs into something greater than themselves.

The train clattered into the railway station, which he learned from Bernie was called *Midan Ramses*. A sergeant with a bullhorn and several lieutenants greeted them on the platform, ordering the military passengers to fall out with their gear and board canvas-covered military trucks lined up in front of the station. The sooner they reached wherever they were going, the sooner they would be fed and watered, so the men jammed in quickly, and, in less than twenty minutes, they'd extracted and filled their canteens and were pulling away from the station in convoy. "Out *Malika Farida* to Heliopolis," Bernie told him. "Then on to Camp Huckstep."

"How do you know?" Hart asked.

It turned out Bernie had been sent to meet the *Nieuw Amsterdam* and deliver a diplomatic pouch, the contents of which he claimed to know nothing about. He told Hart that the camp was fifteen or so miles from Cairo, and Hart confessed that he'd been away from Africa for almost a year and had never visited Camp Huckstep.

"It hasn't been here that long," Bernie said. "The fellow it was named after worked in Ordnance."

But for the dust and sand as their convoy rolled toward their destination, Heliopolis was a modern-looking place. The streets were wide and lined with palm trees and four-story or taller buildings with balconies, most of them brown or tan, like sepia prints. Except for the occasional cultivated garden, a tram line beside the road, and irrigated fields between the outskirts of Cairo and Heliopolis, what struck Hart as they traveled was the sense that the desert was encroaching on the city. Fifteen miles would have made for a tough hike.

They did not break down on the way. There had been no reason not to gulp his whole canteen of water, and he swigged liberally when the convoy approached the barbed wire fence around Camp Huckstep and Payne Field, the adjacent airstrip.

The camp itself was not unlike other bases Hart knew. It was laid out in row after row of rectangular buildings. Military Police stood guard at the gate. When their truck passed through, Bernie told them he'd be reporting back to his own unit but would be at liberty for a few days. Hart pumped his hand and invited him to meet the next evening at the bar at Shepheard's Hotel. This was a last-minute idea. He'd heard of Shepheard's on the ship and hadn't let on to Bernie that his one and only previous trip to Africa had not included Egypt.

"You sure?" Bernie said.

"Yep," Hart said. "You can take the tram, right? Meet you there at seven."

A colonel mounted the reviewing stand wearing crisp suntans the color of the dusty parade ground, where Hart and his fellow travelers stood lined up four-deep with their duffel bags. "Welcome to Camp Russell B. Huckstep," he called out, his voice ringing with emotion as he pronounced the name, making Hart think Russell B. Huckstep, whoever that was, must've died, been the colonel's best friend, or both. "Stand in place until your name is called."

Gordon, Frank Braverman, Wally, and Tim Kelleher, alias *Patrick Packard*, stood waiting near Hart until, eventually, their names were called. A weather-beaten Private First Class with a Brooklyn accent, a Polish-sounding last name, and thinning sun-streaked brown hair greeted them with a welcome and leathery smile, calling them "yous" instead of you. He escorted them to a command car with a canvas top and, when they'd loaded back in, drove them back the same way they'd come. "Where are you taking us?" Hart asked from the back. Gordon sat in front with the driver.

"Heliopolis."

"That's where we just came from."

"There's the Army for yous."

"Have you been in long?" Gordon asked.

"Drafted in the First World War. Drafted again after Pearl Harbor."

"How old are you anyway?" Gordon asked.

"Forty-six."

Hart hadn't known they would draft people that old, but decided not to comment. They were still driving through desert.

Gordon had his eye on the tram beside the road. "I don't see any women on it. I wonder where Lucy and Margie and that Tom guy went."

Hart had been thinking the same thing, but they weren't alone. Not that their driver was a German spy. "Say, who's Russell B. Huckstep?" Hart asked to change the subject.

"Major Huckstep was a real nice guy. Worked in ordnance. Smart fella. Got the ordnance repair shop started. From Iowa."

"What happened to him?"

"Killed in a plane crash."

"I'm sorry to hear that," Hart said.

"That's war for yous."

"But it's winding down, right?" Gordon said.

"You wouldn't know it from all the wounded." The driver shook his head. "I'm just glad we kept Rommel and the Jerries out of here."

Why was it that leaving a new place always seemed to take less time than going? They were back in Heliopolis before four o'clock and soon turned off the wide main street onto a residential area of one-story houses with green lawns surrounded by masonry walls. They stopped at number eight *Sharia Thutmosis*.

"Here you go," the driver said. "Everybody out. Enlisted men's barracks for OSS."

"Where do the women stay?" Gordon asked.

"You mean WACs?"

"No, OSS women."

"Beats me," he said and promised to pick them up the following morning, a Friday, to take them to OSS headquarters. "The guys there'll know."

In comparison to their forty-seven days confined to the *Nieuw Amsterdam*, where they'd slept in stacks on canvas slings, waited in endless lines for grub, and showered outdoors in salt water, the quarters at 8 *Sharia Thutmosis* were unbelievably luxurious. The house where they would be staying had high ceilings, a living room, a dining room, a kitchen, six bedrooms, two bathrooms with tubs, and two Egyptian servants, brothers who both spoke English and who wore white *galibayas* with waistbands and leather sandals. The taller but younger man, named Ahmed, showed Gordon to a made-up cot with an actual mattress. Hart got the bed next to it. Each bedroom had four or five cots, but fewer than half were in use. While Gordon and Hart stowed their duffel bags, Wally, Frank, and Slap were shown to beds in another room.

All the men were filthy from travel and ravenous, not having eaten anything for sixteen hours. Hart took his turn washing up and soaped and rinsed his socks in the sink afterward and emerged to the smell of sausage and eggs. Mustapha and Ahmed brewed hot tea and laid out a platter with link sausages, ripe olives, and scrambled eggs. One by one, the men followed their noses, appeared at the table, and chowed down, all of them full of ideas about what to do next. Frank and Wally planned to walk the neighborhood. Gordon said he would try to make it to headquarters and ask where the women were staying; Hart, who'd already invited Bernie, proposed they all meet at Shepheard's Hotel to celebrate their arrival. He spread his map on the table and asked directions of Ahmed. How would one catch the tram? What was the fare? Where were the markets? How far was the Nile? Were there crocodiles? The questions seemed to amuse Ahmed, but he answered patiently and politely.

CHAPTER TWENTY-THREE

Bella
Yugoslavia, 1943

It always began with sounds from the forest: sometimes birds rising from trees or a kind of rumbling that made her picture bears and wolves from fairy tales, sometimes gunshots. Nura and Abdullah reacted with abruptness, snapping out orders. Sometimes Bella thought their faces showed hope that their son, Adem, would come running up the hill.

There was no way to tell who was coming, so they always made her hide until their visitors appeared over the crest of their wooded hill. One day Nura's lean face creased with an expression like when Abdullah had made the porridge of manna. She muttered to herself and cupped Bella's cheeks in her rough palms. "Sorry, little mouse," she whispered. "You must hide. I dreamed of Adem last night. If he's alone, I will let you out." Abdullah removed bowls from the cupboard so Bella could squeeze in, and then he carefully fitted the planks back in place and slid in the nested bowls.

Bella waited. She no longer pretended to be a mouse. Instead, she wished to grow into a strong woman who could shoot a gun. Where she hid was very dark. She sat on the floor. If someone opened the cupboard, a line of tiny gleams sparked through. Unless she took out one of the floor planks, nobody, not even someone who found the trap door to the cellar and climbed down the ladder, could see up into her hiding place.

She heard Nura run to catch and hide Tišina under the potato bin and heard Cluck call out her *bebukaclukluk* objection to being shut in the henhouse. Then she listened to silence so ringing and vast that her heartbeat became a drum. An engine roared, and she pictured a motorcycle and an automobile and a truck digging tire marks into the hillside. She wondered why Nura and Abdullah did not hide. Chetniks did not come in cars. Neighbors came in wagons or on foot. The Partisans did not come in cars. Only Nazis and Russians had gas.

Bella did not know the German language, but she heard the "Heil Hitler" and stern voices and Abdullah's patient answers. "*Ne*," he answered. Their daughter Esma died of a fever, and their son was killed in the war. Nura did not speak to disagree with his lie about Adem. One of the Germans spoke Serbian. He asked if they were Chetniks. "No," Abdullah answered. "I am a farmer." He offered soup. Much of what he and the Germans said, Bella did not hear. Abdullah used his nicest voice.

Loud footsteps crossed the kitchen floor and the bedroom floor. The cupboard opened. Bella heard the contents spill to the floor and saw a line of tiny sparks where the back of the cupboard met the bottom shelf. She heard the kitchen table move and pictured hands pulling the carpet away from the trapdoor, which opened with a bang.

"Why do you hide your cellar under your table?" a man hissed in the language of Yugoslavia, and she pictured a giant serpent. Other men spoke in the stern tone of giving orders. *Do this. Do that.* But she did not understand their language. Abdullah and Nura would be killed if she were found.

This time Nura answered. "In wartime, there are many thieves."

Bella heard feet on the ladder. Cascades of thuds. She stayed still as a hen, watching a line in the dust. She heard shouts and remembered the time she wet herself in hiding. She remembered when Nazis came and her father moved the mezuzah from high up against the front door frame to the place under the floor where he told her to hide until Abdullah came for her. She remembered the picture of the star of David and the letter *shin* and the picture of a castle. She remembered that there was a holy paper inside. She wondered if it was still in the house where her family had lived.

She pretended to be very far away, but she kept her eyes on gleams of light.

A deafening *rattattat* almost made her call out, but she shut her eyes while the sound rang in one long and high note that seemed never to end. *Do not move*, she thought. The sound was the sound of fever. Be still. *Mama*, she thought. A man laughed. Another barked orders. Boot steps stomped from the bedroom to kitchen to sitting room. The ringing went on and on. She did not hear Abdullah or Nura, but she knew not to whimper. She heard a car start. She heard a motorcycle. She could wait a long time.

Thirst woke her. That and pins-and-needles pain in her foot. There was no light at all, so she assumed someone had closed the cupboard while she slept. For a long, long time, she listened but heard nothing. Not the snore of Abdullah. Not the murmuring of Nura. Or even Cluck's *bebukaclukluk*. She changed positions as silently as she could. This had happened before, though she barely remembered. The thought of that faraway time of sleep and hiding and dreaming only of the sparkle of light under the arches of the stone bridge gave her a bad, bad, bad feeling, like the ringing in her head. She wanted to scream and scream and scream, but in that other time, Abdullah had taken her out from hiding and wrapped her in a tablecloth and loaded her into the wagon that had belonged to her grandfather. She had not spoken for weeks afterward.

She slept, and when she awoke, the sparks of light had returned. Some lined up from the cupboard, others like Abdullah's prayer rug, glowing whether her eyes were open or closed. Her thirst was more than she could bear. She thought of water, of swallows from her tin cup, of rain falling into her mouth. She heard no one. Not Abdullah or Nura. *Mama*, she thought. *Mamika*.

She supposed she would die in the wall, but the thought of Tišina trapped under the potatoes began to scream in her mind as if Tišina were calling her, both of them suffering from thirst that made them pray rain would fall from the roof and stream down the walls. She was both cold and hot, but knew better than to whimper or call *Mama* or kick the back of the cupboard. She wedged herself into one end of her hiding space and lifted the board that separated her from the cellar. She heard no sounds but the scrapes and bangs from opening her way to the cellar.

There was no one to catch her. She lowered her legs through the opening and supported herself with her arms. It was her thirst that made her drop to the floor with a sound so loud anyone in the house would have heard. She crawled into the shadows away from the square of light below the trapdoor, crouched, and listened. If she were a woodchuck, she would dig a new hiding place. If she were Abdullah, she would climb into the light and stride to the well for water, but the ladder had fallen away from the trapdoor, so she could not. If someone had heard her, they would come soon.

The floor was cold earth, black in the shadows, deep brown in the square of light. A shelf on the wall opposite her held glass jars of boiled and pickled vegetables. She crept with all the stealth she could muster, opened a jar, drank the salty tart liquid, and gobbled the wet contents. She heard nothing from above but thought of Abdullah and the woodchuck. Something made her want to stay underground forever, but she was still thirsty.

The ladder lay flat in shadows like railroad tracks leading nowhere. She dragged it under the trapdoor and tried to raise it but, even taking an end and stretching her arms as high as possible, could not make it reach. She lowered the ladder and thought about what to do next. The cellar was a single square room with only two ways out, both higher than her reach. If she were still inside the wall behind the cupboard, she could have pushed her way out, but she had trapped herself by jumping down.

She rested until she had the strength to take hold of a middle rung and lift it and walk her hands rung by rung, propping the rails on the wall and raising the ladder above her trembling arms until its rails banged firm in the opening. She listened and heard no one coming, but an odor worse than the outhouse met her when she stood, gathering her courage to climb out.

CHAPTER TWENTY-FOUR

Hart
Cairo, Egypt, 1943

Hart's plan was to arrive first at Shepheard's Hotel and reserve a table. Thanks to the sign in English over the hotel roof, he found the place quickly enough, a semi-ornate four-story building with palm trees and a broad restaurant terrace large enough to serve crowds. Men in uniform, mainly British, took up most of the space, but a few American Army Air Force officers in summer uniform and floppy garrison caps sat at a round table smoking cigars, their fumes blending with scents from the tables: garlic, mint, bread, lamb, whiskey, and spices. When a group of British officers vacated a table, large enough for him and his friends, he hurried to the *maître d'* but was confronted with an easel displaying a sign reading: *Officers Only, by order of the Commander, H.M. Forces.*

Hart was only a sergeant but reasoned that since he was not in His Majesty's Forces, he shouldn't fall under British command. Mustering bravado, he raised that point with the *maître d'*, who declined to debate. Shepheard's Hotel forbade American enlisted men as well as British non-coms. That was that. All he could do was search for another restaurant. As had been his practice on the ship, he walked along, listening in on random conversations.

As the sun set, oil lamps flickered on horse-drawn gharries, and glowing cigarette tips blinked on and off like fireflies. The streets thronged with local fellahin, and with military men, most in British battle dress. He heard English, Spanish, French, and Arabic, as well as snatches of languages he couldn't identify. When a male voice spoke in German behind him, he made a nonchalant turn without confirming the source, though it could have been one of the men accompanying a uniformed, heavyset rich-looking Egyptian with a waxed mustache who was approaching the hotel entrance.

Though males outnumbered females at least ten to one, he spotted several women in black robes hurrying past him in a small group like nuns, avoiding the soldiers and not speaking aloud. The few bare-legged young women in European garb wore skirts and blouses and were accompanied by men in civilian clothing. He glimpsed and quickly lost sight of a girl who, from behind, resembled Lucy, which made him think of Margie. Prior to his stint at Station S, he'd been offered a spot at Officer Candidate School, which he had turned down for fear it would cost him his chance to go behind enemy lines. He had no intention of changing course, but still hoped he might have a chance with her before he was deployed. He was about to make a second circuit around the hotel when someone called his name from the street, and Gordon, looking travel-worn but cheerful, jaywalked through the traffic, told him he thought he'd earlier glimpsed Lucy and Margie and launched into an unrelated story he'd heard on the tram from Heliopolis about New Zealanders beating up every American they ran into in Cairo. He hoped the others would be careful.

"They won't know Frank and Wally are Americans, so they're safe. I doubt they'd go after an MP like Bernie," Hart said. "What's their beef?"

"Our bombs," Gordon answered and passed on the story he'd heard from an Air Force private on the tram. The New Zealand Second Armored Division had driven through the desert to outflank the Mareth line in Southern Tunisia, and the American Air Force dropped bombs on them. "A mistake, but ..."

"Anyone killed?" Hart asked.

"I hope not."

"I wonder if it's true," he said. "That's the kind of rumor the Nazis would like to spread. Make us fight among ourselves."

Tim and Wally arrived together. Then Frank Braverman with his Eastern European accent. If Shepheard's hadn't been off-limits, they could have sat on the patio and watched for Bernie. Hart glanced at his watch. 7:10. He'd noticed other watering holes open to enlisted men, but had no way to reach Bernie. He scanned the crowded streets, half listening to Gordon, and decided to give him another ten minutes.

Gordon tapped Hart's shoulder. "Margie looked very serious."

Hart was about to ask for details when Bernie jumped out of a black car and rushed to join them.

"How'd you swing the wheels?"

"Hitched a ride with the brass. The colonel's going to meet some bigwig."

"Movie star?" Tim asked.

"Can't say, but look," he said, pointing with his chin at a group emerging from Shepheard's and settling at a large table on the terrace. "There's King Farouk." This was the same group Hart had seen earlier. The heavyset Egyptian with companions.

"Would he have a German with him?" Hart asked Bernie.

"Was she a blonde?"

"No," Hart said. "A man with brown hair."

Lucy

She concentrated on whatever landmarks she could see through the morning jam of honking vehicles, donkeys, and camels. Kim, in the driver's seat, remarked on sights as he, Lucy, and Margie headed toward OSS Headquarters; the Nile below Aguza

Bridge, though mud-brown, glittered with sun and the rolling wakes of boat traffic. The wooden sailboats were called *feluccas* and were lateen-rigged, meaning the triangular sails were at an angle to the mast, Kim told them.

"Over there by the shore, those are houseboats," he said, but Lucy couldn't see much from her spot in the back seat. Soon they were creeping with military and civilian traffic into a neighborhood of large, mostly fenced homes. "I'm going to try and rent something near King Farouk's houseboat," he added, then grew silent, concentrating on house numbers, horn-tooting drivers, and a man leading a donkey with a load on its back.

"Here we are," he finally announced. "*14 Sharia Ibn Zanki.* Did I tell you *Sharia* means street?" Yes, he had, several times, but she thanked him, meanwhile considering the advantages versus disadvantages of being supposed ignorant.

They pulled up to a gate guarded by MPs in uniform. Otherwise, the place might have passed for an ordinary residence: a three-story stucco home with a palm tree in front. The stars and stripes weren't flying, but to Lucy's eye, anyone would recognize it as an American enterprise. *Tom* spoke to one of the MPs, who waved them in and parked behind the building. "I'll walk you inside and see you in three days at the party for King Farouk. If the conference goes as planned and my cousin arrives"—he meant President Roosevelt—"I'll count on you to entertain the king and see what you can turn up. Your roommate, Jill, is getting fed up. In the meantime, noses to the grindstone." Gentleman that he was and still in civilian dress, Kim walked them up a half-flight of stairs to the main floor of the villa, which had a high ceiling and many door-sized windows. A desk inside was manned by a corporal in uniform, who inspected their orders: hers, Margie's, and Kim's. While Kim went upstairs to meet with Commander McBain, the corporal showed Lucy and Margie to the *demi-sous-sol* basement, which was cooler than the ground floor and furnished with desks and chairs.

A lieutenant named Jim Raymond greeted them enthusiastically. Apparently, message traffic had picked up, and his unit had fallen behind. He introduced an Italian woman with dark curved eyebrows and a smile like an entertainer. Lacking a high enough security clearance, Sofia stayed in the outer room, manning a teletype machine, which Jim explained linked to a radio broadcast station run by OSS in the desert not far from Camp Huckstep.

When Jim shepherded her and Margie into another room with more desks and chairs, Lucy's neck began to burn, and she spotted Hart McCann bent over a task involving a stripboard. As she looked away, she met eyes with *Buster*, his presence giving her a kind of lewd jolt. The feeling in her neck intensified. She waited for Jim Raymond to begin his introductions: Jill, the married blonde from the house where she and Margie were staying, was paraphrasing messages and looked up with a distracted smile. Hart McCann, with his familiar nose and kind expression, was next. He grinned, explaining to the lieutenant they knew one another already.

Next, they were introduced to the Hagelin mechanical coding machine, which was the size of a typewriter and surrounded by stacks of papers, as were all of the desks. Someone could have walked off with an armload of pages, and no one would have noticed for days. Jim introduced two more men and finally turned to *Buster*, whose probing eyes she'd felt on her back the whole time.

"This is Gordon Aldrich," Jim said.

CHAPTER TWENTY-FIVE

Bella
Yugoslavia, 1943

Bella gripped a rung, climbed two steps, and the ladder slid sideways and jammed into a corner of the trapdoor above her. She didn't dare call out. Bowls and cups lay on the floor, and the table had been turned on its side. She heard nothing but her own heart and breathing.

She saw no chickens out the window, no cars, no motorcycles, no wagons, or horses. The horse had been stolen long ago. Abdullah was not at the woodpile or spading the garden. The wooden bucket sat on the side of the well with its rope slack. Neither Tišina nor Cluck was in their coop.

She ran across the yard in a crouch and nearly swooned to the ground in a shower of stars when she reached the well. After she got her balance, she cranked down the bucket for water. She thought of rivers and snowmelt and the juice of pears. Her mouth was as dry as ash. She heard the bucket reach water and felt the weight of it in her arms and shoulders. *This I will remember*, she told herself. The lowering of a bucket into water. The bucket rose in turns of the wooden handle, groaning and squeaking, finally close enough for her to grab and swing to the side of the well. The tin cup was missing, so she dipped with her cupped palms and drank, wetting her dry throat with sweet, cool well-water.

When her thirst receded, she crept to the stone barn and listened for sounds inside and stood with the door ajar to listen for car engines or the calling of blackbirds. As before, all she heard was her own breath and heartbeat.

The trapdoor to the barn cellar was still hidden under a covering of burlap spread with straw. She gripped a corner and then a second corner and lifted it back. When she shoved away the trapdoor, a cloud of straw dust rose like the cough of a demon, stinging her eyes and throat. The ladder stood propped against the bottom rim of the opening, just the way it had been the last time she hid inside. Descending the ladder would be like entering a pit of horrors, but this was the place Abdullah would have hidden Nura.

With her feet on the ladder, Bella thought of her mother and of her father and of Abdullah and Nura. She thought of Adem, the Behnam's son, joining the Partisans. She wanted to be strong as a wolf.

When her feet hit the ground, she stepped away from the square of light and waited for her eyes to adjust. "Nura?" she whispered and heard something stir, but she saw nothing move.

CHAPTER TWENTY-SIX

Lucy
Cairo, Egypt, 1943

Lucy, preoccupied with the tension of curlers on her scalp and a green lizard near the junction of wall and ceiling, missed what Margie was saying.

"I had the same dream," Margie repeated.

Please don't turn superstitious on me, Lucy thought. Young Meer had already told her about a monster in the Nile called *Aman* something, *Aman Doger*? Sometimes she didn't catch his pronunciations. "What dream?"

Probably the creature was a crocodile, though Meer explained it as a bad spirit, a kind of devil. *Boogeyman*. Lucy unclamped and unwound the tightest rollers near the nape of her neck, her perm growing out. At least there was no humidity to wilt a hairdo. With the ceiling fan running in their bedroom in the villa, a wash and set could be done in an hour. "The same as what?"

"A child was hiding in a small room. Everyone in the house except the little girl was dead."

Like Margie's real situation, Lucy thought with a pang. Every Jew in Yugoslavia taken by the Nazis. Margie's parents dead, and her overseas family gone too. At Sweetbriar, Margie had clammed up or changed the subject each time parents came up in conversation, but if she was telling a dream, maybe she would share more. "Were you in the dream?" Lucy asked.

"I was trying to get to her, but couldn't find the way in."

"My Uncle Walton once told me dreams were like practice in solving problems. He was a small child in the Civil War. Sometimes he was hungry, but they had a milk cow and a garden and berry patches."

"Your uncle?"

She'd been about to explain Uncle Walton's dreams of foraging for food. "Great-uncle, my grandfather's brother," she said.

"That could make sense," Margie said. "I always worked math problems in my sleep. I think I did better in school when I slept the night before a test."

"Me too," Lucy said. "Uncle Walton met Freud but wasn't too impressed with the idea everything in the unconscious was about sex."

"That's not really what Freud said."

"I know," Lucy answered. "But if Uncle Walton ever read Freud, he never discussed it with me. And he never married. Did I tell you he was in love with Kim's mother?"

"Kim who?"

"Roosevelt. *Tom Murray*. Sorry, I should be more careful."

"No, I appreciate your confidences. Besides, that's not the kind of secret that would give Nazis an advantage." Margie attacked her dark natural curls with a brass-handled hairbrush, giving vigorous strokes that showed the muscles in her arms. "You are so lucky to have manageable hair," she said.

"Did your parents have hair like yours?" Lucy asked.

To her surprise, Margie answered: "Kinky? Yes. That's why my mother was so gentle. Everybody else yanked until I was in tears."

"When did she die?"

"When I was a senior in high school. Shortly before my father."

Lucy felt as if the air had been punched out of her. She

still had a head half-full of rollers and was unsure how much space Margie needed. She ventured a hug, but it was stiff and awkward. "Was that the year before we met?" she asked.

"Less than that. The last time I saw her, she was in an iron lung."

The rollers were metal and clinked into the stamped copper tray on the dresser top. If she were reading Margie correctly, more questions wouldn't be welcome.

Lucy disliked medical things. Gore and phlegm and talk of needles and iron lungs. Could her own avoidance have kept her from seeing what must've been right in front of her? That Margie had lost both parents less than a year before they roomed together?

The message center was bustling when they arrived. They got to work so quickly that Lucy scarcely noticed Gordon Aldrich nearby, though she briefly felt his eyes on her legs. *Tom Murray* was supposed to pick them up at ten and take Margie and her to the British Eighth Army parade, where they were supposed to listen in on conversations and scan for people who might be spying for the enemy. Then on to a party with King Farouk, sort of a warmup for the president's conference with Allied leaders. Margie was paraphrasing, and Lucy decoding a message that had arrived on the Hagelin, the latter activity seeming only like rote until words fell into place. She stood up immediately, glanced around—there was Gordon pretending not to notice—and went to Lieutenant Raymond. "I think this is important," she whispered. "The Germans have intelligence suggesting FDR was transferred onto the USS Iowa somewhere offshore in the Chesapeake Bay."

"I'll take it to Commander McBain." The lieutenant glanced at his wristwatch. "*Tom Murray* should be back shortly. This is in his bailiwick, isn't it? The MPs are working on security, but we've been getting a lot of chatter from the Germans. This could be something we provided to throw them off track. Just keep it up and let me know when you get more specifics."

So back to the grindstone, which no longer felt like a grindstone. There was a kind of relief in giving each message her full attention, no room left over for nonproductive worry. After several hours, Jim asked if she would like to switch to paraphrasing.

Their security protocol was that each message intercepted from the enemy would not be passed along until it was reworded. After it arrived at the next station, they would paraphrase it a second time. Occasional messages, like the one about the president's travel, concerned events in Cairo. Nazis knew about the upcoming British Eighth Army victory parade and that King Farouk would be in attendance. According to Jill Benson, the king was disgustingly plump. He knew she was married but insisted on dancing with her. "What are his good qualities?" Lucy had asked, and Jill apologized for not being more open-minded. "He likes to be called 'the pious king.' He practices his religion."

"Islam?"

"Yes."

"And he's not as fat as they say, but he makes my skin crawl."

When Jim Raymond tapped first Lucy and then Margie on the shoulder to let them know that their ride to the parade had arrived, sounds in the code room hushed in an eerie way that made Lucy feel observed. She'd barely registered the activities of her fellow coders, but the piles of paper had shrunk, and Gordon, Hart, and Wally had their heads down. She rushed to powder her nose (not literally; in the dry air, her nose did not shine), and they hurried to join Kim. After only tea and pastries for breakfast, they would miss lunch. She shouldn't have been surprised that he'd remembered to take their needs into account; he was married to Polly and was Belle's son. He'd brought a picnic brunch, which she could smell, something with garlic, no surprise since Cairo itself seemed scented with garlic and spices.

He'd received a letter from Polly and was brimming with pride at the photo she'd enclosed of his little sons, Kermit and Jonathan, whose sweet little faces she quite genuinely *oohed* over while they ate their picnic on the back steps at *14 Sharia Ibn Zanki*. He passed out grape leaves stuffed with savory rice and flat bread called *eish baladi* spread with mashed lentils and used a pocketknife to cut slices of local cheese called *rumi* because it was introduced by the Romans.

Another group of women coders for OSS would be flying in, but perhaps not for months, he said. Some of the American and British brass, Ambassador Kirk, and King Farouk knew his real last name, but she and Margie shouldn't admit to knowing it except if they needed it as a diversion to throw off anyone who thought the president was coming to Cairo. They should laugh at the idea that their friend had been mistaken for the president.

"Just claim Roosevelt is a common name in the States," Kim told them and segued into a monologue about Ambassador Kirk's views on Egypt. "He's convinced the Egyptians are done with colonialism. He thinks the British have underestimated the native force against it. He doesn't see a state of Israel succeeding either, not unless it's militarily forced on the natives. They've had enough of being dominated."

Margie's face stayed calm, but Lucy saw her hands clench. "Ambassador Kirk is wrong," Margie finally said. "A Jewish state has to prevail. If it takes military force, that's what must happen."

"The Nazis are spreading anti-Jewish propaganda in North Africa," Kim said. "Once that kind of pestilence gets out of the box, it's impossible to stamp out."

Margie raised her chin. "Nowhere in the world is free of anti-Semitism. Is it you or Ambassador Kirk who said what you just said?" She didn't wait for an answer. "You should never use the word 'pestilence' in a conversation about Judaism."

Kim, packing up their food scraps, swallowed visibly and ushered them to the car, where Lucy expected they would both get an earful, but perhaps he would speak to Margie alone.

Hart
Cairo, Egypt, 1943

Their lieutenant was a freckled guy with a boyish face, so enthusiastic about progress in the code room that Hart found himself getting a swelled head. Before long, the previously log-jammed messages were stacked and ready for the brass to draft replies. Hart, determined not to abandon hope about his prospects with Margie, went searching and found out she and Lucy had left for the Eighth Army victory parade. He was so disappointed he could barely sit still, but Jim, seeing his expression, told him and Gordon they'd earned the afternoon off.

If new messages arrived from Yugoslavia while they were away, the others could brief him when he returned. Any random scrap of information might be just what was needed to keep Gordon and him alive. The word was that *Ustaše* and Nazis were blaming their atrocities on Chetniks and Partisans, who already hated one another, ramping up tension between them and increasing the danger. The Catholics, Eastern Orthodox Christians, and Muslims weren't exactly singing in harmony either. Any romanticism Hart used to feel for the knights of the Round Table and the Crusades had bitten the dust when he was in college—no group was blameless—but the Nazis and the *Ustaše* had laid waste to entire villages. He hoped that something like his fate with Margie was delaying his deployment—the wait was excruciating—but he knew she'd been watching him. Not that she'd risen to more than occasional arguments and given him a few smiles, but if he could get her to go out with him before he got deployed, it would feel like a small victory. A fellow risking his life should, at least, have a picture of a girl.

The tram station was a quick walk from OSS headquarters, but the seats on the car were full. Hart and Gordon shoved their way on and rode standing, gripping the same pole as a barefoot *fellahin*, a farmer or some other sort of peasant, who reeked of garlic and sweat. When his stained *galibaya* brushed Hart's arm, something crawled up Hart's sleeve, and he drew back. In reaction, the *fellahin* gave him a look so penetrating and steady that Hart felt his prideful soul exposed. It was as if the man had seen him with eyes like the preacher from the tent revival in his boyhood. His own selfishness, a quality he hid more from himself than anyone else—he knew this—was so much a part of him that all he could do was try to wrestle it down, compensate, and do some good deed. He would rather be a Brit than one of the *fellahin*. Would he have been a Tory during the revolutionary war? No, definitely not, but the look in the eyes of the man on the crowded tram made him ashamed. He wondered how the Egyptian people felt about British troops marching down their streets. Someday the *fellahin* would be the revolutionaries ready to take up arms for freedom. He nodded at the man and tried not to turn away, though his attention was drawn by jaywalking pedestrians dodging cars near the Grand Hotel, where he and Gordon planned to get off and walk. Half the car emptied at the Grand Hotel stop, only to fill immediately while Hart and Gordon pushed out. So many people bumped them that Hart began to worry about pickpockets. They heard distant drumming over the traffic and set out down *Sharia Suleiman Pasha.*

Gordon led the way through the crowd and staked out a spot on the curb where they could see troops marching up *Sharia Qasr El Nil* from the English Barracks. Drummers drummed, bands played, and marched. Hart was hot and preoccupied with scanning the crowd for Margie and Lucy, whom he imagined in a viewing stand with *Tom Murray*. It was a beautiful day with blue sky and dry air. The troops stamping into view had seen real action, and he was grateful.

A division of Polish troops marched by in top-notch formation. They'd served under the British but kept their Polish uniforms. Soon he and Gordon heard bag pipes lilting and droning, giving him chills up his spine. There came the pipers, kilts and all, their ruddy cheeks puffed, making tears come to his eyes as if he were seeing his Highland ancestors, but someone jostled him, and again he thought of pickpockets. It was a boy, no two little boys, one on each side. Both had black hair and alert brown eyes and were pulling at him eagerly. The smaller one smiled. "Chocolate?" he said, pronouncing it in French. His two front teeth were missing, which bothered Hart until he saw the new teeth starting to grow in. Just an ordinary barefoot boy, but Hart kept his hand on his wallet. He had no chocolate with him. Both boys were lean and dirty, but neither looked starving.

"*Laa*," Hart said. "No."

The smaller boy patted his stomach and pantomimed eating. He was quite small, but Hart had been warned about beggars. Meanwhile, Gordon dug in his pocket and gave each boy a coin, making Hart feel like a jerk.

Over the next hour, units of Greeks, Palestinians, and Gurkhas from Nepal, paraded by and, finally, from New Zealand, the Second Armored division, looking so fit that Hart decided the rumor of Americans bombing them by mistake must've been false. The crowd thinned, and the viewing stands, which they could now see, emptied, but neither he nor Gordon caught sight of Margie, Lucy, or anyone else they knew.

"Maybe they're back in Gezira at headquarters," Gordon said. "I'm not giving up, but—" He stopped mid-sentence. "Can't talk about it here," he said and led the way back to *Sharia El Bulaq*, where they boarded the tram. Hart tried to yield his seat to an Egyptian woman, but a man took it, and she averted her eyes.

Frank, Wally, Jim Raymond, and Tim had eaten at headquarters while the others were away at the parade, and there were leftover dates and flatbread with mashed lentils to which Hart and Gordon helped themselves as they dove back into the piles of messages that had arrived while they were away. Margie and Lucy had not returned, and though Hart felt a pang of disappointment, he soon put his full attention into work.

The transmissions from Yugoslavia were filled with requests for supplies. The Partisan group, with their handful of American and British agents, had no backup radio and wanted a new transmitter and radio operator. The Germans had closed in around them several times in narrow escapes. Shortly after Hart decoded the message, which was in English from an OSS operative codenamed *Red Squirrel,* Jim Raymond asked who in the room was good at Morse code. Hart raised his hand and was beckoned into a quiet space to tap out a reply with a timetable for the next airdrops. "I've done parachute training twice.," he volunteered when the message was sent. His heart thudded unexpectedly.

"Noted," Jim answered. "But the Brits don't want us to send any more Americans in, so we're wrangling it out in trade for our supplies. Don't get your hopes up, but I'll put in a word. What languages do you speak?"

"English, Spanish, German, and a bit of Nakota Sioux."

"How good is your German?"

"Fair, and I can read French. I bet I could pick up on Serbian pretty quickly."

CHAPTER TWENTY-SEVEN

Bella
Yugoslavia, 1943

The darkness in the cellar under the barn lay below her as solid as the blade of a shovel, but as Bella descended and her eyes adjusted to the shadows, she could see that the silent lump in the corner was not Nura. She patted the dirt floor, raking the ground until her fingertips reached feathers, and she could scoop Tišina into her lap. Tears of relief came to her eyes, but the body was as hard and still as a turnip. *Don't be afraid*, she said with the silent voice in her mind. *I will take care of you.*

She crouched in the shadows, listening, smoothing Tišina's feathers, but the little body did not curve against her. It was as if Abdullah had carved a bird from wood and dressed it in soft plumage. She heard her own heart. *All I ask of you*, she whispered to the feathers in her arms, *is to stay alive*. She said it again in Ladino and looked up into the darkness, where the shape of the trapdoor glowed like an echo of the real light from the barn.

When she closed her eyes, she saw her mother's face shining, beautiful and kind, with a picture frame around it. *All I ask of you*, said her mother, *is to stay alive*. The face floated in the darkness and reached into her chest as if the life from her mother's heart had come into her own, which now beat with the force of an axe splitting wood.

Bella was unsure what to do. With her lips but not her voice, she said, *I will try*. She tied Tišina in her apron, climbed the ladder, laid her silent friend on the barn floor, and covered the trapdoor with straw. When she was done, she made a nest and tried to set Tišina on it, but the little hen was so stiff that she only lay on her side.

A terrible fear rose within Bella as she crept away from the stone barn. The dirt road curved from the forest as it always had, and the trees at the edge of the woods stood straight like soldiers. A cuckoo called faintly and reminded her of the clock in her grandfather's house. She thought of her mother's face and ran as quickly as she could past the woodpile to the potato frame. She ducked to her hands and knees and cleared away the thatch of weeds at the opening, which was nothing more than the woodchuck hole covered with boards and dirt.

Again, she thought she heard a sound, but it was only her own rustling as she crawled into the dugout. Abdullah had left a jug of water there, and she was able to sit up straight, but the underground room was empty. She drank stale water from the jug and sat hugging her knees, but if she were to stay alive and get help for Tišina, she would have to find Abdullah and Nura.

For a while, she lay on her side and slept but awoke shivering. Once more, she saw her mother's face and thought of what her mother had said. She would have to go into the house for a blanket. She would have to get Tišina from the barn to keep the Nazis or the Partisans from eating her.

She felt her way through the woodchuck hole to the outside, where stars shone like the glitter of snow. The moon was beginning to rise. She crept across the barnyard to the stone house and slipped inside, quiet as Tišina, and followed her nose to the shadowy bedroom, hoping for no more than an uncovered chamber pot. You need to *be* alive, she thought, but Abdullah lay face up on the floor, his mouth gaping as if he were screaming. Nura lay face down beside him. For the third time, Bella thought she heard a sound, faint mewing like the cry of a small animal.

"Who is there?" she whispered.

She heard a moan and saw Nura's hand move and then her shoulder, but she was afraid Nura was a ghost.

"Are you alive?" Bella asked.

"Shh," said Nura and pressed her hands to the ground and rose as if she were only bent over in the garden, each movement stiff because she had old bones and was not spry. She embraced Bella, and they wept silently, but Bella's chest rose and fell, and she could not stop from making the noise of a dying woodchuck or of a baby rabbit in the jaws of a fox.

CHAPTER TWENTY-EIGHT

Lucy
Cairo, Egypt, 1943

"Tennis would've been more fun." Lucy meant more fun than viewing the hours-long parade. As soon as the words were out of her mouth, she realized she should have kept mum. Soldiers had risked their lives and deserved acclaim for defeating Rommel.

Margie frowned, and *Tom Murray* raised his eyebrows. They were in his car, almost back to the villa.

"I take that back," she said. "The men were impressive, marching like that in the hot sun, but the stands were uncomfortable. It was good to see Americans represented." She meant the small unit of American MPs carrying the Stars and Stripes. Still, she would have preferred staying at the villa and visiting in the kitchen with Mahmoud Meer.

"That's the spirit, Lucy," *Tom* said, making her more determined to live up to his expectations. "I'm sure you and Margie will dazzle King Farouk tonight."

She didn't think she would dazzle anyone and was reminded of President Roosevelt's visit to Uncle Walton and Aunt Edith's house when Simon, the family cook, had allowed her to pass cookies and the president had flattered her. His visit to Cairo for negotiations with Churchill, and Chiang Kai-shek, if it were to happen at all, was months off, and might take place at Ambassador Kirk's second residence near the pyramids, a secret she would not have known, except she and Margie had been helping Kim brainstorm about things the president might want: A spare wheelchair, a large tub, soft towels, fruitcake, martinis, Camels cigarettes, and blueberry syrup.

"What should we wear tonight?" Margie asked. The party for King Farouk would be at Ambassador Kirk's home in the city, the place they'd visited earlier. Margie, Lucy, and Jill would be expected to socialize with the king and keep their eyes open for anything suspicious. That was all, but Lucy couldn't help thinking about her conversation with Margie on the train to Chicago. Surely the war didn't rest on some false romance with King Farouk. He was married, as was Jill. And what would be the point? As far as she knew, he had no Nazi secrets. Perhaps she could have approached the event in a better spirit, but Jill's complaints had stirred up a kind of revulsion that reminded Lucy of a situation when she was twelve, almost thirteen, and attending junior cotillion. All the girls had decided that they were disgusted by a stocky boy named Douglas. As far as Lucy could tell, there was nothing wrong with Douglas, except he wanted a girl to practice the foxtrot with him. Word of his flirtation had spread with the result that most of the eighth-grade girls had spurned him. One evening she'd sat on the sidelines, ashamed of being a wallflower, and he had stood in front of her and asked for a dance. His face had been all at once sad, tender, and hopeful. What had the others seen wrong in him? She'd accepted his offer and box-stepped around the cleared-out auditorium, discovering him to be both polite and kind. Jill's disgust at King Farouk did not have to mean he was a person of no value.

Lucy missed Tom's answer to Margie about what they should wear. She would ask later, though it seemed obvious she should wear the best dress she had packed. He went on, explaining that other OSS people would be present, including Hart McCann and Gordon Aldrich. "Be kind to them tonight," he said.

Lucy poured herself a half glass of room-temperature tea with mint from a ceramic pitcher on the kitchen table. "Meer, have you met King Farouk?"

After much rattling of cubes into a bowl, Meer plunked several into her glass and poured the rest into the pitcher. "No, ma'am, but my older brother worked in the house of one of his friends."

"What do they think of him?"

Meer busied himself with wiping around the sink. "He's a king."

"But what does he want? I mean, for Egypt."

"I think I cannot say."

"Then I shouldn't ask, should I? I was just thinking about my country and the American revolution, when we overthrew the British. They were our relatives, but we didn't appreciate being taxed and governed from afar."

Meer gave her a keen look, analyzing, but didn't elaborate on his answer. He had a sweet face, usually very innocent and sincere, though he was obviously questioning something, and it made him look older.

"Your king wouldn't hurt me, would he?"

"Oh no," Meer said. "He's devout in his faith."

"Islam?"

"Yes, of course."

"Are you Muslim, too?" She'd wondered if he were Coptic Christian. There was a church nearby that she hoped to visit.

Meer agreed that he was Muslim and, with great care and respect, explained to her the Five Pillars of Islam: There is no God but Allah, the same one God worshipped by Christians and Jews. Muslims were to pray five times a day. During the month of Ramadan, they must not eat or drink while the sun is up. Each year they must give to those in need. The fifth pillar was a pilgrimage to Mecca, which he had not yet made. "The King adheres to the Five Pillars," Meer said with an earnest expression.

"And when is Ramadan?" Lucy asked.

"This year, September." Meer explained that, all month long, King Farouk and all of the faithful would forgo food and drink while the sun was up, but they would have a hearty meal after sundown. Meer seemed to enjoy teaching her. He was going on enthusiastically when Margie peeked to signal the tub was available. Time to dress for the party.

When Margie and Lucy emerged in their party clothes, Kim showed them a letter to his wife, Polly, with a camel stamp he hoped would please his little sons. As a member of the Armed Services, he was eligible for free postage, but stamps worked in the service of his cover as a civilian businessman, and he was cheerful about the purchase. He complimented both Margie and Lucy on their outfits, black dresses with swingy skirts. Margie had found an ivory-colored shawl with black embroidery, which looked quite becoming, though neither of them had brought jewelry other than barrettes for pinning up their hair. Kim seemed interested in playing Cupid and told them that they should pay special attention to Hart and Gordon.

"Why is that?" Margie asked once they were in the car and underway.

"They won't be around much longer."

That sounded ominous to Lucy. "Are you allowed to tell us why?"

"Maybe it's that I miss Polly so much. When you're fond of someone and going into danger, it's helpful to have them know. It gives a fellow something to hold onto."

She and Margie exchanged glances.

"Who's going into danger?" Lucy asked.

"Our people in Yugoslavia been asking for radios and backup operators; Hart'll be parachuting in with the Partisans."

She saw Margie wince.

"What about Gordon?" Lucy asked.

"If the British don't block us, he'll drop in with the Chetniks." He gave Lucy a piercing look. "The Brits have pretty much given up on General Mihailović, but our people say he's brave and loyal to King Peter, though we have reports of collaboration between Chetniks and Italians and Nazis. Your fellow Gordon may have to go over on a fishing boat if the Brits keep putting us off."

She and Margie exchanged glances. *He's not my fellow*, she was about to say, but Margie's expression and then a thought of Douglas from grade school stopped her.

"There he is," Jill Benson said. She was wearing a pale blue silk dress draped at the neck and looked to Lucy like a movie star of the innocent ingénue type. "Henry, don't leave me alone with him."

"We have to greet him at some point," her husband answered. "Would you like a drink first?"

"Water, please," she said.

Lucy put on her best smile and took water for herself, too, trying to ignore whatever was going on with the Bensons. King Farouk, though heavy for a young man, wasn't nearly as fat as described by Jill and Henry. He wore his tarbush, the red felt hat that Egyptian men wore even indoors. His belted military uniform looked like wool, too hot for the clime. Perspiration had beaded on his forehead.

Tom guided her with his hand briefly on the small of her back. "I think," he said, "you should stick close to Hart and Gordon. I'll introduce you to King Farouk in a moment."

Hart and Gordon had arrived together, both of them with a sort of expectant expression, searching the crowd, Gordon so dashing and radiant that everyone must have noticed his entrance. Ordinarily, she avoided looking at him, but she could barely imagine the depth of regret and sorrow she would feel for avoiding him if he were to be killed on his mission. Even the thought made her ashamed.

She made herself focus on his face. Though she was not ordinarily a woman who blushed, her skin heated up as she strode toward him while Margie, at her side, walked straight toward Hart.

"Hello, Lucy," Gordon raised his arched eyebrows so hopefully that she felt like holding her palm over her heart and had the silly thought it would be like saying the "Pledge of Allegiance." She smiled.

"I'm so happy to see you," he said. "Is there a chance you'll dance with me this evening?"

"You're a poet," she said, grinning. Chance and dance.

He seemed not to realize he'd rhymed and looked befuddled. "Is that a *yes*?"

"Yes, but I think we're supposed to greet King Farouk," she said. "Would you stay with me while we go through the receiving line?"

King Farouk glanced at her face. "Do I know your father?" "I don't believe so, your highness, but you might have met my great uncle, Walton Moore, when he was Assistant Secretary of State. My father didn't have the honor of meeting you. He died when I was a schoolgirl." She gave her best smile, but when the king noticed Jill, he turned away in pursuit. At a loss about how to intervene, Lucy let Gordon guide her away.

Tom had mentioned that King George of Greece would be at the party. Except for Farouk, all the Kings living in Cairo were in exile, thus not reigning kings: King Peter of Yugoslavia, King George of Greece, King Zog of Albania, and King Victor Immanuel of Italy. Only King Farouk and King George, who lived in a villa behind OSS headquarters, were in evidence at the party.

"We could go meet King George," Gordon said with a questioning expression that she read to mean that he didn't want to but would if she chose. He seemed to her quite vulnerable, though perhaps it was only that she knew he would soon be risking his life.

"I don't think anyone would mind if we got to know one another better," she said. "It's about time I heard your life story."

"It's only just starting," he said.

"I won't use your past against you, *Buster*," she said and immediately began to worry she'd touched a nerve.

He guided her into a corner, his hand lingering on the small of her back. "My mother was a librarian," he said, "and my father was a fisherman."

For some reason, that made her happy, though she wondered if he'd made it up. "Did your father take you fishing?"

"Of course." He gave a little wince that made her ask if his parents were living. He said they weren't, and that he was already aware that she'd lost her father when she was fifteen. When he was the same age, his father's boat with two others aboard had gone missing in a storm and never was found. With more questions, Lucy found out his mother had died of the influenza during his sophomore year at Harvard. Since Station S, Gordon, like his friend Hart, had considered Cairo a waystation to service behind enemy lines. "Lucy," he said. "I have to apologize."

"For what? Knocking over my construction project?"

"That was *Kippy*." *Buster* grinned, giving her tingles. "I apologize for hitting you."

"You didn't hit that hard."

"But your face?" He grazed her cheekbone with the light touch of one finger.

"Your slap wasn't hard. I banged my cheek on the window when I climbed out."

"You looked awful."

"That doesn't do much for a girl's ego," she said, and he apologized and led her onto the patio, where they could hear music: Glen Miller's "Stompin' at the Savoy" from a phonograph or radio.

They passed two other couples and then Margie and Hart sitting side-by-side on a garden bench, bent toward one another in intense conversation. Margie glanced up and then back at Hart, as if trying to convince him of something. Lucy hoped she wasn't trying to get him to take her with him to Yugoslavia, but the rhythm and Gordon's palm pressing her waist took back all of her attention. The memory of his touch burned her cheek.

He stepped back and held out his arms. "Dance?"

CHAPTER TWENTY-NINE

Bella
Yugoslavia, 1943

Bella lugged the bucket of water to where Nura sat with her wounded leg outstretched on the kitchen bench, her face like thunderclouds waiting to send lightning and rain. Neither of them had said Abdullah's name. Every time Bella tried to speak, her throat squeezed shut. No one had brought in the washrags and apron and sheets they'd boiled and hung to dry the day before. Daylight had arrived, but no blackbirds had spoken.

Bella brought in laundry and dipped a bowl of water for Nura to drink, and turned away to find the bar of lye soap in its carved wooden dish. She did not want to see rain slipping from Nura's eyes. Her own hands dunked a rag in the bucket. Though she could feel the cool water and the slippery foaming soap as she dabbed the red gash where a bullet had grazed Nura's leg, it was the ghost of her mother who moved her hand. She heard the slosh of water, her own breathing, and Nura's breathing. The water in the bucket grew pink and crimson. Without Nura asking, Bella wrapped a cloth apron around Nura's leg and tied it with the apron strings.

Nura set her lips. "Pour out the water and bring more."

When Bella returned with a full bucket, Nura was not in the kitchen. Water sloshed over the sides. Bella did not want to go back into the bedroom, but the ghost of her mother was with her, and she set down the bucket and straightened the kitchen.

"Bring the water and the linens," Nura called, and that is what Bella did, and she became her mother and helped Nura strip and remake the bed. They lifted Abdullah onto a hammock of sheets and hefted him onto the bed, where they removed his clothes and covered his nakedness with cloths. Nura showed Bella how to help squeeze his body to empty the fluids, how to place towels, and help with each step. Lift his arm. Push here on his chest. Kneel on him here below his ribs. Bella became a phantom watching her mother and Nura wash Abdullah's skin with soapy water and pat him dry and wrap him in sheets, and all the while, Bella prayed her mother would stay with her.

"We have to leave," Nura said, and they spent the rest of the day getting ready. Bella carried the remaining jars of food up the ladder from the kitchen cellar. They replaced the trapdoor and laid the carpet over it, and lifted the table back into place. They boiled water on the stove and prepared balls of grain, some of which they ate with pickled beets. They toasted the rest in their oven and wrapped the remaining jars of cooked cabbage and the *zganci* in napkins.

"Where are we going?"

"To find Adem."

They dressed in their warmest clothes and slung their provisions over their shoulders, but when they went outside, Bella heard a spirit calling her. It was late afternoon but shadowy in the barn. Though Tišina's skinny body had stiffened, her feathers were soft as a breeze or as the breath of a ghost, and Bella knew that Abdullah and Tišina needed one another.

Nura followed Bella back to the house and, without a word between them, pulled back the sheet around Abdullah so Bella could tuck Tišina beside him. Bella kissed both Tišina and Abdullah, but Nura kissed only Abdullah and leaned on a stick, limping and grunting as they left the stone house.

They made their way down a path that Bella had not known. It led to a small stream where they dipped in their tin cups and drank. It did not seem likely to Bella that they would find Adem. If he were close, he would have come sooner. They had not seen him in a long time, but Nura whispered his name, and Bella wondered if Adem would come to Nura the way her mother came to her.

With every step, Bella called silently to her mother, but the face beside her belonged to Nura. It was old and weathered with lines and texture like the surface of the water over stones and the streambank of bent roots. Sunspots danced on the water and on the floor of the forest. They climbed a small hill and rested beside a flat rock with a face like a giant sleeping wolf.

Nura led the way, and Bella followed, silent as Tišina. As they walked, the woods grew darker. At times, they stopped and listened and heard rustling and sometimes the voices of birds, but the blackbirds were silent, and they did not hear voices or motors or anything that sounded like Partisans or Chetniks or wolves or Nazis.

"Stop here," Nura said and held Bella's shoulders and turned her so she faced a gap in the trees. "If you see anyone, hiss through your little teeth as if you are steam from the spout of a pot."

Bella stood as she was told and watched a pink glow spread across the sky and onto a small meadow. The treetops were half-lit with gold, their trunks silhouettes of branches and evergreen shadows. It was so beautiful it stopped her breath.

"We will see if he's been here." Nura bent over a pile of sticks beside a large rock on the hillside. When she raised a bare branch, Bella saw that it was attached to other branches that moved with it. "Help me, Little Mouse."

Do not call me little mouse, Bella thought to herself, but she took hold of the other side, and they tilted the interlocking sticks to one side, revealing a mound of leaves and, beneath it, short planks like at the entrance to the hiding place under the potato frame. Without a word, Bella removed enough boards to see the darkness of a dugout cave.

"Adem?" Nura called, but no one answered. She sat on the big rock, stretched out her injured leg, and began rubbing it.

The cave was dark and smelled like mushrooms, damp earth, and the sweat of men. Nura sniffed loudly, handed Bella her stick, and told her to poke it inside, which Bella did. She wondered if Abdullah had dug the cave, but she did not want to say his name. As Nura directed, she crawled inside. She tapped the underground stone walls and the roof of boards until she knew the shape, which was smaller than the space under the potato frame and larger than her space behind the kitchen cupboard. Adem was not inside, but the walking stick tapped rocks on two walls and something hollow that made the sound of wood. Without Nura asking, Bella crawled to the hollow thing, a box, and carried it to Nura, who opened it and placed her handkerchief inside. "You will wait here," Nura said. "I am going to the village."

Bella handed Nura back her walking stick, but she did not ask when she would be back. Perhaps she would never come back.

CHAPTER THIRTY

Lucy
Egypt, 1943

"King Farouk again. I'm exhausted." Jill wore a funny expression as if swallowing a secret, but then Lucy had secrets to keep too. They all did.

"I can hardly keep my eyes open," Jill added pointedly. Her husband had given Lucy and Margie a ride back from headquarters while Jill snoozed beside him like a sleepy child. Now she'd changed into an ivory evening gown and carried two other gowns into Lucy and Margie's bedroom for them to borrow.

"Did you get enough sleep last night?"

"I seem to need twice my normal amount of sleep." She patted her nearly flat stomach, pressed her back against the wall, and glanced at Lucy with those sea-blue eyes of hers sparking.

Was she pregnant? Lucy raised her eyebrows, ready to receive an announcement, but Jill launched into her favorite subject, complaints about King Farouk, who'd cut in at the last party while she was dancing with Jim. Farouk's hands sweat, he reeked of garlic, and he kept running his fingers like a spider on her back. "He mentioned you."

"What did he say?"

"He had the idea you were an Egyptian British girl with

an Egyptian father and English mother, but when you told him about your father, he thought it might be the other way 'round, Arab mother, American father."

It was her nose. Lucy knew it, the Roman nose like Uncle Walton's. She had the biggest nose in her family. Though her close friends told her she looked elegant, she doubted she had the élan to turn a Roman nose into an asset.

She supposed the fact that nobody had disabused Farouk of the notion of her Arab ancestry offered her some sort of opening, but she was sure she didn't appeal to him. Gordon had boosted her confidence, though. He'd taken her dancing twice that week and told her she was beautiful, which somehow enhanced even her reflection, though his looks compared to hers were as Franklin Roosevelt's to Eleanor's.

Hart

Gordon and Lucy made a nice couple, he thought, both with striking looks and both analytic thinkers, Lucy slender and graceful with a long neck, good jaw, and well-proportioned aristocratic face. Thus far, she'd shown the kind of patience and restraint that Hart believed ideal for an OSS girl. She would survive Gordon's mission, whatever the outcome.

He and Margie didn't make such a bad couple either, but he was concerned with how she would cope while he was away. She was beautiful, brave, and smart, except when carried away. Apparently, she'd befriended a girl from a nearby villa occupied by Jewish women from Palestine, some of whom had parachuted into Yugoslavia and brought out Jews. If they could do it, Margie argued, she could. She'd threatened to resign from OSS and emigrate to *Eretz* Israel, the land of Israel in Palestine. She didn't speak Serbo-Croatian, her Spanish was worse than his—though she didn't know it—and any Jews left in Yugoslavia would be few and far between.

The idea she would succeed in throwing herself into danger left him so stirred up that he'd let her goad him into an argument without ever telling her he loved her. Admittedly, her unpredictability was part of what made her so tantalizing, that or her sweet Southern accent and the fact that she and Lucy were hobnobbing with royalty, which should have made him feel like a cheap social climber, but he was curious and didn't see why royalty would be better than anyone else.

He'd been invited to a bash the British were giving at the Gezira Club in unofficial honor of King George of Greece, and possibly that would be his last chance to get closer to Margie. Although he once glimpsed the King's brother Prince Paul getting into a car with his wife, Princess Frederica, and King George had been at the party for Farouk, Hart hadn't yet spoken to any of them. The princess, he'd found out, was descended from Queen Victoria and Kaiser Wilhelm II and was a native German speaker. The point of his own invitation, Hart supposed, was an unofficial sendoff by *Tom Murray*, who had known that he was in love with Margie and that Gordon was pursuing Lucy. *Tom* expressed hope Hart could talk some sense into Margie, or at least distract her. "Take her dancing again," *Tom* whispered in Hart's ear the week before. "The last time you took her out, she glowed for days."

Hart

"Lucy and I have been asked to play doubles with Princess Frederica and her coach," Margie said when Hart caught up with her by the tennis courts. She was dressed in a sleeveless ankle-length pale-blue gown offering a tempting view of the tops of her breasts.

"Tennis in high heels?" Hart asked.

"Of course not," she answered quite earnestly, her skin so pale and smooth he imagined stroking her décolletage right there in the open. Close up and in the evening sun, he could see fine, colorless hairs glowing on her cheeks and a snag in the fabric over her left shoulder as if she'd once worn a broach there.

He offered his arm in imitation of the other gentlemen, and she took it, walking into the party with him. He hoped she'd taken his earlier input to heart and would lay off her efforts to work behind enemy lines. "You look like a princess yourself," he said. "I'm the luckiest guy here."

"Jill lent me the dress," Margie said.

"Blue suits you."

"Thank you."

"You'll be playing tennis with royalty while I'm away."

She frowned. "Let's trade places."

"You're needed here," he said.

"I know what you think."

"Do you know what I feel?" he asked.

"I think danger has a feeling, don't you? It makes everything intense."

He took a deep breath. *Now or possibly never.* "I was referring to loving you."

She blushed and turned to him. "What did you say?"

"I love you."

She looked shocked, her eyes flashing something he couldn't read. His heart stopped in his chest. Never before had he declared his love to anyone but his mother, sister, and a college girlfriend. The girlfriend had dumped him. Whatever Margie said next could come out of pity or jealousy, but he might not live much longer. She looked up at him, her hazel eyes searching his face. "Let's go back outside," she said.

He held out his arm again, hoping she would take it, but she walked ahead of him, back to the French doors, past a group of British officers at a punch bowl, and outside with him following. Lifting the skirt of her gown high enough to show her impossibly tempting calves and ankles, she led him onto a patio past a stone planter containing some variety of small palm with a crumpled cigarette pack wedged in the leaves. There, she stopped and faced him. “Some people say that to get a girl into bed.”

He tried to read her face but couldn’t, and the last thing he wanted was to be pushed away, so he stood silently, as if before a firing squad.

“Well?” she said. “I’m not loose, you know.”

He held out his arms. “May I?” He felt his chest constrict around his words, but she stepped into his embrace, and he felt her breasts press his chest, her arms encircling his neck. “I love you,” he said.

She stepped back and looked up at him expectantly. He waited for her to say something, anything, but she closed her eyes with their long lashes. He kissed her gently and then with more force, expecting her to pull back, but her lips were soft and pliant, and she kissed back and hugged him tightly.

“Have you been avoiding me?” he asked. Almost every time he’d approached her at work, she’d hurried off somewhere with *Tom Murray*.

“No,” she said with the tip of her tongue pointing through her teeth. “Kiss me.”

“For a while, I was afraid you had something going on with *Tom*,” he said.

“He’s married.”

Hart knew she wasn’t going to say she loved him, but some small voice inside him told him not to hesitate. He might not even be alive in a week. “Will you marry me?” he asked.

“I suppose you should ask my uncle,” she said. “My parents aren’t living.”

He didn’t know what she meant. Was she putting him off?

CHAPTER THIRTY-ONE

Lucy
Cairo, 1943

Lucy, already in her nightgown, looked up from a letter she was writing to her mother. "You look like the cat who gulped the goldfish. Did you have a good time with Hart?"

Margie raised her palms to her cheeks. "He proposed."

Jealousy was a terrible emotion, but there it was. Lucy had imagined waiting until they were both in bed and confiding that Gordon seemed attracted to her and she regretted having shunned him for so long. Now, no time was left, and nothing would happen between them. She would be a childless old maid while Hart and Margie planned a life together. "What did you say?"

"I told him he'd have to ask my uncle for my hand."

"Best wishes, my friend," Lucy managed. "He's a lucky man. I'm happy for you both."

Margie beamed.

"I want to know. Tell me exactly what you told him."

"He knew I was saying *yes*."

"Because you said *yes*?"

"Not exactly."

"Do you want to marry him, or were you putting him off?"

"Of course I want to marry him," Margie said.

"And you didn't tell him *yes* straight out?"

"He's not stupid, Lucy."

"No, he's not, but he's putting his life on the line. If he's distracted by trying to figure you out, he's more likely to make an error."

The anxiety radiating from Margie became a stone in Lucy's throat.

"Now I won't be able to sleep," Margie said. "It's too late to go over there."

"Meer's brother works at the men's quarters, but he's probably asleep," Lucy was thinking aloud, often a bad idea. "We could ring him up." Maybe Gordon would answer. She hugged herself, trying to console herself with the memory of his arms.

Hart

Hart had hit his cot like a flat stone, skipping across sleep's surface until he finally plunked underwater, if that was where deep sleep sent a man. Bernie shook him awake from a dream in which Margie rode a camel, and he was trying to get her attention. It took Hart a moment to register that he was at *8 Sharia Thutmosis* and remember that Bernie had transferred to OSS from the MPs. "Someone's on the phone for you."

"Is the Halifax ready?" He meant the long-range bomber meant to carry him to the drop site in Slovenia, close to Germany and Italy.

"It's a woman asking for you."

He forced himself awake and felt his way past Bernie to the phone in the living room, wishing for the first time he could have a few more weeks in Cairo to convince Margie to marry him. He half wondered if he were crazy, but he didn't care. He was crazy about her and also half asleep and happy after an evening of kissing behind the potted palm. He wouldn't be able to choose the time when he'd leave. "*Meem?*" he said, meaning *who?* and not wanting to give himself away quite yet.

Let the caller think he was the houseboy.

"Margie," she said and explained she wanted to tell him something.

He cleared his throat, but she didn't wait.

"My answer is yes."

In one breath, he was wide awake, heart in full stampede. "You'll marry me?"

"Yes," she said.

"I thought you were putting me off."

"No," she said. "But I really do want you to write to my uncle."

"And if he says no?"

"Hart," she said. "I'll still say yes."

Lucy

While Lucy's father was ill, her mother had played solitaire beside his bed to stay calm. For Lucy, decoding messages with the strip board occupied her mind well enough to accomplish the same. It was only when they stopped for lunch and Margie excused herself that Lucy's inappropriate jealousy surfaced. Even then, she suppressed it because Margie and Hart had become dear to her. Day by day, under the tension of Hart's pending mission and Gordon's training, the idea of her friends as a couple became more pleasing. Twice, Hart disappeared without notice, troubling Margie, only to appear again when his parachute drop was aborted.

Somehow Lucy's unease around Gordon became an intense crush—maybe absence made her heart grow fonder. He'd been sent for training jumps, and she hadn't seen him for days. She had trouble deciding if her missing him was less legitimate than Margie missing Hart. She supposed it was, though since the party for King Farouk, Gordon had been attentive. That was the way of soldiers and no guarantee her feelings would be requited. At the party at the Gezira Club, she'd realized part of what was troubling her. Gordon had gotten under her skin as *Buster*, but she hadn't realized her distaste for him was so close to attraction. Now that she'd accepted the hold he had over her, it seemed as if she would lose him to the war or to another woman. The latter being preferable because she couldn't allow herself any negative wishes toward Gordon. Or Hart.

Headquarters in Cairo had replacements in the works for both men—replacements, not substitutes—which signified they might not come back. Bernie was an MP. Hart had met him on the train, thought he had potential for OSS, and arranged for his transfer to their signal intelligence area. The other new man was a soldier recuperating at Camp Huckstep, and Margie was training him. As soon as his leg injury was better, he would be joining Bernie, whom Lucy had already taught to use the one-time pads and strip boards.

One-time pads were thought to be the only unbreakable code method. There were duplicate pads at headquarters and in the field. After agents in the field used a page for coding, they destroyed it. Bernie was getting the hang of the system but was supposed to ask her for help when he hit a snag. Men didn't like doing that, so Lucy kept an eye out. Margie must have slipped out to lunch with Hart. Gordon was at parachute training. It was time for lunch, but Lucy figured she'd calm herself down by taking on a new message. She was much quicker than Bernie, of course.

Usually, she wrote out the letters using the strip board before she read a message for content, but since Margie was off training the new recruit, Lucy would be doing the paraphrasing, which obviously couldn't be pulled off without a close reading. The message turned out to be more bad news. In retaliation for the blowing up of one Nazi car by the Chetniks, the fascist *Ustaše* had lined up and shot to death more than a dozen civilian women. The agent had seen their bodies. This was where Gordon would be deployed. She doubted Hart would be any safer, though he would be with the Partisans, not far from where Winston Churchill's son Randolph was serving.

She didn't want to dwell on the women's deaths. It wouldn't bring them back, but it made her wonder what she would do if she were in Chetnik shoes. Would she cease attacking for fear of provoking atrocities? Towns had been burned. Children killed. Nazis and *Ustaše* didn't obey ordinary rules of warfare. Ceasing attacks on them might prevent some horrendous acts of retaliation, but it might also prolong the war.

"Did you like the new recruit?" Lucy asked the next evening after supper while she sewed on a button.

Margie stuck out her hand. "Look what he got for me."

"The new recruit?" She glanced up, saw the diamond ring, and knew Margie meant Hart, not the new recruit. Margie was beaming, her wet hair backlit by red sky through a tall window in their bedroom.

"I'm so happy, but Lucy, we're in the same boat." Margie thrust her hand closer, solitaire diamond sparkling in its gold prongs.

Not completely, Lucy thought, though, yes, both of them were in love with men who might be killed. She *oohed* and *aahed* over the ring and let Margie tell her about how Hart had made her climb up with him on the Great Pyramid. When they were several blocks up, he'd gotten down on one knee and slipped the ring on her finger.

"Do you think they might delay his mission so you can get married first?"

Margie shook her head. "I want to go with him, but nobody wants to let me."

Lucy wished Margie would get that out of her head. "I think we'll be more help here," she said. "How's the new fella doing?"

"He's smart, but I think he's in pain."

"What happened to him?"

"He was shot in the leg. If he's still there after Hart leaves, I'll take you to see him."

CHAPTER THIRTY-TWO

Hart
Yugoslavia, 1943

When the Royal Air Force sergeant disappeared into the cockpit, Hart's throat tightened. His hand began shaking. The latter might have been caused by vibrations, but even allowing for the possibility the sergeant had made up stories to impress him with the need to attach his snap-hooks, the report of the last chap's chute not opening was not reassuring. There was no way he could sleep. He'd been deployed with so little notice that he felt the way he had in Oklahoma when a tornado destroyed his uncle's barn while they sat in the storm cellar. Except worse: out of nowhere, he had the idea that, if he thought about Margie, it would be dragging her out of the bomb bay with him.

After a bone-jolting and seemingly endless flight through darkness—Hart's mind kept circling back to the innate aloneness of the human condition—the sergeant reemerged, frowned, and folded back a wooden door, revealing a circular bomb bay about four feet in diameter and three feet deep. Wind would be rushing past the opening with as much force as he'd felt standing at the door on his practice jumps from other planes, but he felt none of it. This was like the blimp, like proposing marriage or a silent plunge off a cliff. The sergeant clipped the snap hook on Hart's webbed static line to a ring beside his shoulder and told him to dangle his legs. Hart gripped the edge to lower his feet into the slipstream but felt nothing. He peered into a well of darkness that unsettled his stomach. The static line lay coiled at his side. He tested the end clamped to the plane—yes, attached—and groped behind him to feel the connection with the parachute on his back. The sergeant must have been thinking the same thing. He checked the static line at both ends. As they neared the drop area, a red light was to come on. When the navigator spotted Morse code blinks from a flashlight on the ground, they would jettison supplies. Hart's signal to jump would be a green light.

The sergeant busied himself moving cargo to the edge of the hole; he attached the static lines for each package to rings on the plane. They felt the aircraft slow and hush and the effect of dropping altitude on their bodies. Hart braced himself, watching for the light. The engines surged, and they rose again, banking in an abrupt turn. The Halifax was a bomber. He was the bomb, one with legs dangling into invisible, absolutely black night.

Perhaps he should have been thinking of strategy. What would he do when he hit the ground? All his concentration was on the hole through which he would have to drop without banging his head or smacking his elbows. He rechecked his static line, the red light came on, and the sergeant shoved out the cargo.

Hart tugged the line attached to the plane, rechecked the end attached to his parachute, and held on to the rim of the hole. The green light came on, and his heart sped up. When the sergeant signaled thumbs-up, they met eyes, the sergeant shouted an encouragement, and Hart dropped into violent turbulence. Feet first, he thought instinctively as if he'd been dumped from a raft into white water. After several seconds of unstable free-fall, he turned onto his belly and spread his arms and legs, still tumbling as if the force of rough seas were carrying him toward a beach. His body tilted, and his chute popped open, yanking with a wallop that made him swing violently. *Margie, Margie,* he thought. The lights could have been Nazis signaling. It had happened before. Other men had been captured or shot as soon as they landed.

There was no moon, nothing to see but the shape of his dangling legs and boots. A soldier could break a bone landing on one leg, so, as he'd been taught, he moved his legs and feet together and held his knees slightly bent. He gripped the risers tight, arms raised to protect his head, and squinted at the dark terrain below. A dim meandering line could have been a river. The silence aloft lulled him, and he took deep breaths, thinking soon he would spot the cargo chutes. With no warning, the ground smacked him too hard for him to do anything but react. His knees and waist buckled as his canopy collapsed over him.

He heard his plane whine away in the distance and felt muddled and abandoned, but uninjured. He rose to his hands and knees in what seemed to be plowed farm field with the stink of manure. Shouts reached him from a distance while he struggled out of the harness. When he was free, he signaled with his flashlight. He didn't think the exuberant hollering he got in return would be from Germans, but his first view was of two men with rifles slung over their shoulders rushing toward him, and he experienced a moment of panic. The field was a rough terrace on a steep hillside, and they appeared from below, head and shoulders first, but one of them called out, "Welcome, chap," in a heavy accent. The other pumped his hand, gathered up the parachute, and said something that started with a *d* and had a *b* and Russian *r* sound.

"Welcome," the first one said. "*Dobrodo*šli!"

The third man spoke English with an accent like Wally's, though thicker. He introduced them all around, but Hart's ear couldn't make out every name. The English speaker said he was Andrej, named after Prince Andrej from *War and Peace*, making Hart wonder if the name was chosen by parents or, like the name of the Partisan leader, Tito, had been assumed for the war instead. Pearl Harbor had intervened before Hart had the time to read the novel, but he was embarrassed at his ignorance and threw himself into relating to his Partisan comrades to cover up. If he made it back, he would read *War and Peace* and make some kind of guess of what it meant for someone to be named after Andrej. At least he knew *War and Peace* was by Tolstoy.

Some of the men gathered up the silk of the parachute canopies to use for bandages; others hefted cargo containers and directed him down the steep hill. The packages contained radios, batteries, ammunition, plastic explosives, blankets, wool uniforms, and some packaged rations. It was a cool night, vivid with stars, the date chosen because there was no moon and the Partisans thought they could make it to that particular rendezvous without German interference.

Hart took out his knife and pierced the silk of his chute with the point to rip a section in case he might need a bandage for himself. Other men bustled to clean up the landing site, and soon he was following all of them down the hillside along a rocky path that overlooked a valley. One of the men pantomimed eating and pointed toward a hill in the distance. Hart's last meal had been with Margie, and he missed her intensely. If he saw her again, he would tell her about this moment, landing and thinking of her, but it was time to put her out of his head.

CHAPTER THIRTY-THREE

Lucy
Egypt, 1943

Margie's hand rested on her lap, where her diamond caught light from the arched window in their room. "I should have gone with Hart," she said without looking up.

Lucy, still in tennis whites borrowed from Jill, concentrated on untying her shoes. Should she suggest Margie leave her diamond behind for their first excursion in disguise, or would that sound as if it arose from envy? Probably the latter. Besides, the ring had become a kind of talisman for Margie. With a bit of care, the flowing sleeve of the black *tob sebleh* would cover it, and the two of them would look like a pair of nuns. Meer, whom *Tom* had suggested they take with them on their travels, would be their altar boy, though they'd be traveling as Egyptian women and he would be either their son or servant.

Meer was unambiguous in calling himself the least favored son in his family and more than willing to help them, though Lucy saw several flaws in relying on his keeping secrets from his brothers. He was of an age when changes in commitment were common, his face wouldn't be concealed by scarves or veils, and his culture valued honesty. Any member of his large family would recognize him. *Tom* had recommended Meer go as himself but without his red *tarbush*. It was Lucy's intent for their first trip to serve the triple duty of introducing her and

Margie to the *souq,* or market, trying out their new disguises, and making a clandestine pickup from the tailor working for OSS—the same man who had made clothes for Hart and Gordon to wear in Yugoslavia. She and Margie would carry a bag with black *tob seblaat* they could don over their street clothes. Meer would stow his red *tarbush* and sash in the bag while they traveled. She and Lucy would stop at the Gezira Club to change clothes.

"He landed safely. I could have, too," Margie said.

Lucy removed her socks, then Jill's tennis clothes, and set about choosing a clean blouse and skirt to wear under her Egyptian disguise. It was to their advantage that Lucy had substituted for Jill in a doubles tennis match there that morning as Princess Frederica's partner. Lucy and the princess had won, and the princess, her checks flushed with the heat, had thanked her politely and rushed away to her adorable children. Lucy could refer to the match if anyone stopped her and Margie on their way to the locker room. No doubt the staff paid close attention to royalty. This was a bit like the practice at Station S. *What were you doing in the building? I can't find my watch. I thought I might have left it here after my tennis match with Princess Frederica.*

"How does the princess feel about a Jewish state in Palestine?" Margie asked as Lucy zipped her skirt.

"I have no idea except that she's German. Did your Palestinian friends say anything about her coming from Germany?"

"Not a word."

They found Meer at his station in the kitchen, ready with a grocery list and bubbling with excitement to be part of some game of American espionage. He kept nodding and smiling as Margie related the rest of their plan. They'd already let his cousin, Mahmoud the cook, know they wanted Meer to be their guide while they shopped. Everything beyond that, Meer had insisted he would keep secret.

If their venture in disguise to the *souq* went well and Meer proved reliable, they might wear them to travel to Mena House several days hence to help with the set up for the president's conference. Meer was quite willing to check out their disguises. He followed them to their room, stood in the hall looking both proud and meek, and, after they'd transformed themselves, entered to inspect their *tob seblaat*. Lucy was concerned their shoes would give them away and had come up with the idea of letting their leather flats get dusty and wiping them off when they switched back into western guise. Meer didn't think that was necessary.

"What did your mother wear on her feet?" Margie asked.

He hesitated, looking very sad, but seemed quick to realize the question was about disguises, not about his deceased mother. He gave Lucy an earnest glance and explained to Margie that both his stepmothers wore sandals or flats when they left home but had high heels for parties.

Meer waited under a palm tree at the gate of the Gezira Club while Margie and Lucy strolled to the women's locker room in ordinary dress with shopping bags over their shoulders, hoping not to be questioned. They were lucky. No one was inside. They threw the *tob seblaat* over their heads and shoulders, examined their passable reflections in the ornate mirror, and slipped back outside. Their plan had been to walk differently, perhaps with their eyes downcast, but when they were halfway back to Meer, a fire-engine red car drove past him. "Don't turn your head, but I think that's King Farouk's car," Lucy said, casting her eyes toward her robe-obscured feet and then away toward the golf course.

"He has someone with him."

"He always has someone with him. It isn't Jill, is it?"

"There's a man in the back seat with him," Margie said.

They kept walking toward the gate. "If anyone gets close enough to overhear us, say *shukran* and then hush."

As Lucy had been reminded, *shukran*, thank you, was all she could say with a passable Arabic accent. Fortunately, the rest of the way was clear, and Meer popped up, seemingly from nowhere, to carry the bags. Then onward toward the bus stop.

"Was that King Farouk?" Lucy asked.

"Yes," Meer answered. "That was Mr. Eppler with him."

"You mean the German spy?"

Meer nodded solemnly, giving Lucy a sinking feeling because she knew the spy had been caught passing counterfeit bills and jailed. He wouldn't be riding around with the king. The boy was too young, all full of daydreams and unrealistic ideas. If they weren't careful, he might involve them in unfounded misperceptions and become too involved to let go. She was already fond of Meer and had even briefly imagined adopting him and bringing him back to the States, a fantasy a mite more realistic than one of marrying someone as handsome as Gordon.

After an uneventful, successfully incognito bus ride, the market in Old Cairo—*souq*, Lucy reminded herself—greeted them with exotic sights, sounds, smells, and the amplified call to prayer from a muezzin. Meer led them down narrow streets lined with small shops with hand-woven tribal rugs, perfume, ivory whatnots, and artifacts from Egyptian tombs. Leather goods, clothing, and fabrics were hung and piled on tables, clotheslines, and portable racks. Arched doorways led to warrens of spaces occupied by working coppersmiths and silversmiths and vendors with barrels of grains and spices. Small children with beautiful faces, wide eyes, and tattered clothing scurried this way and that or hung onto the skirts of women selling fruit and colorful vegetables. She could hardly take her eyes off them. A wizened old man roasted ears of corn. They passed meat sellers and fishmongers without anyone giving them a second glance. Meer stopped at a stall to buy lentils and potatoes and held up a potato. Margie, who'd mastered the glottal stops of Arabic when she studied Hebrew, said, "*Na'am, shukran*," meaning *yes, thank you*. A child no older than two tugged on Lucy's robe and might have crawled under her skirt if Lucy hadn't looked down. The potato seller gave a toothless grin, and Lucy smiled back, wishing she could ask if the child belonged to the woman. Was she the mother or grandmother? This child, though in rags, looked happy and well-fed, in contrast to thinner urchins who begged from soldiers and European shoppers. Later, Lucy would ask Meer if they lived with parents or had to fend entirely for themselves.

CHAPTER THIRTY-FOUR

Bella
Yugoslavia, 1943

All night she shivered in her blanket, longing for Tišina and praying Nura would return. A mouse would have nibbled dry leaves for a nest under the huge folds of wool, but the blanket was too thin to keep Bella warm, and she was too cold even to leave her tiny spot of body heat. In her dream, her mother had called soundlessly, her face always in shadow. Bella was afraid to come out of hiding. An owl hooted and startled her awake, making her glad she was not really a mouse.

Needles of light pierced the entrance of the hiding place. For a while, she imagined Nura outside preparing food, but the only smells were damp earth and forest, so she decided to sip water and save her remaining *zganci* for later. Soon she needed to tinkle. The more she thought about squatting in the forest, the more she needed to do it. She crawled to the entrance, lifted the cover of thatched branches, and gasped at the rays of mist beaming through dark green pine tops. She had entered a land of magic, rich with the smell of spice and pine. She had never seen anything so beautiful. Birds warbled, whistled, and hopped along a ground carpeted with needles and vivid green moss. Once again, she imagined shrinking to the size of a little mouse and living off seeds like giant nutmeats. One *zganci* grain cake would last all winter, but a mouse would have to hide in darkness.

When she climbed down the hill, she saw that the cave where she'd slept was well hidden. Even with the cover pushed aside, the opening was out of sight. She listened. The birds sang, and water trickled over rocks in the brook below, but she heard no tromping of feet.

After she tinkled, her thirst and hunger grew, and she carried her tin cup and followed the sound of water. Nura had told her to cover her cup with her square of lace and submerge it in the water to keep out the dirt. The tiny clear pool where she stopped did not look dirty, but Abdullah and Nura knew more about the forest than she did. Mud swirled from the bottom of the stream when her cup touched it, but the water she dipped was clear and cool as well water, and with each swallow, she felt stronger.

She gathered pine needles in her apron and spread them in the corner of the burrow for a bed. Once Nura had roasted pinecones until the scales tipped open. They'd sat at the kitchen table collecting the seeds, which they ate with wild greens.

On her second day, Bella ate a *zganci* and filled her stomach with water from the stream. She searched for pinecones and found some with their wooden scales raised but no seeds beneath them. Most cones were already nibbled to the core. Unlike the magical river in the village where she had lived with her mother and father and grandparents, the little stream had no fish, or, if it did, they were very good at hiding. The God of Abraham did not send mushrooms for her to eat, and her belly clenched in hunger, but never in her life had she felt so free. The little stream glittered and rushed over stones, and sunlight lit the morning mist in glowing shafts. That night, stars shone like the jewels she imagined in the crown of Queen Esther, and when she finally crawled into her burrow, she slept soundly on her bed of pine needles.

In the morning, she was very hungry and ate one of the two shriveled apples Nura had packed. When she crawled outside, she saw that the sky was gray and dim. God's magic had left the forest, making her afraid that Nura was not coming back or that the Nazis would march up the mountain and kill her. Her mother needed her to stay alive. If Bella hid without food or water, she would die. She took a shortcut from the path to the stream that trickled into the little pool where she had first filled her cup. After she drank, she ventured to the edge of the forest where she could look down on the valley. Far in the distance, a woman and a man, small as ants, were walking along the path. The woman was using a crutch.

CHAPTER THIRTY-FIVE

Lucy
Cairo, Egypt, 1943

"I didn't tell you about his injuries," Margie told Lucy *sotto voce* on their way to Camp Huckstep. They were jolting along in the back seat on their way to see the new OSS recruit, Mike Gold. Their driver, Private Al Mozinsky, had just delivered Kim Roosevelt to the nearby Mena House hotel and was trying to entertain them with stories about practical jokes. Lucy was sure the phone calls to tobacco stores wouldn't go over well with Princess Frederica, a descendent of Prince Albert and Queen Victoria. *Do yous have Prince Albert in a can? Well, let him out.* The dead fish under the hubcap prank Al described was cruel, though the idea of sending unwary soldiers out to buy "elbow grease" had the kind of appeal her brothers would have appreciated as children. She supposed all practical jokes appealed to some inherent unkindness based on jockeying for rank or resisting it.

It took her a moment to switch gears. It was only Al's accent and enthusiasm that made him funny. When she tapped him on the shoulder and pressed her finger to her lips, he met her eyes in the rearview mirror and nodded. "Excuse me," she said to Margie. "Were you going to tell me about our new recruit's injuries?"

"Yes," Margie answered. "Mike Gold. I didn't mention his amputation."

"How is he doing?" Lucy asked and waited for Margie to tell her what had happened and which limb. From his name, she'd already guessed he was Jewish. From the fact he'd been chosen for OSS and ready for her to test, she assumed he was smart. Sergeant Gold had been shot down in Italy and developed a festering leg wound that led to amputation below the knee. He would have been sent home, but he was determined to serve and well recommended by others, including Bernie, the MP she'd been training at *Sharia Ibn Zanki*. "Not bad at chess," Bernie had said, "and a really nice guy who wants to be sure we beat the heck out of those Nazis."

"When will he be joining us at headquarters?" Lucy asked.

"As soon as he gets a better fit on his artificial leg and can manage steps. He said he can go up and down on his you-know-what, but he has a blister on his stump. The doctor won't release him until it heals. In the meantime, we wanted you to give him some lessons. You're better at ciphers than I am." They were early, Margie said, and suggested they visit some of the wounded.

They had a duty to visit, Lucy knew. She and Margie were in perfectly good health, playing tennis and socializing with royalty in venues with exotic food, servants, and palm trees. Kim said he was making progress with his plan for housing OSS women in a houseboat on the Nile. Jill, it turned out, was pregnant. Soon there would be a baby in their villa. But what about Meer? Where would he live? What about the children they'd seen at the *souq*? Lucy hadn't joined the OSS to live the high life. She had an obligation to help others.

She'd had no idea that so many wounded men were in treatment at the Camp Huckstep hospital. Many had been transferred to Morocco, but hundreds remained, housed in hospital tents and attended by busy nurses. During those last weeks when her father got pneumonia on top of his blood cancer, she'd realized that nursing was too revolting for her. Remembering his rattling of phlegm, she took a deep breath and followed Margie into a barracks-sized tent filled with cots and stinking of antiseptic, bleach, and something rotten that the other smells failed to mask. The nurse was busy and sighed. Perhaps they weren't welcome. Who were they to pop in unannounced? But Margie insisted they divide the beds, with Lucy visiting each cot from the side they entered and Margie starting from the other side. They would meet in the middle and go on to another tent.

"I couldn't stand the moaning," said an earnest-faced boy who looked about sixteen. He'd lost his left arm and had recently been moved from a tent in which the other patients cried out. Lucy listened to what he volunteered and refrained from asking more for fear of causing him further anguish. He thanked her, and she moved on to a lean man with a flank wound, who asked her to read a letter to him. It was from his mother and filled with spelling errors: his mother had visited a tent revival where the preacher had told her that her son would come home filled with the spirit of the Lord. The next man was asleep. She touched his forehead, which was hot and dry. "I think he has a fever," Lucy said, and the nurse told her she knew.

They stayed away from the closed door of a tent with a man sobbing. Thank goodness for the nurse ministering to him. At the next, Lucy wrote a letter for a man in bandages. He was from Wisconsin, had lost a brother, and wanted his mother reassured that he would be all right. Before they ever got to Mike Gold, Lucy was exhausted. She wondered how exposure to all these injuries would affect Margie and her determination to go to Yugoslavia. But Hart was there, and if the British would provide transportation, Gordon soon would be too.

"Like most of us, Mike Gold is stubborn," Margie said before they entered the barracks where he was quartered. "Just subtler about it."

Lucy, already lightheaded from the medical smells and troubled by the tent they'd bypassed, didn't see herself among the stubborn. She considered herself the converse, overthinking half her decisions based on how they would impact others. Gordon, for instance. She wanted time with him, but he was intent on his mission and wouldn't want her to interfere, pro or con. Margie walked ahead and greeted Mike Gold. As Lucy approached, he stood up, using one crutch and the edge of a table for leverage, his eyes first on Margie, then on her.

His nose, she noticed, was long, narrow, and pointed, and the rest of his face boyish, though slightly horsey, his dark hair parted at the side and falling limply. She got the impression he was studying her and eager to show off what he'd already learned about coding. They made small talk as she quizzed him about *Playfair*, which could be used in the field as a fallback. Mike had it down pat. She tested him on the strip board. He was quick and accurate, with the kind of concentration he would need. He encoded a message and tapped it out in Morse Code on the tabletop using light taps for *dits* and hard taps for *dahs*. He'd met both Hart and Gordon before Hart's deployment and was very focused on getting his spot at OSS headquarters.

After Lucy gave Mike her thumbs up, he produced a hint of a smile and told her Gordon had asked about her.

"About me?"

Mike was halfway through telling her that Gordon was stuck on base, waiting for a time window to be deployed, when—speak of the rascal—Gordon tapped "Shave and a Haircut" on a metal bedframe and came up behind her. "Just the dame I've been looking for," he said with that chin dimple, too-handsome face, and eyes telegraphing mischief. He led her for a quick walk while Mike quizzed Margie about the stairs at headquarters. "I can manage," Mike was saying as Gordon pulled Lucy out the door and around a corner, where he took her in his arms and squeezed the breath out of her. Anyone passing could have seen them, but she hugged back with all she was worth. Gordon was the one who leaned away but only far enough to look into her eyes with that magnetism she'd felt and resisted from the start. "I was hoping you wouldn't mind."

He hadn't been deployed yet, he explained, averting his eyes in a way that made her wonder if he shared the shame other men mentioned. As if lack of combat experience made them guilty of cowardice. Her own cheeks were still hot from being near him, and she felt a bit outside of herself as he told her about how the British kept promising to drop him in but delaying and delaying. Yugoslavia was their operation, and the Yanks were just observers, which sounded safe, though she knew it wasn't. Some of the wounded she'd just seen had been paratroopers.

It turned out Gordon was coming along to Mena House with her and Margie.

"What will you be doing there?" she asked.

"I want to look at the pyramids with you."

"That sounds romantic, but I think I'll be working."

"The terrace has a view. I want a picture of you there to take with me when I go."

She was about to say she'd like one of him too when Mozinsky told them to get the show on the road. He would drive her, Lucy, and Gordon. Kim Roosevelt was already at Mena House.

CHAPTER THIRTY-SIX

Hart
2001

The sailboat beyond Hart's house was lateen-rigged, its sheet at a slant on the mast, evoking feluccas on the Nile. He stood on his dock watching, his shirt flapping against his chest, squinting to see who was tacking in on the blue Rappahannock. Just a tanned neighbor boy on a Sunfish with a hull no longer than a paddleboard. For some reason—maybe because he'd been awash with sentiment since he lost Margie—Hart couldn't get Egypt out of his mind. Or maybe it was the attacks on his country and that Meer, who had promised to visit, hadn't yet appeared. Three weeks had passed since Hart had called on the "burner" phone, and he'd been experiencing peaks of angst that reminded him how tenuous life could be. He hoped Bin Laden's group didn't have the bomb.

Waves lapped at the sand and splashed against the dock posts, too loud for him to hear tires on gravel but not loud enough to banish his anxiety. What was he afraid of? Not death. The boy sailed aground on a patch of beach several houses away, and Hart glanced up at his own blue-shingled, sea-weathered house. He started up the steps, thinking of Meer and huffing and puffing more than he would want anyone to see. He heard a car door slam. Could be Jim back to check on him, dang it. He hated being dependent and was put out at Meer for standing him up. By the time Hart's head and shoulders crested the hill, he saw it was neither Meer nor Jim but Bella, still lean and strong but gray-haired.

She met him with a hug. "I don't know what it is about this place that feels so magical," she said. "Driving in here through the woods, I felt I'd been let out of a cave."

The driveway was through five acres of pine forest. "Did you see the wild turkeys?" he asked, poured iced tea for her, and invited her onto the screened porch to talk and look out at the river. She hadn't seen turkeys on the way in, but she'd noticed an Osprey V-22 fly over.

"Have you seen Lucy?" he asked.

"Of course, but she doesn't know me." Her large eyes were expressive as ever. He felt he could see down to their depths, the loss, the hopes, her whole history.

"There are lots of ways to know people," he said and almost added that Lucy had been searching for her, but had she? She'd wanted Gordon. And had been thinking of Bella and Meer, but how had he come to that conclusion? He sat in the rocker Margie bought at an estate sale, creaking back and forth because the motion felt good on his new knee.

"I came to tell you Muhammadu was assaulted."

"Who?"

"Meer's son." A crease deepened between Bella's eyes as she explained that Muhammadu's nose had been broken, his arm fractured, and he'd suffered a concussion. His assailants told bystanders he was a terrorist but ran off. The police had transported Muhammadu to an emergency room, where he was forced to stay under a green warrant.

"A what?"

"Mental warrant. The doctors wanted him admitted, and he refused, so they kept him in a psychiatric ward."

"I wonder if that's why Meer didn't call me back." Hart explained about the recent notes from Meer, who had become a naturalized American citizen at a ceremony he and Margie, and Lucy and Gordon, had attended sometime after Nasser died. Everything had changed since their Egypt days. Sudan, where so many Nubians lived, was no longer part of Egypt. Yugoslavia held together as a Communist country until Tito died in 1980 but broke up in 1992. The Nazis were gone, but their atrocities echoed in one war after the other. Hart saw it as wrongs piled atop one another. Nothing stayed the same. Vengeance begat vengeance. Bella listened patiently and let him ramble on about the years when he and Margie lived in North Africa, Yugoslavia, and Turkey. Sometime along the way, Meer had married Muhammadu's mother and moved to Somalia. Muhammadu had never become a US citizen, though he'd stayed in touch with other freed captives and provided intelligence to the CIA.

Once, in the 1990s, Meer told Hart that his brothers still didn't believe in the Holocaust. They'd thought the Nazis had simply shipped Jews to Israel. But Meer knew that Bella had found her parents' names on a list of the exterminated. All that loss, and Bella was letting Hart vent, probably because she knew he would take Muhammadu's beating as a terrible turn of events.

"Meer knows he's under surveillance," Bella said.

"Is he? Our Meer?"

She did mean Meer, but wouldn't explain how she knew. It reminded Hart of the teetering-on-the-edge angst of Partisans revealing their distrust of the Chetniks. He doubted he would live to see the end of that dynamic. "Did the police know what happened to Muhammadu in Somalia?"

"About his kidnapping?" Bella shook her head no. "They suspected he really was a terrorist. Anyone from the Mid East or Africa."

"How old was Muhammadu then? Twelve?"

"When he was kidnapped? Thirteen and living with his grandmother."

"How long was he with them?" Hart meant Muhammadu's

time with the soldiers in Somalia. Meer had flown back to Africa to search for him and, in the end, had paid a ransom to get back a confused boy who wouldn't talk.

CHAPTER THIRTY-SEVEN

Bella
Yugoslavia, 1943

Bella lay prone, watching as the man and limping woman plodded up the hillside. Despite her clothing, the woman was too tall to be Nura. The man was lean and bent under a pack, and the woman leaning heavily on a staff. They both had rifles slung over their shoulders. When the droning of an airplane reached Bella from someplace out of sight, the man and woman disappeared behind a ridge with rocks and small pines. The plane never appeared. After the sounds faded, the man and woman resumed their slow pace.

As they came closer, Bella became more afraid. Nura would have told her to stay in the cave and not to make a sound, but that was impossible. If she moved, the leaves around her would rustle, so Bella lowered her head to the ground and prayed she would not be seen.

She imagined them coming closer and closer. She heard leaves crackling under their footsteps and the thump of the staff against the ground. She heard heavy breath and prayed that the man would be her father speaking Ladino and that the woman would not be Nura but would be her real mama, whose face she could not remember. She wished her mama would ask her, *De mi quieres?* Do you love me? And she would answer, *A ti quiero*—I love you—and bury her face against the woman's shoulder.

"We're near," said a man's voice in Serbian.

Near what? Bella wondered. Did he know of the cave dug into the ridge?

"She must be hiding," whispered a different voice, like gravel plunging to the bottom of a well. They were so close Bella heard the rustling of skirts. She opened her eyes but dared not move. Had the Nazis disguised themselves as ordinary people. Why would a man dress in a woman's clothes?

"Esma!" a voice called. A man's voice, but not Abdullah's. She had no memory of her father's voice. She thought of Adem. He had not liked his parents hiding her and would blame her for Abdullah's death. The voice coaxed, but she kept her lips closed and tightened her every muscle to keep still.

The people discussed the cave. She heard them move sticks away from the opening. "Too small." Their sounds dropped to murmurs like the flow of the stream. She imagined them eating the last of her food. The shriveled apple. The jar of rosehip jelly. Her jar of pickled cabbage. If she'd made herself small, her provisions would have lasted all winter.

She edged out from under the brush and leaves with clatters and crackles so loud she knew she'd given herself away and they would shoot her. If she were lucky, they would ask if she were a Jewess or a Roman Catholic or a Mohammedan or Eastern Orthodox. They would want to know if she were a Croat or a Serb, and she would give the answer Nura had instructed: "I am a girl." That would make them laugh. But she was afraid to speak and froze in a crouch, hoping they would spare her life.

Their rustling was louder than hers, the barrels of their rifles like tunnels filled with the darkness of all the hiding and all the loneliness she could bear. She did not mean to weep. She did not mean to let loose even a tiny whimper, but her chest bucked, and a dry squeak escaped her throat.

"Who are you?" the first man demanded.

She shook her head because the spirit of Tišina had taken her voice.

Two men stood over her. The one who had dressed as a woman looked her straight into her face, judging. "Are you Esma, daughter of Nura?" he asked. He had removed his scarf, his shawl, his skirt, and his apron, beneath which he wore Army trousers and a wool tunic like the one Adem had worn, though he was too short to be Nura and Abdullah's son.

Tišina had never spoken, even as a chick. Bella imagined the hen's feathered body vibrating against her own and said nothing.

"Your mother is very sick. She gave me her clothes for a disguise, but she couldn't come back herself. She told us you could help us."

"I am a girl," Bella whispered, but no one laughed. "I am eight years old.

"Will you help us care for the wounded?" the first man said without laughing, his eyes boring into her, his gun barrel lowered to the ground.

Lucy

The conference would take place at Mena House, Kim explained to Lucy and Margie on their way from Camp Huckstep. President Roosevelt and Prime Minister Churchill would stay with Ambassador Kirk. The driver, Private Mozinsky, who tended to be deferential when a civilian rode in the front seat beside him, hadn't been told that Kim was a grandson of a president, an Army private, and an OSS agent posing as an international businessman. Lucy sat in the back between Margie and Gordon with her feet on the hump, thinking Egypt, with its horizons of hills and dunes, made the perfect backdrop for layers of secrets and meetings between world leaders. Fine sand rose in mysterious clouds from under the tires of the Jeeps ahead, blurring palm trees into reminders of *Arabian Nights*. When she and Margie visited the *souq* at *Sharia Al Muski,* she'd almost bought an oil lamp like Aladdin's to summon a genie and wish for the very moment she was experiencing: Gordon stroking her hand tenderly, naming pyramids, and promising to someday take her for a camel ride and tour of the great pyramid. If she'd allowed herself, she would have swooned into believing it was already happening.

For the time being, the fleeting moments and view of the pyramids from Mena House grounds would have to do. Kim, once again playing matchmaker, had engaged a photographer, who promised prints by the next day. He'd done the same for Hart and Margie, but they were engaged. Lucy regretted she had avoided Gordon for so long. She leaned her head on his shoulder, and, ever so gently, he put his arm around her. She was tempted to close her eyes. Though it was too hot and she should have sat up straight for politeness, she stayed snuggled close to him as they rumbled toward the hotel.

Only when they approached a checkpoint outside the entrance gate did she sit straighter to take in the sight of the whitewashed building, the ornate porch, the gardens, and the terraces. After Private Mozinsky let them out, Kim led them for a tour and walkthrough of the space for the meeting. They paused on a terrace with oleander bushes, where the English photographer with the bad front tooth snapped a photo of her and Gordon and one of each of them alone under a trellis with fragrant, climbing roses. The landscaping and plantings made it seem as if palm trees and flowers were all that stood between them and the pyramids, but when Lucy climbed steps to have a better look, she was greeted by a somewhat flat golf course stretching out to meet first a line of military trucks and beyond that a bare hillside of sand, above which rose the plateau with the Giza pyramids.

The MPs had already made their assessments. Both British and American troops were busy closing off a compound that included Ambassador Kirk's second residence and Mena House with its many whitewashed guesthouses. If all went well, the location of the meeting would be kept from the Germans, though Lucy found that doubtful and said as much to Gordon, who agreed and told her about Hart once having overheard someone near King Farouk speak German.

Lucy's farewell to Gordon midway through the tour was most unsatisfactory, but there was nothing to be done about that and very little, beyond her moment-to-moment actions, that was in her control. At the very moment that Ambassador Kirk joined them, Gordon was summoned to Camp Huckstep. It wasn't until Private Mozinsky arrived to drive her and Margie back to their villa and Lucy had a moment to think that it sunk in that Gordon's deployment was imminent. He'd been so convinced the British were throwing deliberate roadblocks to his going that he'd complained to Kim and suggested that the deployment of Americans to help out Chetniks might be added as a fine print item to the conference agenda. Then, he was gone, and her mind taken up with the plans for her and Margie to converse with guests and help move them along, so the more important dignitaries could confer and the lesser ones be made happy. She was to speak with Jill about King Farouk and, if possible, learn how she might appeal to his vanity, which gave her a sinking feeling. She might be able to pose as an Egyptian woman, but when she imagined bleaching her hair to appeal to him, she could only think of an intoxicated floozy she'd once seen on the streets of Washington, DC. Brassy curls, black roots, rouge, and eyes lined with black. King Farouk liked pale blondes, Jill said, and his knowing that Jill was married and now pregnant hadn't put him off.

They arrived at headquarters in the late afternoon, not hungry after lunch at Mena House but parched, and drank from the pitcher of ice water and lemonade in the code room. Jim Raymond soon filled them in on the latest from Hart, who was requesting batteries for the radio, clothes for the Partisans, socks for himself, and medical supplies and antibiotics for the Partisan wounded. The need for antibiotics was urgent.

CHAPTER THIRTY-EIGHT

Hart
Yugoslavia, 1943

While Andrej and an MI-6 Corporal by the name of Danny supped with him on thin but savory porridge served to them by a peasant family, the rest of the Partisans kept moving with the parachuted supplies. The family members—a gaunt mother with a chapped, worried face; an old man, who might have been eighty or ninety; and two small boys with blue eyes and brown hair—sat watching them eat. The woman, he learned as Danny translated, was in her twenties, and the old man, who also had blue eyes, was her husband's grandfather. The little boys were five and four years old.

The stone cottage where the family lived crouched in a wooded valley a six-day hike from the mountainside where Hart had landed. Though he was bone-tired after hiking twenty hours straight and going thirty without sleep, he set up his radio and strung the antenna out a loft window onto the red-tiled roof. Using the first page of his one-time pad and silk square conversion table, he painstakingly coded the Partisan's request for supplies. While Danny and Andrej kept watch, he tapped his message in Morse code. If the enemy appeared, his group would have to hightail it back into the mountains. It was hard to concentrate. He was afraid he'd made errors, so he tapped out the same message a second time, which doubled the risk that the enemy could locate his signal. In his sleep-deprived mind, the possibility of enemy retaliation against the family made the process into a nightmarish battle between his heart and his fingers.

On the way into the valley, they'd passed a bombed-out village with a damaged stone wall and a smoldering orchard burned by the Nazis as punishment after a Partisan was discovered hiding in the little church. Hart, who did not speak Slovene, was spared the details, but the faces of the few townspeople made it clear that many villagers had perished. In particular, he couldn't shake the sight of old women digging graves.

Danny and Andrej spoke the Slovenian language, and while Hart was taking down the antenna wire, they conferred with the family, pointing at themselves and then Hart, occasionally translating for him. Despite knowing the likely consequences of harboring enemies of the Germans, the woman continued to insist they stay the night. Hart already felt guilty taking some of their supper, but he was exhausted, and a large blister had formed on his heel and was bleeding. The woman made him a bandage and darned his sock. He was reminded of his own mother, who, during the Depression, had always been willing to find something for a hungry visitor. A fried egg. Bread. They hadn't had much, but they hadn't needed to worry about Nazis.

The Slovenian woman shook her head vehemently when he told her with gestures and pidgin German that she and her family would be safer if he and the others left. She pointed with her calloused, chapped hands to the loft, herself, her sons, and grandfather-in-law, and then to him, Danny, and Andrej, and to the padded benches on three sides of the main room, which were white-washed plaster over stone. There was a crucifix on one wall, a sturdy wooden table, a cupboard, and an oven in the corner. The loft was a third the size of the room, supported by large wooden beams, with access by a hand-hewn ladder, its rails bigger around than the shafts on a horse-drawn wagon.

After the radio and battery were stowed, Hart, Andrej, and

Danny went outside to confer in the barn, which housed two oxen, a goat, and several chickens. "Shouldn't we head on anyway?" Hart asked, though he felt close to nodding off and longed to sleep.

"Too fatigued," Andrej said. Danny chimed in that this was the dilemma they faced continually. Their presence was a threat to the peasants, but the people were behind them and wanted to help. "Chetniks, they collaborate with *Ustaše*. We Partisans don't do," Andrej said with a shake of his head and started back toward the cottage.

Hart, hoping to kneel by his bed and pray for the family, was about to follow when Danny stopped him to ask if he knew any Jews. Almost asleep on his feet, he responded that his fiancé was friends with women from the Jewish Agency in Cairo and had been raised in a family with both Sephardic and Ashkenazi roots.

"Where did she live before the war?"

"Virginia." Even in his half-asleep state, Hart realized he was confiding too much. What if Danny were a collaborator?

"In America?"

Hart didn't answer, but Danny held his shoulder and confided that he was a Jewish Palestinian in the British Army, working as an agent of the Jewish Agency in Cairo, the same organization Hart had learned about from Margie. Margie's new friends didn't approve of mixed marriages, but it was too dark to read Danny's reaction.

The mission for the Jewish Agency, Danny told Hart, was to reach German concentration camps by the time the Allies won the war, so survivors liberated from the camps could settle in a new state of Israel. Behind Danny, stars like spilled crystals lit a moonless sky, evoking the star of Bethlehem and the Bible, and awakened deep longing for Margie, his mother, and his sister, and for the Holy Spirit. "Are many of you with the Partisans?" Hart asked.

"A few, if you mean Jews."

"And with the Chetniks?"

"Dunno," Danny said. "Partisans hate Chetniks more than they hate Nazis. They just know they won't get British support if they don't stop the Germans."

Hart felt he was walking in a dream. He'd known about the mutual distrust between Partisans and Chetniks. He'd also heard secondhand that Palestinians and most Arabs firmly opposed a Jewish state and resented the Jews and the British. It seemed better not to share the latter, but after he'd lain down on one of the padded benches and Danny's and Andrej's breath had slowed into the rasp of sleep, he said a silent prayer for Margie, for his mother, and for his sister. And then he knelt by the bench and prayed for peace and for the safety of the Slovenian family.

CHAPTER THIRTY-NINE

Bella
Yugoslavia, 1943

If the limping man had worn the skirt and draped the shawl back over his head and shoulders, Bella might have pretended she was walking through the light-stippled forest with Nura. But the man, whose name was Dusan, reeked of sweat and tobacco. He wore filthy trousers and the tunic of a soldier and leaned heavily on his stick as he walked. The other man, who was not quite as smelly, was called Matija.

Ghosts had sometimes seeped through walls to visit Bella in hiding but had rarely come to her outdoors, so she was unsure how to understand what happened next. She was trudging the mountainside trail behind the two hard-breathing men when she felt someone come behind her. She looked, but no one was there, and she decided that it was the ghost of Abdullah, hurrying her along. When they were almost to a rocky crest, so narrow that the trees stood single file, they stopped and sat on a flat boulder. Dusan carved off a portion of cheese for each of them. While she ate, she again felt the ghost of Abdullah. This time she saw a fawn lying against a fallen log, as still as if it were made only of leaves and wood itself. Perhaps it was a trick of her eyes. She said nothing, and the men seemed not to notice it. If they had, they would have slit its throat and skinned it to take the meat.

After walking for hours along a narrow trail, Matija grunted and stepped behind a boulder; he gestured for Dusan to follow him. Dusan crooked his finger at Bella and whispered for her to come along too. The two men crossed a flat rock and made their way to another patch of forest, where they threaded through the trees to a small meadow that smelled of cigarettes and wood smoke. She looked at Matija to see where he was leading them, but said nothing. Soon they reached a large boulder with a grassy hill against its side and stones piled in a mound over the grass. Matija showed them a door on the side of a hill, which did not surprise Bella because she was used to hiding in such places. What surprised her was how large a room was hidden under the earth. It was as big as the main room at Abdullah and Nura's home. The walls were stone, and the ceiling was wood and high enough for Dusan and Matija to stand upright. There was a stone oven in the corner and a chimney that emerged from the pile of stones.

Matija explained that this would be a hospital and that Dusan and Bella should stay, and he would bring a doctor. He unloaded a sack of grain and a round of cheese from his pack, but he did not say why the house smelled of cigarettes. The oven had been used, and there was a stack of wood beside it. There was no well, but a spring-fed pool overflowed into a stream bed of rocks that disappeared down the mountainside. Bella knew that Abdullah's ghost would have liked this place. She could have brought him food and water while he lay on one of the wooden cots inside, though he would have preferred Nura, and he would have wanted Bella to ask why Dusan had been wearing Nura's clothes.

CHAPTER FORTY

Lucy
Cairo, Egypt, 1943

"You have to come with me to Tolumbat," Margie said as if she were in charge. Ambassador Kirk's organizers had summoned them from Mena House to his nearby villa, both properties cordoned off with barbed wire, warning signs, and enough military trucks and soldiers to signal the meeting location to anyone who knew that Roosevelt, Churchill, and Chiang Kai-Shek were going to meet. From cipher traffic at the message center, she knew that the Nazis had found out somehow that President Roosevelt was on his way. From Kim, she'd learned that the president would stop in Tunis where his sons, FDR Jr. and Elliott, were stationed; Perhaps he was already there. Meanwhile, the risk that the enemy would discover the specific route and meeting details was escalating.

And now Margie wanted to go someplace Lucy hadn't heard of.

"Come where?" Lucy almost snapped, though she didn't mean to be impatient. After a full schedule the day before, she'd fallen into bed well after midnight and risen before breakfast for their ride to Mena House. "Tolumbat–is that where the Generalissimo and Madame Chiang Kai-Shek are staying?

"No, Tolumbat is the camp for refugee children. It's near

Alexandria. We can't go now. I mean after the conference."

That sounded more than fine. Lucy loved children and wanted to help in whatever way she could. Possibly young Meer felt the same way, though he'd not been told about the conference. He'd seemed so pleased by their practice spy venture, but there'd been no more sleuthing after Kim Roosevelt called a halt to going about in disguise. Kim had been skeptical of Meer's sighting of Johann Eppler in King Farouk's car and decided there was too much risk King Farouk would sniff them out and become offended. It was much more likely the Germans had learned about the conference from someone else.

That morning, Meer had seemed disappointed when they left. "What is it?" Lucy had asked.

"I want to help," he said so earnestly, that her eyes stung.

"You do help. And thank you for serving us this scrumptious breakfast." They hadn't had time for more than a taste, but she'd wondered if the part about her gratitude for his serving them had offended him. She'd added it to a mental list to address when they returned, but they wouldn't be home for supper. Word was out at headquarters that Churchill and the Chiang Kai-Sheks had arrived the day before. Perhaps, if she could think of something for Meer to do and send him a message, it would make him feel more useful. Or would she be sowing the seeds of his discontent? She had no problem seeing herself as a cog in a wheel. Wasn't that the role of any human, fitting with others, doing something useful in the service of a greater good? But Meer was just a boy and needed purpose.

One of Bernie's MP friends was planning a run back to pick up the Bensons, and she printed a note for him to deliver:

Dear Meer, Please draw me a map of Heliopolis &
mark places where you could hide a message if
need be. Don't worry if we're late tonight. We'll get
supper on our way. The lemons were delicious.

Lucy

"Lemons were delicious" was a prearranged cue for Meer to use lemon juice invisible ink if he had a message for her. She hoped he would work on the map and stay away from King Farouk and the person he thought was the spy, Eppler, who was actually in prison. The lemon juice would give him something to do and possibly cheer him up.

Lucy and Margie inspected one another for grooming flaws. Despite the heat, Lucy's permanent waves had kept their bounce, and the skirts on their silk shirtwaist dresses flared gracefully. Margie looked lovely. The driver who shuttled them to Ambassador Kirk's residence a mile away whistled and gave them a grin and a promise not to do the same to Madame Chiang Kai-shek. "Did Kim tell you she learned American English living in Georgia?" Margie whispered. "On top of that, she went to college at Wellesley."

Well then, Lucy thought, the Chinese Generalissimo's wife wouldn't be shocked by a whistle. Offended, certainly, but not shocked. As Lucy and Margie had been told by Ambassador Kirk, Madame Chiang was her husband's cultural advisor and translator and would attend the conference, though neither President Roosevelt nor Prime Minister Churchill was bringing a wife. The security was as high as Lucy had seen it, almost, but not quite enough to block the view of the pyramids, which, no doubt, Alexander Kirk would expound on to his guests, Egyptology being one of his favorite topics. The house, gardens, and palms were exquisite, as were the architectural details of the whitewashed house with its arches, cornices, and furniture inlaid with ivory and mosaics of colored ceramics. Kim met them inside as himself, not Tom. Looking preoccupied and glum, he shepherded them into a corner for a briefing.

"Is he here?" Lucy asked.

The president had arrived by plane that morning, Kim said, not long after the fighter escorts that were supposed to protect him had worried everyone by returning to base without locating his plane. It turned out the president had detoured south and followed the Nile northward. General Royce, the US Commanding General for the Middle East, and his chief of staff, Brigadier General Cheaves, met him at Cairo West, the British Royal Airforce field, and arrived at Ambassador Kirk's villa by midmorning, bringing along the president's valet and cooks and stewards.

"So, you don't need tasters?"

"It wouldn't have been your job anyway," Kim snapped.

A deserved putdown for conjecture unbecoming to a public servant, but she didn't know *what* their job was supposed to be, so she waited for Kim to explain that she and Margie were to put a human face on what General Donovan had already requested from the president: pressure on Churchill to provide air transportation to deploy OSS men to Yugoslavia.

Lucy needn't have been proactive about introducing herself as Uncle Walton's great-niece. President Roosevelt either had remembered her or been briefed, more likely the latter. As in their very few previous encounters, he was kind and charming, engaging her with interest in his gray-blue eyes. He looked older, his face more lined with bruised circles showing under his wire-rimmed glasses. He sat in his wheelchair, examining a pile of papers that ruffled under the steady turning of a ceiling fan. In his teeth, he held a cigarette holder with a cigarette twining smoke but laid it—holder, smoke trail and all—in a long, narrow brass tray next to a pack of Camels.

"Of course, I remember you, Lucy." He inquired about her mother, mentioned his visit to his sons in Tunis, and expressed his gratitude to her and all of the younger generation for serving. "Your Uncle Walton used to say that you and your brothers were like grandchildren to him." What he said was true and made her homesick.

"I hope you'll be kind to young Kermit." The president meant Kim.

She nodded, wondering why he'd brought that up.

"Kim's mother didn't want to tell him while he was traveling, but I agreed to play it by ear."

"Tell him what?" Was traveling a euphemism for serving in the war?

"I trust you can pledge secrecy about the circumstances."

She placed her hand over her heart, which strained under the forewarning of she knew not what.

"Kermit, Senior, took his own life. He was drinking again. Belle asked me to break the news. She thought someone here should know." The president explained that when Belle received word that he had delivered her letter to Kim, she would tell Polly, Kim's wife. Yes, the president had already given Kim the letter, and though it had understandably thrown Kim off his game, he'd kept to task and asked Lucy and Margie to review the OSS request for more assistance from the British in getting to Yugoslavia.

Margie had been waiting patiently outside the door with some of the president's guards. Lucy would not be able to tell her why she'd been excluded but invited her in, and they explained to the president that the British had kept delaying Gordon's deployment, which confirmed other indications that MI-6 did not want Americans interacting with the Chetniks, but Chetniks would be evacuating wounded Americans and helping Jews out of Axis-occupied territory. Margie's voice broke when she said Jews, but she cleared her throat and put on a good face.

"And how do you know this?" the president asked.

"We work decrypting messages," Margie said. "My fiancé is with the Partisans."

"Donovan said there was foot-dragging from MI-6." The president meant General Donovan of the OSS. "Winston and I should be able to get around that."

CHAPTER FORTY-ONE

Lucy
Egypt, 1943

The waiting was terrible. Lucy knew she shouldn't unburden herself to Margie and Kim, but the dead space between Gordon in the air, Gordon parachuting to the Chetniks, and a message back was agonizing. Meanwhile, Kim was grieving for his father, whom he loved and resented for his drinking and infidelity, and Margie was toughing out her worries about Hart and the Partisans.

It had been three days since Gordon's drop. When she was alone, Lucy got down on her knees and prayed. Every morning at headquarters, she riffled through the messages that had arrived in the night, hoping Gordon had radioed something to be decrypted.

By the third week, she found herself thinking of her cousin, whose husband had been missing in action for more than a week before the awful visit from an officer announcing he hadn't survived. Lucy prayed for courage. She prayed for hope. But mainly, she prayed that Gordon would be safe.

Hart's messages were lists of requests: Another radio, another radio operator, batteries, a new pedal-operated generator for charging the batteries, warm clothes for the Partisans, plastic explosives, ammunition, antibiotics, bandages, and rations. His repeating requests made it clear he hadn't received anything.

When she asked Jim Raymond why, he explained that drop-offs were extremely risky. They had to wait for moonless nights, so the planes wouldn't be spotted and shot down.

"There was no moon the night Gordon went out, was there?"

"No, let me finish," he said. "Our people on the ground are careful to find a location without Nazis. After they choose a site, they have to wait and hope it will still be safe when there's no moon."

Something must have shown on her face because he interrupted himself:

"Lucy, if this is too much for you, I'll assign you to something else. I'm beginning to think we shouldn't let you look for Gordon's messages."

She protested, and Jim resumed explaining:

"Gordon won't be able to signal us without stringing up an antenna in a site far enough from the enemy to tap out a message before they triangulate on it. That means he'll have to keep moving to find a spot in the clear."

She knew that, of course, but only thanked Jim and resolved to keep more of a poker face. Instead of working extra hours and brooding over the absence of messages from Gordon, she would go with Margie to visit the displaced persons camp at Tolumbat.

Meer volunteered to accompany Margie and Lucy. His cousin, the other Mahmoud, had given him the day off, but, at first, Margie objected, hoping to get a ride for her and Lucy with one of the Palestinian Jewish friends from the nearby villa. When that fell through, she agreed with Lucy that it would be safer to travel with Meer, who had a rough idea of the area. He could translate, and his presence would make them feel safer. With all that in mind, the three of them left from the railway station at *Bab El Hadid*.

On the train, Lucy made conversation with Meer, asking

many questions, which he answered in his earnest way, pointing out sights and answering questions about his hopes for Egypt. Margie sat beside her, so she did not ask about his fellow Muslims' objections to a Jewish state. They'd discussed the bare-bones objection, but not the reasons, in an earlier conversation. She wondered if seeing the children at Tolumbat would soften his position.

On the strength of their affiliation with OSS, they were allowed in, but the camp for unaccompanied children was clearly a British operation with mostly English nurses and teachers attending to the children, who were cute as buttons—were buttons cute? Cuter than puppies. One does not compare children to dogs, Lucy thought, though they had in common sweetness and a predilection to snuggle that tugged her heart. Most of these sweet children were too thin with expressive, large eyes in soft faces with bowed lips. The tents they lived in were identical to the hospital tents at Camp Huckstep. Though most of the children were not physically wounded, a few had bandages or walked, like Tiny Tim, on little crutches. One meek child had lost her right hand, and nurses in their white garb were trying to make her laugh by popping up, saying peek-a-boo. Meer tugged Lucy's sleeve and took her to a boy, about eight, who was alone on his cot, weeping silently and sucking his thumb. Lucy addressed him in English, and he squeezed his eyes tight as if trying to shut out the sound of her voice. Meer tapped the boy's shoulder and looked at him straight on with an expression she read as, *You can do it, little man.* Though it was wordless.

Inside some of the tents were rows of metal white-slatted cribs, most containing small children. The nurse for the tent was not sure of the exact ages, but the youngest was able to stand up but not walk. The oldest looked about three years old. They were all malnourished and being fed medically prescribed cereal so as not to tax their systems. Most of the nurses seemed very kind but complained about the lack of supplies.

Some seemed to have favorites; others seemed quite numb and business-like. As Margie and Lucy went from tent to tent and to tables where meals were served and laundry washed, they glimpsed so many yearning faces, some sad but many smiling and hopeful, that Lucy found herself remembering a Christian missionary who had given a talk at her church and who had adopted an orphaned child in the country where she had served.

A British nurse, dressed in white garb that made her look like a nun, explained in a hushed voice that the parents of most of the children were from the Balkans and had been executed or taken to camps by the Nazis. Many of the refugees in the other sections of the DP camp, which held families and adults, had reported "troubling events." If the families of these children were found, that would be miraculous. The nurse handed over a solemn toddler with wide brown eyes and a Buster Brown haircut like the one Lucy herself had worn as a child. The girl laid her head on Lucy's shoulder, a moment that she savored off and on over the next few weeks.

CHAPTER FORTY-TWO

Hart
Virginia, 2001

"I have something to ask you," Bella said. She'd driven all the way to the Northern Neck to take Hart to see Meer and, if possible, Meer's son, who was still recuperating. Her voice usually strong, unfaltering, and deep for a woman, came out like a girl's: "Did your wife oppose my adoption?"

"What do you mean?"

"Did your wife oppose the adoption of Semitic children by gentiles?"

Hart tapped his chest. "She married a gentile. But if you mean immediately after the war ..." He let his words trail off. "Yes, she did oppose it." Margie believed people should not be ruled by what might have been and had not wanted him to bring up the effect of her opposition. She had loved him passionately and then industriously, always working for what she thought was right. Occasionally, in his worst moments, he'd said to himself about her, *often wrong but never in doubt*. But that was wrong. She'd been wrestling with uncertainty her whole life and regularly took corrective action, though some things, once set in motion, did not turn around.

"It feels as if I've lost every mother I knew," Bella said. She was driving and did not take her hands off the wheel. Three and nine o'clock. Her knuckles white.

Hart never knew how to respond when women said things like that, so he said nothing. Occasionally he'd quoted Freud to Margie: "What do women want?" But he'd learned to expect a comeback along the lines of, "What kind of fool would think women want only one thing?" If Margie were with him listening to Bella, she would have kept her chin up but wept in private.

They stopped in Fredericksburg for lunch. Almost every car in the lot had a magnetic flag like the one he'd bought after his knee replacement. People seemed to meet eyes more often than before, exchanging looks that meant, *We're in this together. What next? Is this the start of World War III?* A family with brown skin, who spoke English with a Hispanic accent, sat at the next table, shrinking from pointed staring by a man who looked like a villain from the movie *Deliverance.*

Driving on, they listened to public radio from Washington. Tapes from Lyndon Johnson's presidency, and then, on another station, personal stories about escaping from the twin towers, accounts so intense that he and Bella ceased speaking until they pulled up at the Virginia hospital where Muhammadu had been transferred after his beating.

"It's thrown him back to Somalia," Bella said.

"Did he know you?" Hart asked.

"I haven't seen him since he was injured, but he recognized his father."

"I have to confess, it's been so long I'm not sure I could pick him out of a—" The car radio was still going, and Bella switched it off, which gave Hart time to censor himself. *Group, not lineup.* Without Langley intervening, Muhammadu might've been in the clink.

Bella's hands, he noticed, had weathered and looked as if they belonged to an older woman. Her previously glossy hair was threaded with gray and grayer at the roots.

"We're hearing a surge in anti-Semitic propaganda," she said.

"From where?"

"*Pravda. Al Manar.*"

"Russia and Muslim Palestine? What are they saying?"

"That Israel had advance warning and no Jews reported to work at the World Trade Center. I personally know four Jews who died in the World Trade Center on Nine-Eleven." Now Bella was shaking her head the way Hart had been earlier.

Meer met them in the hospital lobby and embraced Hart. "My friend," he said in his deep voice and patted Hart's back. "I fear this will be a hard time." He thanked Bella, who looked solemn but had lost the poignant vulnerability that was part of her beauty as a young woman. They sat for coffee in the hospital cafeteria, as they wouldn't be allowed in to see Muhammadu for another hour.

"That'll give us a chance to talk," Bella said. "I was planning to retire and stay in the States, but now I don't know. I may go back to Tel Aviv."

"It's worse than when we were children." Meer had aged into a solid man. His close-cropped hair, like Bella's, was graying.

Bella's expression betrayed her disappointment in Meer. "Not that bad."

Hart knew Meer had meant his childhood in Egypt, not Bella's in Yugoslavia, which Meer recognized with a nod at her and gave them an update on Muhammadu's injuries: his broken nose was healing, his arm was in a cast, and the doctors had found no bleeding under his skull, but he had heard the voices of his captors in Somalia ordering him to shoot the men who beat him and had told the doctors.

"He was almost silent in Ankara," Hart said, thinking of

when Meer brought Muhammadu to stay with him and Margie after his rescue. He'd been twelve or thirteen and stayed six months.

"He's stubborn," Meer said. "He fears the men who kidnapped him will kill him if he doesn't do what they order."

"But that was before 1985."

Meer didn't answer.

"Have you spoken to Lucy's daughter?" Hart asked. "She's a neurologist. She would know about concussions, and I remember she did a psychiatry rotation when she was in training."

"That's a good idea," Bella said. She'd finished her coffee and had left a smear of lipstick on the Styrofoam cup.

"When I was a boy," Meer said, "Lucy and Margie took me to a camp where there were Jewish children. I think they wanted me to see that the children were suffering. I did feel sympathy for them, but they seemed well cared for. I had the idea the Nazis had made them leave Germany. For a long time, I thought the camps in Germany that people talked about were places with white tents like Tolumbat, where families waited to be deported."

Bella pinched a piece off the rim of her Styrofoam cup and dropped it inside. "How did you learn the truth?" she asked.

"Years later, Lucy and Gordon took me to see Auschwitz and Birkenau."

CHAPTER FORTY-THREE

Bella
Yugoslavia, 1943

Dusan was stoking a fire in the oven, which warmed the dugout. He did not answer when Bella asked what had happened to Nura. Soon he would ask her to toast the *zganci* she had made from soaked grain. He'd shivered all night and sweated in the morning. She heard his teeth rattle and his grunting as he propped his wounded leg on top of his good one.

"She wanted us to help you," Matija said from his seat outside the open door, where he was keeping watch. Bella saw only his boots and legs.

Bella wanted to ask how they would help her, but because of them, she was warm, toasting at her back and cool on her face. They had walked with her through the living forest and taken her to this place, where they expected soon to shelter soldiers wounded fighting the Nazis and *Ustaše*. Matija had brought a sack of grain, hard sausage, cheese, and a bottle of wine.

"Why is your beard so long?" Bella asked.

"I vowed to God I would never cut it until the Germans are driven from our land."

"Are you a Chetnik?" she asked.

Matija laughed. "Yes and no."

"Are you a Partisan?" she asked.

"I am a Partisan," Dusan bellowed. "Matija is a yes-and-no. His mother was a Catholic and his father Orthodox, and his sister married a Muslim."

"I brought you here, didn't I?" Matija said.

Bella stooped near the entrance to see him, his breath swirling around his face as if he were a ghost. For a moment, she could see the image of Nura in the vapor.

Matija looked into Bella's eyes. "My sister knew Nura."

Nura is dead, Bella thought, though he had not said that. But there was Nura's ghost, and Matija carried no message from her. Perhaps his sister was dead too. "Is your sister alive?" Bella asked. Her cheek touched the cold stone doorsill at the opening to the dugout house as she peered outside to see his reaction.

"My sister was shot by the *Ustaše* after one of their trucks was blown up."

"Then you should blow up a thousand of their trucks," Dusan called. He was sweating again and had moved away from the fire.

"If I destroy one truck, they shoot a dozen innocents," Matija said. "I will help the Americans, and after the war, they will help us."

CHAPTER FORTY-FOUR

Lucy
Egypt, 1943

"Don't tell them," Lucy heard someone say as the door to the message center opened. She scanned faces: Bernie, Tim, Jill Benson, two new women, and Mike Gold with his artificial leg in a shoe and olive sock standing unattached by his chair. Margie was behind her. For a moment—before Lucy felt the eyes on her—she thought something might have happened to Hart. Jim Raymond came to her, and Hart led Margie aside.

Lucy didn't bother to ask what had happened. Jim ushered her out the door and past Sofia, their Italian receptionist, who, for once, looked solemn. For the ten long seconds it took to walk to the small office upstairs, Lucy believed Gordon was dead, but the first thing Jim said was, "He survived the jump."

She waited with every muscle tensed.

"The radio was damaged in the drop, and they had to keep moving. He's with Chetniks."

If Jim hadn't looked so concerned, she would have let herself feel relief, but she waited, and bit by bit, he explained. Gordon had landed in a tree and had to cut himself down. He'd been spiked by a branch, resulting in a wound that infected his foot. He was lucky they'd gotten him to a doctor, Jim said, "But ..."

She barely listened because Jim was offering details about

the transmission. Too much static. The radio operator had a faltering hand. They weren't sure of everything. "But he's alive?" she asked.

"Yes," Jim said. "He's alive."

It made no sense to go back to the villa early. Lucy knew that. Jim knew that. Everybody in the war knew you had to keep going. If you stopped every time someone you knew got wounded, or worse, nothing would get done. Besides, the news had been good. Gordon was alive.

"Of course, I'm up to working," she told Jim. She must have looked awful for him to even offer to send her back to the villa. Everyone looked up when she went back into the message center, though even Margie knew not to do more than tilt up her face to offer an exaggerated stiff-upper-lip expression. Bernie winked, and Lucy mustered her concentration and took a page from the top of the stack to decrypt.

When she got far enough to see that the message was from Hart, her finger began tapping of its own accord on her knee. A report and list of needed supplies. Some of the Partisans with him were miners. They'd succeeded in using the plastic explosives dropped with him to blow up a bridge, but they needed more. They wanted blankets, more sacks of flour, batteries for the generator, and ammunition. He'd heard word of an American who parachuted in and was injured and needed antibiotics. Need for antibiotics urgent, he wrote.

CHAPTER FORTY-FIVE

Hart
Yugoslavia, 1943

He, Andrej, and the miner, Janez, tromped beside the tracks, ready to skid down the hillside if they felt vibration on the rail. They'd already used up almost their entire supply of plastic explosives to destroy a stone railroad bridge; the diversionary attack beforehand on the Germans had cost the life of one young Partisan. Hart prayed silently for the boy as they walked. The death had merited a solemn minute, but no time for burial. Something about the clouds massing above the mountains and the smell of rain made him imagine the boy's soul tailing them.

Janez jabbered something too fast for Hart to understand, but Andrej translated. "We find curve soon."

As Hart understood the plan, they would most economically use their remaining plastic explosives to derail a train. A section of straight track could be easily repaired, and a train might jump across a missing section without mishap, but if damage occurred on the outside rail of a curve, momentum could carry an engine off the track. The more cars derailed, the better. Any disruption to the Axis transportation infrastructure would seriously hinder the Nazi supply line to Italy and France.

Every once in a while, Andrej spoke in his heavily accented bass. He explained that the British wanted the Partisans' every effort to go into killing Nazis and destroying tunnels and bridges but that it was also necessary to keep the enemy away from the wild areas where resistance fighters could live through the winter.

They trudged on, step after weary step, mostly silent, hoping each turn of the tracks would reveal a mountainside curve where they could pack a mine with their remaining plastic explosives and set it to detonate under the weight of a locomotive.

Thunder rumbled in the distance, and Hart stooped to feel the rail for vibration. The curve they sought had to be close. The little river below them lay in shadow, but enough light escaped the clouds to make them squint and for him to wonder if the silvered sky and shafts of light meant something profound—it felt that way—or if it meant something about the boy who fought fiercely but lost his life to gunfire from the bunkered Nazis. All of them were tired, had blistered heels, and were hungry. The straps from his pack bit into his shoulders. He shrugged and readjusted his rifle to relieve the pressure. Since he'd joined the Partisans, most of every day had been devoted to covering ground on foot. Hart guessed he'd lost fifteen pounds.

As the drop-off beside them grew steeper, they took to the tracks and began walking on the ties, which required looking down to place their boots. With the sun behind the clouds, he no longer had to squint. The hillside across the track was thickly forested, but he thought he saw movement in a rocky gap. Something two-legged, ant-sized in the distance, darted across the clearing.

"Do you see someone up there?" he asked. "Halfway up the slope ahead."

Andrej huddled with Matija and gestured to the tracks and back at the mountain. "First, we set mine." They'd reached the perfect place for a derailment, the track curving sharply, the bank beside it dropping away in a steep slant, almost a cliff.

When they'd spaded enough gravel away from under the outer rail to wedge the mine underneath, Hart warmed the packet of plastic explosive under his arm and knelt to pack the mine. Andrej kept watch as Janez prepared the trigger.

Hart looked up when he was done but didn't spot anyone on the hillside. They were sitting ducks, completely in the open. The two-legged creature had been too skinny for a bear.

"Now I see," Andrej growled.

"*Pripravljen*," Jenez muttered, which Hart thought meant "ready." He'd learned a smattering of Slovene and a bit more of Serbo-Croatian but still couldn't come up with a complete sentence in either language without jumping rails into words and phrases from French and Spanish.

"Ready," Andrej translated and pointed to the mountain. He'd seen the person too. "We can surprise."

Hart doubted that the three of them could be quicker than the man he'd seen, but at least Andrej and Janez had a plan. They led him down the slope opposite the loaded mine and picked their way down a switch-backing path until they, too, were in the forest. Then back they skulked, like foxes, until they reached a stretch of track with a large pipe beneath it high enough for them to crouch through to the other side and follow a deer path to a collection of head-high boulders. Janez held his forefinger to his closed lips. They unshouldered their rifles and settled in to wait.

Both Janez and Andrej carried Carcano carbines, Italian rifles captured in battle and delivered to Partisans by the British. Ammunition for those could be obtained more easily than for American rifles like Hart's, but Andrej had been complaining about being saddled with weapons left over from the First World War. Hart could say the same about his American M1917 Enfield. He hoped he'd convinced Andrej. They could have swapped if they had more time, but it made no sense to trade rifles for arms they'd never fired. And the more the danger, the more a man could come to love his gun. Hart was reassured by the feel of his Enfield, the grace of the oiled wood stock and handguard, the heft of the rifle across his forearm.

Each of them faced a different way from their cover among the boulders. Andrej had the best view of the tracks. He could easily have picked off anyone tampering with the mine. Janez faced the mountainside, and Hart looked down onto a shaded patch of forest dappled with sunlight. Several times he heard rustling and raised his barrel, but none of them said a word.

A twig snapped, and Hart's pulse accelerated. He heard rumbling and couldn't tell if it was thunder or a distant locomotive. He tilted his head to listen. His back was to the others, but he could feel their alertness through his skin.

He heard a loose rock tumble off the roadbed behind him but kept his eye on his patch of forest, trusting Andrej and Janez to watch his back. The sound of a locomotive grew unmistakable. They would need to move away from the tracks before the mine blew. Lightning flashed, but he kept his eyes on his patch of forest and counted the way he did when he was a boy. At three-one-thousand, thunder rolled in like an avalanche, blending with the clatter and roar of the approaching train. He was on his feet. If the train derailed, it could smash them all. Andrej and Janez were at his back, still sitting casually but with rifles raised. Andrej looked up, amused. Janez shrugged and gestured to the woods.

The train sounded much closer. Hart was sure he would see it if he looked down the track. Yes, his companions were seasoned combat veterans, and he was a novice, but the train could be loaded with enemy troops, and his fellows needed to get back to the other side of the tracks before their mine blew. He said as much to Andrej, shouldered his rifle, and pushed past to lead the way to the pipe where they'd crossed. All that crouching in wait for the man who hadn't appeared had made his joints stiff, but he managed a sprint across the open stretch and into the pipe under the track. He heard Andrej's and Janez's footfalls echo behind him, but the roar of the locomotive was bearing down.

The opening of the pipe looked out on forested mountainside. For an instant, it struck him as an opening into Montana, a sort of time machine into the world of his boyhood. He ran straight through, skidding downhill on gravel. His foot caught something, and he plummeted forward, already mid-fall before he realized he was falling. He turned midair to land on his side with his arm up to protect his head.

When Hart finally looked up, it was to three pointed rifles. One barrel followed his skull as he rose. The others were Andrej's and Janez's carbines aiming at the man who'd tripped him. The language shouted above the thunder of the coming train wasn't German or Italian. He guessed Serbo-Croatian rather than Slovenian and that they were talking about him, the American. Andrej was answering in the same language. The owner of the rifle that was pointed at him wore a British tunic. His waist-length beard made Hart think Chetnik, though the British had ceased sending Chetniks uniforms or much of anything else.

Andrej and Janez held their rifles aimed at the stranger. Hart pointed at the train. "The mine will ex—" he yelled, but an explosion obliterated his word before they, all four, hit the dirt.

CHAPTER FORTY-SIX

Lucy
North Africa, 1943

"We'll get Gordon back," Jim said. "It's a logistics problem. In the meantime, the Brits are packing the same medical kit for each drop. That way, they can be ready to go."

"Is there penicillin in the kits? Or any of those sulfa pills?" she asked.

"I don't know."

They hadn't heard from Hart in more than a week, but that wasn't unusual. Not even Margie seemed concerned, though she was spending more time with her Jewish Palestinian friends. A British officer in the field with Tito reported that Hart's group had derailed a train. Someone in the group had been injured, only a minor wound, but a peasant family had been executed in retaliation, and they were lying low.

"Can the British fly Gordon out?" Lucy asked.

Jim shook his head. "There's no way to make that happen. He'll be smuggled out by fishing boat."

"What does that mean? He's not at the coast, is he? How will they transport him?" She could see Jim's eyes register her question and reflect his search for an acceptable answer.

"Will they hide him in a farm wagon?" she asked. "I can't imagine them carrying him down a mountainside on a stretcher."

Jim was too diplomatic to say his guess was as good as hers, but that was how she read his face. He gave her a kind look and sent her back to work. One of the new women, a wiz at ciphers nicknamed Lettie, looked up and winked when Lucy went back to her desk in the code room.

"Do you want me to play the net?" Lucy asked and rolled the ball to her opponent. After a full day of ciphers and weeks of worry about Gordon, Lucy wanted nothing more than to slam some good hard balls into the extreme reaches of their opponents' court, but her partner, Princess Frederica, was intermittently watching her five-year-old, Sofia, who was on the next court in a white frock with an enormous bow in her hair, under the supervision of a tennis coach, who was showing her how to bounce the ball with her racquet, while Meer, in a white galibaya, hitched up at the waist, retrieved stray balls.

Princess Frederica beamed her usual sunny smile, scooped the ball with her racquet, and backed up behind the line to serve. "No, thank you. I'd like to practice my groundstrokes."

The sky was a brilliant clear blue, and they faced west, where the sun beamed straight at them, making spots in front of Lucy's eyes. The other children, little Prince Constantine, whom Lucy had only met once—he was three—and the baby, Irene, were with a nanny, but their mother obviously kept them in mind. To Lucy's gratitude, Princess Frederica showed interest in Meer and praised him for retrieving balls.

Also, to her credit, the princess had been shopping at the *souq* and confided in Lucy her concern about the welfare of the street children in Cairo. The slow-paced series of lobs and groundstrokes allowed for conversation between points and, on Lucy's part, a wandering of attention. A red limousine she believed might be carrying King Farouk arrived—yes, she was correct. "Could that man with King Farouk be the spy John Eppler?" she asked in English.

Princess Frederica shaded her eyes with her hand. "Isn't he in prison?"

"He's supposed to be," Lucy said. "But I supposed the King can do what he wants."

"I doubt any king can do just what he wants," Frederica said. Her brother-in-law King George certainly couldn't. "When we're done with this set, I think I'll ask him."

CHAPTER FORTY-SEVEN

Hart
Virginia, 2001

"I'll freshen up and meet you by the elevator," Bella told Hart when she'd finished her coffee. He didn't like waiting in hospitals—it reminded him too much of Margie's last days—but if Meer wanted him to see Muhammadu, so be it.

As soon as she left, Meer asked if Hart remembered that back in the day, he, Meer, had been the one who noticed that King Farouk had been furloughing the spy John Eppler from prison and taking him to the Gezira Club for lunch.

"I was still behind enemy lines, but I do remember. I heard you told Queen Frederica, and she walked right up to him and spoke to him in German."

"She was a princess then. Lucy was playing tennis with her against two British women, and I was fetching balls when we saw King Farouk get out of his car. I rolled a ball over near him and overheard King Farouk asking Mr. Eppler's opinion about the Muslim Brotherhood. The King was concerned that his people would think he was too involved with the British."

"I didn't realize you did that with the ball. Was it deliberate?"

"Yes, to get me over there. Eppler had a German mother, but he was an Arab in his soul," Meer said. "I understood him because I love this country, but part of my soul is in North

Africa. He was split the way I am split."

"Were you there when Princess Frederica confronted Eppler?"

"I was," Meer said. "The princess was a fine woman. By that time, the King and his friend were sitting at an outside table. I'd managed to get close enough to overhear. Eppler was so grateful for the opportunity to be in the open air after all his time in prison that he wasn't careful. They were talking about what might happen after the war. They were strategizing how to end colonial rule, but King Farouk didn't know if he would keep the backing of the people after the British left. Eppler believed there would be a new elected government with the Muslim Brotherhood in power."

"They were speaking in Arabic?"

"Yes, but then Princess Frederica walked up with her little daughter, Sofia. Frederica smiled that sunny smile she had and addressed Mr. Eppler in German. He was a very charming man, but his hands began to shake."

"What did they say?"

"I don't know. I don't speak German."

Bella emerged from the ladies' room before Hart's conversation went farther, and they took the elevator to the floor where Meer's son was recuperating. After tossing aside his earlier idea that Muhammadu would be at Alspy House, Hart expected to find a twenty- or thirty-someone resembling Meer in a hospital bed with his face bandaged and perhaps a leg in traction. Instead, he was faced with a locked ward that required pushing a buzzer and speaking to a nurse on an intercom to gain admittance.

It reminded him of a ward where he'd once visited a CIA colleague who'd been given LSD. Muhammadu could barely look at them and held himself so rigidly it gave Hart pain in his chest. Muhammadu's mother had been lighter-skinned than

Meer and resembled the Syrian nurse Fatima at Alspy House. Muhammadu himself resembled both parents, lighter-skinned and taller than Meer, but his expression reminded Hart of a scene in Slovenia, one too painful to revisit. He gathered his resolve and faced Muhammadu. "Can you tell us anything about the men who beat you? Did you recognize them?"

Meer winced. The look on his son's face, a flash of sheer terror.

Moments later, a nurse proclaimed the visit over, though Meer was allowed to stay a few minutes longer than Bella and Hart, who felt inept and guilty and immediately apologized when Meer reappeared.

"He makes no sense," Meer said. "These men who beat him were not from Al Qaeda or Taliban. They were not the source of his information, but he fears they disguised themselves as Americans and punished him to warn him against talking."

"Did he know in advance about the attacks?"

"His handler asked him to seek someone out, but he was in Somalia. He barely made contact. He was brought back several weeks before the attacks."

"Did he go to Alspy House?" Hart asked.

"I don't know," Meer answered. "But he came back to the States using an assumed name."

CHAPTER FORTY-EIGHT

Hart
Yugoslavia, 1943

Hart, Andrej, and the Chetnik had been walking for hours; every inch of his body ached, though in phases. For a while, his left heel throbbed, and then his right ankle and both knees. When he breathed, his ribs ached. The straps from his pack bit into his shoulders, but it hurt his right elbow to adjust them. His ears rang as if he'd spent a day on the rifle range with no ear protection. He wasn't sure of the Chetnik's name: Kosta something that sounded like Kalabić.

The explosion had made him at least a temporary ally, and he seemed respectful that Hart was American.

They'd been lucky that the train tumbled away from them, leaving the Nazi passengers occupied with saving themselves. As far as Hart and the others could tell in their scramble uphill into the forest, there had been no prisoners onboard. That had been one of Hart's worries. If anyone had been killed in the explosion, he wouldn't know it, though, and that was a source of both reassurance and nagging, unfocused guilt.

When they had hiked for almost an hour, they came to a ledge where they could look out from under the scrub without being seen. The engine and four cars had derailed, though a few rear cars remained upright, and the train looked otherwise intact. Many men, presumably Nazis, were scurrying like ants on the side of the derailment, some as far below as the little river, a ribbon of silver. So far, no one seemed to be coming up along the path where Kosta had led Hart, Andrej, and Janez up the mountainside on a route a bloodhound would have been hard-pressed to follow. They backtracked across little streams, trekked off-path around boulders, and skirted a pond on their way to a secluded hut, where Kosta, with a gap-toothed smile through his oily beard, claimed that an American, who'd bailed out of a fighter plane shot down by the enemy, was recuperating.

Gordon's plane had not been shot down—Hart knew that much—so it was unrealistic to hope to run into his friend, but he wasn't so tired that he couldn't pray silently for the American and for those he injured when the train went off the track.

Before sunset, they made their way through tightly spaced trees and came upon a large mound of stones. Kosta called out, and a weak male voice responded. After some chatter with Kosta, Andrej explained that they had reached a one-room hut constructed by shepherds and that the American was inside.

"Hello!" Hart called out. "We're friends. I'm American." He ducked inside after Kosta, pausing to adjust to the dim light.

The room was round, with a dirt floor softened by mounds of pine needles. Immediately opposite the open door, an American GI lay with his head and shoulders on his pack and one leg outstretched and splinted. He accepted water from Hart's canteen and explained he'd bailed from a burning Tomahawk aircraft, had grown up in Pennsylvania, and had broken his ankle trying to hike out. The Chetnik, Kosta, had carried him partway on his back.

"The ground comes up fast, doesn't it?" Hart said.

"No joke."

The airman was named S.K. Kelly. His friends called him "Skip," but S.K. didn't stand for anything, and the Army Air Corp called him S(only) K(only). "Just don't call me Sonly Konly," he said.

Hart hadn't packed the radio, but he promised to send out a message when he reached it and a pedal-operated generator a two-day walk away. The others had crowded in by then and conversed back and forth in their native languages, with Andrej translating to English for Hart and Skip. "How about loaves and fishes for supper?" Hart said, meaning they would share what meager provisions they'd brought. A can of Spam. Cheese. *Zganci.* One apple, cut in quarters. Despite wariness between the Chetnik and the two Partisans, they communicated well enough to talk about delivering wounded Americans to the coast. Kosta did not know Gordon, but he had an idea where he might have been taken. If Hart and his friends would help take turns with the stretcher, they might be able to get Skip to the next hospital on the same route.

CHAPTER FORTY-NINE

Bella
Yugoslavia, 1943

Bella wished for a hollow place inside the wall, so she could burrow into darkness and enter the world of tiny stars and ghosts. The man the Chetniks brought had a leg wound that smelled like a dead animal, and each time he changed position, he growled. When he tried to drink, his water sloshed and spilled. Once, he yelled in a language she did not know and hurled his tin cup at her. She refilled it with spring water but was so frightened of his groans that, unless Dusan was nearby, she waited until his eyes were shut to creep close and set the water beside him.

Though Dusan still limped, the wound on his leg was healing, and he no longer shook or sweated day and night. Neither he nor she knew how to speak the talk of the new man, whose name was "Gordo," though he was not fat. Nor was he as lean as Dusan or Matija. Dusan expected him to die.

While Dusan was in the woods setting a snare for a badger, Bella squatted in the door of the dugout, watching the man sleep. She did not want to touch him. An hour before, he had been shivering, but in the short time since she had refilled his tin cup, he had begun to sweat and throw off his covers.

He opened his eyes, and she crept backward. "*¿Que pasa, chiquita?*" he called. "¿Tienes miedo?"

Papa, she thought. "*Si, tengo miedo*," she said. Yes, she was afraid, but the moment she told him, her fear left her. She crept back to his side and held the cup for him to drink. He was smelly with stubble on his cheeks, too short for a beard and too long for no beard, but his face was handsome.

"*Bella*," he said, and she wondered how he knew her name. Matija and Dusan called her *Esma* because they thought she was the *hija* of Abdullah and Nura. He asked her about her mama and papa. What were their names? But all she could think was Mama and Papa and the song her mama taught her:

Dos y dos son cuatro
cuatro y dos son seis
seis y dos son ocho,
Animas benditas
Me arrodillo yo.

There was more, but she did not remember. *Two and two are four ... Blessed souls, I kneel myself down.* She had not seen her mama and papa for a very long time.

Wiping Gordo's sweating brow calmed her. She dipped her kerchief in spring water and wrung it out and mopped his brow, but she was afraid to take the stinking bandage off his foot. At night, she lay between him and Dusan and listened to the sounds of the forest: the cry of the lynx, the hoot of an owl, and other calls that must have been from souls roaming in search of their families. Nura seeking the real Esma.

Sometimes she wondered if the soul of her father had entered Gordo. He was American, Dusan told her, and if that were true, he could not be her father, but his voice in her old language made him seem like a father. She did not want him to die. She tried to feed him broth and rice when he roused, but he slept more than he was awake.

The day Matija returned with the doctor, they sent Bella to the spring for water. The doctor was old and white-haired and more wrinkled than Abdullah. She lugged her bucket into the dugout and, as Dusan ordered, left to sit near the spring, where she heard terrible sounds that made her think they were killing the American. She hid behind a large rock and made herself small. From her hiding place, she saw Dusan emerge through the door with her bucket and splash the crimson contents into the woods.

She shut her eyes and tried not to hear, but the sound of spading into the earth was more than she could bear. She hoped they would wash him as Nura had taught her, but she did not want to help them. She crept into the forest where souls floated among the trees and made her way down the mountainside, following the stream.

Thickets near the rocky streambed clutched at her arms and legs, and unexpected drop-offs sent her skidding downhill. Through the pine needles and leafless treetops, the sky grew as flat and blank as a hung sheet and so quiet that all she heard was her own breath. Even the water stilled and became as silent as the ghost of Tišina. When Bella lay back to rest, snow began to float over her. Moist lace collected on the valleys of her skirt and sleeves and on branches and pine boughs. She knew no one would call her back. No one but Tišina.

It was not hunger that forced her back. Nor was it the chattering of her teeth, the ache in her fingers, the darkness, or a sound from Dusan, Matija, or the doctor. They were in hiding; if they had called, a Nazi might have heard them.

An owl flew overhead among the snowflakes, silent as Tišina. Every pine and every stone in the valley was silvered with moonlight. Seeing such beauty, Bella thought of her real mother, who once told her the story of children in the woods leaving a trail of breadcrumbs to find their way home. They hadn't counted on their trail markers being eaten by crows. Bella wouldn't have left a trail of crumbs; she'd have eaten any bread she had, but the little stream that led her away would show her the way back. Her mother would not have wanted her lost or alone, so she followed the stream uphill toward the dugout. The snow had covered any trail she might have left, and climbing uphill was much harder than walking down. She slipped and fell and sometimes crawled on her hands and knees. Sometimes she ate snow.

When she reached the clearing with the little spring, Bella was shaking the way Dusan had shaken and Gordo had shaken, but she was not sick. She was cold and tired and bruised and scraped. Smoke was rising from the stone chimney of the dugout, and the wooden door was shut, but she remembered their knock. Three and two and three.

Like magic, the door opened. Matija frowned and complained, and she hung her head. She was afraid to ask if they had killed Gordo.

"Come warm yourself by the fire," the doctor said. "But be careful. We have taken your apron for Gordon."

She did not speak but crept closer to see for herself that they had not buried Gordo and that he was alive. His breath was raspy and slow, like a knife scraping a whetstone. His eyes were shut, but they flickered when she touched his warm hand.

"¿Que pasó?" she asked, but it was not Gordo who answered.

"We had to take his foot," the doctor said. "It was very infected, but we gave him medicine. Now he needs a nurse. You must be a nurse, Esma."

CHAPTER FIFTY

Hart
Virginia, 2001

"I don't eat chicken, brother," Bella said to Meer, but Hart already knew that—or once had known. His memory was not functioning at its most efficient level after the drive and visit to Muhammadu. He'd been relegated to the back seat, his choice because he'd thought he could elevate his leg. Bella's rental car did not permit a passenger to ride unfastened, though, not without an alarm dinging incessantly. Meer and Bella were discussing places where they could dine after visiting Lucy.

"Sister," Meer said. "Their vegetables are good, but we can have dinner in the cafeteria."

Hart had never heard them *brother* and *sister* one another that way before, but it didn't surprise him and was touching. Gordon and Lucy would have liked that. Perhaps it was new, a kind of 9/11 solidarity between Semite and Muslim. Or they'd suppressed it around him when Margie was alive.

"There's a nurse named Fatima here," Meer told Bella. "She looks the way Lucy looked when we were in Cairo."

"When we were children?" Bella asked.

Hart didn't hear Meer's answer. It seemed strange to him, but everything had seemed strange since Margie's death. He had always believed himself to be a sensible, practical person, but he'd recently found himself talking to ghosts, something

Margie used to do. Or at least she'd talked to herself, which in her mind, was the same as talking to her dead parents.

While they parked, Bella brought up chicken again and told them she'd helped hatch chicks at the farm where she'd lived with a Muslim couple during the war. One that didn't peep had imprinted on her and followed her everywhere. "I don't know why I said that," she told Meer. "This situation with your son, maybe."

It seemed like a non-sequitur to Hart. But then life was chocked with events that seemed unrelated yet were connected: Yugoslavia like a pressure cooker after the war; Tito of the Partisans siding with the Communists and governing with an iron hand. Was that necessary? Hart hadn't thought so at the time. What astounded him was how good, brave, patriotic people misjudged one another's motives and, expecting more horrors, created them everywhere. When and how does a nation intervene to prevent genocide? What means were acceptable? Hart's life had been spent studying these questions, and yet he felt as ignorant as ever and didn't like the idea of being useless.

"Watch your step," Meer said. They'd parked and were approaching a curb near the back entrance of Alspy House. Entering the building was like going through an airlock, glass sliding doors, stale air, camera, intercom. Yes, they would be admitted. He'd seen the bank of monitors behind the front desk and knew they were being watched.

They presented their IDs, signed in, and rode an elevator to the floor where he and Bernie had stayed after their knee replacements and where Lucy now lived.

"Where does your friend Bernie stay?" Bella asked.

"He has an apartment upstairs," Hart said. Meer's expression said he already knew.

Lucy was in a wheelchair at a table with another elderly woman dressed stylishly in narrow slacks, pink flats, and a patterned blouse, Lettie Nash from OSS, Cairo, Hart realized. When they approached, both looked up, and Lettie asked Lucy who the people were.

Lucy looked up and smiled broadly. “My children,” she answered.

“Those aren’t your children,” Lettie said, her voice almost unchanged from their time in Cairo. She wore her characteristic small hoop earrings.

Lucy’s face was striking, her eyes still large and expressive. She was grinning at Bella. Meer took her hand, and she looked up at him like an overjoyed child.

Bella bent close. “Do you know what’s happened?”

Lucy, who had been beaming, glanced at Meer and Hart, and her smile faded. “Are we at war?” she asked.

When Bella told her about the attacks on the World Trade Center, Lucy frowned. “Do you know what the man is going to do?”

“President Bush?” Hart asked.

Lucy shook her head. “No,” she answered, and Hart couldn’t get more out of her, though he was sure she didn’t mean Cheney, Meer, or her son.

“Do you mean Gordon?” Bella asked, and Lucy looked distressed. She shook her head.“Leave her alone,” Lettie said.

They chatted for a few moments more and found out nothing, but Bella placed a call on her cellular phone and reached Bernie, who invited them up to his apartment for drinks. Meer led the way. Obviously, he’d been there before, which piqued Hart’s curiosity.

The visit with Lucy had set Meer and Bella to reminiscing. “Gordon only got angry with me once,” Bella said when they were seated with drinks in hand, wine for Bella, brown ale for Meer, and a whiskey sour for Hart. “It was in a field hospital in Yugoslavia. He was feverish and sick all over his shirt. I washed it in boiling water to get the smell out.”

“Was he cold without it?” Meer asked.

"I didn't find out until a long time afterward that he'd hidden a picture and a silk square for decoding in a secret pocket in the lining of his shirt."

"The square should have stood up to boiling," Hart said.

"It did," Bella said. "But the picture turned to pulp. I found out later it was of Lucy."

CHAPTER FIFTY-ONE

Bella
Yugoslavia, 1943

"No, little one. My name is Gor-doN," he told Bella, dragging out the *n* with a groan that made her believe she was hurting him. Her job was to remove his bandage, wash his stump, and rinse and boil bandages for him to use again. The doctor had demonstrated the first few times, coaxing her to see that the wound had been sewed with a flap of skin but needed to drain and be kept clean. Matija would give Gordon an injection of medicine, and when the pupils of his eyes shrank to small dots, she was to work on his stump. After a week, the medicine ran out, and Gordon moaned at night. Although he seemed more awake than before the doctor removed his foot, he sometimes shivered, and at other times sweat blistered and ran off his body.

Each morning Dusan cracked the ice on the spring. When the ice became too hard, Bella melted snow in a pot in the oven. They were happy that it was too cold for the Nazis to come on foot, but when they heard planes, they put out the fire and hoped the smoke would float away.

Gordon liked to tell stories to her in their secret language. He told her about a small girl who entered the house of a bear family and tried every chair and every bed to find which fit her best. It seemed strange that a small girl would be able to choose what she wanted. Sometimes Bella pretended she would be allowed to choose her father from among the men in the dugout.

Once or twice in her pretending, she chose the doctor, but every other time she picked Gordon because the soul of her real father had settled inside him. Snow still lay on the ground when he started hobbling on crutches. Inside the dugout, he crept about on his hands and knees. He asked Bella to knit him a sock for his stump. She did not know how, but when the doctor returned, he brought yarn and taught her to make rows of slip knots on one needle and wrap a strand around the other and poke through with another needle. Bit by bit, she learned to knit well enough to make a scarf that she could stitch into a sock like a soft bag for his stump.

The doctor brought him a wooden foot that did not fit because it had belonged to someone else, but Dusan set about adjusting it, carving the inside to make room for what was left of Gordon's leg. Matija spoke about taking Gordon to the sea to meet a fishing boat that would take him across the sea to the north of Africa, where his friends lived. Hearing that, Bella turned her face to the wall and wept silently because she did not want Gordon to leave her.

Not long after the doctor's visit, a man named Kosta delivered a parcel of food with grain, hard cheese, wine, potatoes, and a packet of meat. That night, Bella awakened to the sound of shouting between Matija, Dusan, Kosta, and Gordon. The following morning, she asked Gordon why they had argued, and he asked her if she would like to come with him.

"*Si*," she told him. "*Me gusta*."

"*Entonces*," he said. "I will insist. It will be a long journey with much walking. Bad men may shoot at us."

Gordon could barely walk to the spring and back. Bella wondered how he could go on a long journey with much walking. She was too small to carry him, and he was too big to be carried. When the Chetniks brought him, it had been on a stretcher carried by two men in rotation with two other men. She said none of this, but looked into his serious face.

His beard had grown full, and his brown eyes glittered in the firelight. He patted his chest in the spot where he had a secret pocket and where her washing had melted a picture of his girlfriend into a formless wad. Bella's face felt hot with shame. She looked at her feet and waited for him to tell her she was bad and he did not want her to come. "You are a child, and I may not be able to keep you safe," he said. "*¿Entiendes?*"

She understood that no one could protect everyone, but the soul of her father was inside Gordon, and what she wished more than anything in the world was to stay with him.

CHAPTER FIFTY-TWO

Lucy
North Africa, 1944

Why did men feel they needed to give advice along with bad news? Lucy noticed that the only one who hadn't offered it was Mike Gold, who'd been in Gordon's shoes and lost his leg. If Gordon lived, the Chetniks would try to smuggle him to the coast. From there, they would ferry him across the Adriatic Sea in a fishing boat to rendezvous with a friendly vessel.

During their break, she asked Mike about his journey across the mountains, and he told her farmers had hidden him in the back of a wagon. They'd ridden until the road ended, and from there, a group of Chetniks carried him on a stretcher. On the way, they'd stopped at a hut where an American tapped out a coded message on a radio powered by a treadle-operated generator. They'd taken gunfire from a Nazi machine gun nest as they made their way down a path with many switchbacks and had hidden behind rocks until moonset that night.

"They risked their lives for me. I'll always be grateful." He shook his head. "It's a terrible war. The *Ustaše* want to wipe out the Serbs, and some of the non-Serbian Chetniks collaborated so they and their families would be spared. No good choices."

"I think there are," Lucy said. "There have to be."

"But what do you do when your family is at risk?" Mike asked.

"Fight for them," Lucy said without hesitating, though she understood his point. How would one weigh protecting a family member against collaborating? If she could guarantee Gordon's safety by helping the Nazis, would she do it? No. It made her think again of the story of Abraham obeying God's command to offer his son Isaac. Young Meer had told her the same story with touching earnestness, only in his version from the Qur'an, Abraham's elder son, Ishmael, was offered. Both versions, she thought, were about the very situation she and Mike Gold were discussing. Circumstances forcing a person to choose between duty and beloved family. Would she help Hitler to buy Gordon's safety?

"It's too painful to think about," she said aloud. "Especially when all I can do is pray."

"That's not all you can do," Mike answered.

She thought he meant she could go on with her work at the message center, encrypting and decrypting and paraphrasing messages, but he went on:

"Put yourself in his shoes," He tapped his artificial leg. "He might expect you to reject him."

"Because of his leg?"

"If you lost your leg, mightn't you think that?"

She had to admit, she wouldn't be surprised by a man rejecting a one-legged woman. She hadn't heard that Mike had received a Dear-John letter, but perhaps he'd kept a rejection to himself. Lettie Nash seemed interested in him, though. More likely, he was the one dissatisfied with his patched-up body. It seemed too intrusive to ask, though she might ask Lettie about it later on. But it was out of the question that she would reject Gordon because of a lost limb.

After the birth of the Bensons' new baby, the OSS women moved to a houseboat on the Nile, where sunrise regularly cast dazzle on the wall of the cabin Lucy and Margie shared. Each morning Lucy prayed, sometimes with her eyes open to watch the dance of miniature suns, for that's what they were, tiny images of the sun. On that particular morning, she'd been praying for Gordon's safety, for her mother, who'd written that she'd been coughing like hounds in pursuit of a delivery truck, and for Aunt Edith, who had, by the report in her mother's latest otherwise upbeat letter, begun dragging one leg.

The adjacent houseboat was owned by King Farouk, though he used it for entertaining rather than as a dwelling. While she was absorbed in the reflections on the wall, the shadow of a gull or some other bird crossed the space she was watching. From where she knelt, her face was at the level of a porthole. When she turned her head, she saw someone moving around on the pier by King Farouk's boat.

Margie was rousing but not up. Lucy covered herself with a robe and crept onto the deck to look. Two of the men she saw were in uniform, the other in Egyptian garb. When she glimpsed the face of the Egyptian, she thought for a moment that he might be the German, Johann Eppler, whom Princess Frederica had confronted before she and her family left for South Africa.

He smiled at Lucy with a charming expression and gaze of physical intensity that made her blush. She regretted coming outdoors in her robe, but, given her duty to investigate and report, she called out. "Are you Herr Eppler?"

By this time, Margie and the occupants of the other cabins, including their new coworkers, Lettie, Penny, and Liz, had dressed and joined her on deck. The man smiled at them also. "I am under guard," he said in English, "doing some work for the King."

One of the men in uniform nodded and tapped his pistol, and the other stepped closer to Eppler. Lucy had been correct. Margie also recognized the German spy.

"I will be going back to prison when I'm done," he said. "I hope you know it was not my choice to work for Hitler's government. I would rather have helped out Princess Frederica of

Hanover. Now I serve King Farouk."

One of the guards spoke to Eppler in Arabic, and Lucy understood nothing but the words for *where* and, in Eppler's reply, *but*."

"What are you doing for him?" Lucy pressed.

"I think you should ask him yourself," Eppler said. "I believe you will be invited to his party next week." He gave a partial bow. "I'm sorry to say my escorts have informed me I must return to my confinement."

As predicted, an invitation was delivered to the occupants of the OSS houseboat next to King Farouk's. During the intervening few days, there had been no news of Gordon, and Lucy began sleeping on her side with her back against the wall of the cabin, imagining him spooning with her, as if the dream would keep both of them safe. Margie seemed tense, but Hart had sent his regular reports. A young Partisan serving with him had been killed, and Hart would soon meet with Tito and Randolph Churchill, son of the Prime Minister. Lucy and Margie had reported Eppler's presence on King Farouk's houseboat, but they were not told what use, if any, was made of the information.

Kim had revealed his true identity to King Farouk, thus would be coming to the party as himself, and had declared that the women on the houseboat have new dresses made for the occasion. At their own expense, of course, though women weren't paid as much as the men, and Lucy was concerned about the expense. She'd returned Jill Benson's dress, though, and had no choice, though something ready-made would be preferable.

There had been no excursions in disguise since the trip to the *souq* with Meer, but he'd been assigned to live on the boat with them and assist when he could. His eager presence was a comfort, although the situation—a boy looking after adult women—seemed backward to her. At times she thought that if Gordon didn't survive, she would adopt Meer as her son after the war and remain in Cairo.

She and the other OSS women had grown used to traveling together without an escort, but she asked Meer if he would prefer to stay behind with his cousin, the cook who lived elsewhere, or if he would like to accompany them to the dress shop. As she predicted, he was eager to accompany them, but Lettie, Penny, and Liz decided to go later on, and that left the three, Lucy, Margie, and Meer. Margie had already bought a dress and was due for a fitting.

"Is it inconvenient to have me along?" Lucy asked.

"I'm not superstitious," Margie said as they stepped off the dock onto dry land.

Lucy wondered what Margie meant but didn't comment, nor did Meer, but when they arrived at the dress shop, Margie sent Meer out to buy pastries. The owner of the shop was French, but the seamstresses were Egyptian. One of them recognized Margie and rushed into a curtained area to fetch the dress she had ordered.

The seamstress returned with an unusually long dress bag, which she unzipped and hung in a private area. The reason for Margie's wide grin became apparent as the dress was uncovered. It was shining white silk with a fitted bodice and a full skirt. The veil was fine Egyptian lace. The neckline off the shoulders. A few adjustments, and the beautiful bridal gown Margie had ordered would be ready to go.

"Don't tell," Margie said. "I'm going to have it stored."

"Not a word," Lucy promised. "Now we just need this war to end and our men to come home."

The dress Lucy ordered was not a wedding dress but a black ankle-length sheath and gold-embroidered velvet jacket, ready well in advance of the party. From what she saw of her reflection when she tried it on, she looked as glamorous as an old maid could. The German spy had not appeared again, but Meer learned from dockhands that King Farouk had previously entertained his Jewish mistress, Irene, on the houseboat, but she had returned to Europe. The king's father, King Faud, who died when Farouk was a teenager at school in England, had also engaged in a long-term affair with a Jewish woman who was married and a leader in the Jewish community.

Lucy and Margie had hoped to be free of any obligation to flirt with King Farouk, but Meer's information about Irene reminded them of their train trip to Chicago and their late-night conversation about the Biblical story of Queen Esther and the Persian King. The other tidbit gathered by Meer was that the British High Commissioner for Egypt, a man named Miles Lampson, had been pressuring King Farouk to abdicate.

Lucy had not realized the king was so young and had succeeded his father when he was seventeen. No wonder he was so childish. Jill Benson had said he often balled up bits of bread and tossed them at people in restaurants.

The night of the party, a great deal of pedestrian traffic moved along the pier, which was strung with lanterns, that cast rippling reflections. Lucy, Margie, Lettie, and the other women had decided to wait for escorts: Mike Gold for Lettie, Kim for Margie and Lucy, and young Meer as a chaperone for the others. Bernie and Jim were also attending.

Kim came onboard slightly before the designated time, briefed all of them in a quiet voice, and asked for questions. Lucy, also *sotto voce* lest they be overheard, asked how King Farouk had gotten along with President Roosevelt, Prime Minister Churchill, and the Chiang Kai Sheks.

"He didn't meet them," Kim answered. Lucy felt her eyebrows bunch with worry. Would the king be dealing with another snub?

"He had an auto accident." Kim explained that the king had broken ribs and spent days in the hospital, but offered no conjecture.

"The red car?" she asked. Kim didn't know which car, but her mind mulled over possibilities. King Farouk usually had a chauffeur. If he were at the wheel driving after a meeting with the British High Commissioner pressuring him to give up the throne, he might have been stirred up enough to speed recklessly.

A half-dozen other guests had already arrived when the OSS girls and their escorts boarded the king's houseboat. Though the king was Muslim, Lucy quickly discovered that the fruit punch was spiked with Cypriot brandy. After a few sips, she emptied the remainder of her glass into the muddy Nile. King Farouk, well into his role as host, wore his Royal Air Force uniform and usual tarbush, though Lucy thought he looked disappointed, as if he were searching for someone who hadn't arrived. She boldly approached him and, along with her thanks, made a point of passing along Jill Benson's message. *Please, mention my regret to King Farouk*, she'd said.

"Jill reminds me of Gerda, my Swedish *au pair*," the king told Lucy. "My father only allowed a one-hour-a-day visit to my mother. I spent a lot of time with Gerda." He went on to describe what sounded like a very lonely situation, an *Our Gang* comedy of one. Mischievous prince pouring vinegar in tea and placing tacks in chairs. He frustrated his tutors with pranks. With minimal encouragement, he told Lucy of taking two horses into his mother's quarters. The resulting manure had not pleased his mother, Queen Nazli, who had been entertaining a visiting queen from Romania.

CHAPTER FIFTY-THREE

Bella
Yugoslavia, 1944

Bella's boots pinched her toes, but she knew their journey had been harder on Gordon than on her. They walked day after day until his stump bled into his knitted socks. He wouldn't let her pull them off, even the night Dusan found shelter for them in a shepherd's hut.

Gordon leaned hard on a staff as he limped along, trying to keep the weight off his false foot and looking down to keep from tripping. He grimaced with each step down the rocky path. Twice when she and Gordon were near Dusan and Matija, they hid in a ditch while Italian soldiers rode past in trucks. That night Dusan and Matija slipped away, and the next morning Bella and Gordon set out on their own.

They had been walking for hours when two men on horseback appeared in the valley below them. Gordon was so slow following Bella into hiding that she was afraid they'd been seen. The men led a third horse, something that seemed impossible because horses were scarce. Before their journey, Dusan had told her that all the horses had been made into goulash and eaten by Germans.

She and Gordon lay beside the path until the men on horseback were close enough for Bella to see that the man in front was Matija, mounted on an almost black mare. Dusan rode behind him on a gray horse with its head down. The third horse had no saddle. There were no enemies in sight on the path, but soldiers could appear suddenly, so her fear took only one step back as the horses came nearer.

The horse with no saddle was a bay with a healed wound on its neck and white hairs that grew over its hooves. As she rose to her feet, it twitched the muscles on its neck and shoulders and turned its head to watch her. She stood waiting while Gordon spoke to it. It was a mare named *Ri*, which meant new, though the mare was not new; she was old and very patient. Dusan told Bella not to walk behind any of the horses because they might kick.

Ri wore a bridle but no saddle, so there were no stirrups for Gordon or Bella to step into. Matija led the mare beside a large stone, and Dusan helped Gordon onto her back and handed Bella up to him. When she patted the mare's warm neck, *Ri* blew through her lips, and her warm hide twitched. Bella had never ridden horseback before, but Gordon made her feel safe, and they went clopping off after Matija down a winding trail.

Even on horseback, Bella's shoes pinched her toes, but after several hours she took them off, tied them together by the laces, and held them in her skirt. They stopped briefly by a stream and allowed the horses to graze and drink. Matija climbed a hill to look for enemies, but they were lucky. Getting back on *Ri* was hard for Gordon. She knew from his sounds that he was in pain, but soon they were on their way. At times, she slept and awakened amid strange dreams to find herself starting to slump off of *Ri's* back, but Gordon always caught her.

When they were all too tired to ride on, they tied the horses, and Matija laid Bella on the ground to sleep under the stars. The voices of the men murmured nearby. Though her eyes kept closing, she overheard that they were going to Albania, which was occupied by Mussolini's Italian Army. The king of Albania, King Zog, was a friend of King Peter of Yugoslavia, and they both were in exile. Mussolini's army and their Nazi friends controlled the ports on the Albanian coast, but the townspeople were friendly to the Chetniks. Albanians liked to stick together, Matija told Bella when they stopped the next night in a barn. The Muslim family who lived there brought them cold supper, including bowls of creamy yogurt. These people had helped Jewish neighbors escape to the sea. Now they were helping Chetniks evacuate wounded American soldiers like Gordon. The mother talked softly as she cut away the toes of Bella's leather shoes, and that night, sleeping in the hay, Bella dreamed of Tišina.

Their first glimpse of the sea was from the mountainside, a line of glitter beyond a valley of whitewashed houses with red-tile roofs. They would need disguises to get past the Italians. The hut where Matija and Dusan left her and Gordon belonged to an old woman, who chopped her garden with a hoe while they watched from inside. The old woman did not have a basement or hiding places in the walls, but miles of road stretched out below them. If enemies drove up the hill, she would see them before they arrived and would sing a song she had chosen because it made the Italians homesick and because they would be less likely to kill her if they were missing their mothers.

The song was called *Mamá*. When the woman hummed it for them without words, it made Bella sad, but she did not cry because Gordon was with her. He would not let her unpack the blood-soaked wrapping from his stump, but after Matija and Dusan left on their horses, he removed his wooden leg, sat beside her on the floor of the woman's hut, and put his arm around her.

Bella awoke to the sound of footsteps and the racing of her heart. Gordon strapped on his leg, but they heard no singing, just a soft *psst* from a boy and his sister, neither one much bigger than she was. The woman gave Bella and Gordon clothes that belonged to fishermen. Bella would pretend to be the grandson of a fisherman named Vjosa. She would go to the village with the boy. At sunrise, they would set out in Vjosa's fishing boat and rendezvous with a larger boat that would take Bella across the sea to Alexandria, Egypt.

Gordon would accompany the woman down a side trail, where Vjosa's son would meet him and carry him by horseback to a sheltered spot where a rowboat could land. Vjosa's son would row Gordon to a fishing boat, and he would hide under a pile of fish until the fishing boat could deliver him to a third boat.

"Will I be on that boat?" Bella asked.

"No," the woman said. "You will be on a different boat, but you will cross the same sea."

The old woman rubbed Bella's skin with the juice of dried fruit until it stung and was stained red-brown. Bella squeezed her eyes shut as the woman snipped with heavy shears. Hair dropped like spiders across Bella's face and down her shoulders and onto the floor. The woman dressed Bella in trousers, a rough-knit sweater, and a cap belonging to the real boy, Arlin, who was brown from the sun. When Bella saw him next, he had changed into clothes belonging to his sister: a headscarf, a dress, and a white apron. Bella knew she must not say a word as she followed him. She was Arlin, grandson of Vjosa, and the actual Arlin pretended to be his own sister, who stayed at the old woman's house. They crept single file down a rutted path through bushes on their way into town. If she needed help, she should cough once. If an Italian soldier spoke to her, she should cough three times and pretend to be sick.

Bella was used to silence, but she was not used to being away from Gordon. His absence had left an aching hollow inside her chest, and she would not allow herself to imagine beyond their crossing the sea in different boats to find one another. She followed the boy toward the town, and as they entered, he pointed out his grandfather and disappeared into a doorway.

The light of the sun scoured the seaside village with such intensity that Bella was forced to squint and keep her head down as she walked beside Arlin's grandfather, her shoulders barely reaching the level of his waist. Whitewashed buildings crouched against the hillside, across which cobbled streets wound toward a crescent harbor with docks and many boats, including a military vessel anchored offshore. On their way to Vjosa's boat, a small dog in a patch of sunshine looked up hopefully and thumped his scraggly tail against the dust. She smelled fish and salt air and a background stink that seemed almost pleasant. Soldiers yelled something to Vjosa. He called back and they asked him to bring them fish. She understood that much. He handed her an empty bucket and pushed her by the shoulder toward a boat that was painted blue and red. When she was on board, a man in uniform called out, and Vjosa answered him. She shaded her eyes with her hand to see his leathery brown face. His eyes glittered like wet stones.

Vjosa barked orders she did not understand, handed her a length of net piled in a stinking mound beside his boat, and pantomimed sewing. She had no needle, but tied a knot where a cord had snapped. She felt soldiers watching her back as Vjosa shoved away from shore and started his engine. The net in her lap was heavy and dirty, but she picked through it as if she knew what she were doing.

They headed across the sparkle of the harbor, and—at first—the boat reminded her of the rolling gait of the horse with Gordon holding onto her, but he was not there. The boat vibrated, bucked, splashed, and belched the smell of machines. She kept her face down as they passed the Italian boat and headed deeper. She had never been to the sea. Looking down into the waves was like looking off the side of a mountain into a deep valley, or off a cliff into a ravine.

Vjosa spoke calmly to her, but his voice was thick, his language hard to understand, so she had to look into his dark shining eyes and watch his old hands to tell what he meant. Though the sky was bright blue, clouds like ash-stained snow piles moved across it. The farther they got from shore, the higher the waves rolled. Below her was a world of spirits different from the ghosts of the forest. She felt the presence of swimming ogres and beasts with fierce jaws that could swallow a girl in one gulp.

CHAPTER FIFTY-FOUR

Lucy
Cairo, Egypt, 1944

"Don't tell them," Lettie was saying as Lucy and Margie entered the new headquarters. With the arrival of so many new coders, OSS had outgrown the space at 14 *Sharia Ibn Zanki* and relocated to a three-story in Garden City, where the communications branch was allotted six rooms in a large English basement.

"Tell them what?" Lucy asked, catching up. The MP stationed outside the hall winked and let them through.

Lettie tapped her lips. "Shhh."

Something secret, Lucy assumed, though she was Lettie's supervisor and should know what Lettie knew.

The new headquarters on *Rustum Pasha* stood a block from the British Embassy and two blocks from British Headquarters and the English barracks. Security was tighter, and a masonry wall ran around the property with an iron gate and guard at the sidewalk. Another MP was posted outside the communications branch.

New coders arrived every week and, hearing about Hart and Gordon, greeted Margie and Lucy with so much sympathy, it was difficult to tolerate politely. When she, Margie, Lettie, and the other old-timers joined the newer woman in the area to paraphrase deciphered messages, Lucy overheard whispers and asked. "Don't tell whom what?"

"No need to worry," Lettie said.

"Something about Hart or Gordon?" Margie asked.

"We heard from Hart. He had his meeting with Randolph Churchill, who apparently has a hollow leg, but that's not it."

Lucy heard "leg" and for an instant thought of Gordon, but Lettie moved on from the Prime Minister's son's problem drinking to an impromptu paraphrasing of Hart's report on his meeting with Tito, head of the Partisans. The messages were invariably chocked with compliments about the courageous Partisans. "If Hart's report isn't 'it,'" she asked, "then what *is*?"

"The Brits were hoping to meet an Albanian fishing boat with one of ours, but he didn't arrive. There's been a storm."

She studied Lettie's face. "Tell me the 'one of ours' isn't Gordon."

Lettie kept a poker face, though Lucy could tell it *was* a poker face, slightly too blank.

"This goes with the territory," Lucy said. "Every one of our relatives back home has to wait for news. I have a great-aunt who didn't want me to leave Virginia because she didn't want my mother to be stressed." She winced. "I sound preachy, don't I?"

"Yes," Lettie said. "We don't know for sure, but we suspect the missing man is Gordon."

Jill Benson tapped on the door and poked her head into the room where Lucy was teaching some of the new OSS recruits. "An invitation for you and Margie," she whispered.

Lucy slipped into the hall to hear the rest.

"My Jim and I are having a little party for King Zog and King Peter. They're back in Cairo."

"I'd be glad to help. Would you like me to bring something?"

"I'd be most grateful if you'd keep an eye on King Farouk.

Sometimes I think he's his own worst enemy. And I thought you'd like to meet King Zog. He's from Albania. Maybe he could offer some help for Gordon."

This time it was Lucy who had to maintain a poker face. Had Gordon been captured? She asked Jill if she had news, but the answer was no. Her suggestion was because Gordon's Chetniks were supporters of King Peter of Yugoslavia, who was a friend of King Zog. Jill thought Gordon might need local doctors before he could leave wherever he was hiding out, and the king of Albania might help. When Lucy's shift was over, she would insist on being told.

"Did you find out anything about Gordon or Hart?" she asked when she found Margie in the ladies' room.

"Some Czech-American recruits dropped into Czechoslovakia were captured by the Germans." Margie frowned. "Remember Tibor?"

Hart and Gordon had taught Tibor and his group ciphers and radio operation. "Did anything happen in Albania?"

"A British vessel picked up a Sephardic boy from an Albanian fisherman. The boy kept asking for an American named Gordon."

"Has anyone located Gordon?"

"Not yet. He may not have even set out to sea. There was a storm."

CHAPTER FIFTY-FIVE

Bella
Egypt, 1944

She huddled below deck with her eyes shut, gagging into a tin bucket. Fumes from the engine and the terrible rolling of the English gunboat made her feel as if even a sip of water would bring up yellow slime.

"Lad, abitto gingatee. Ifyekannadrink, givasneff." She didn't understand what the man meant, but he held a steaming quarter-full cup under her nose and placed it in her hands. She inhaled, touched the contents with her tongue, and poured it into the bucket. Her head hurt, her stomach hurt, but the biggest hurt was that Gordon was not with her. We will cross the same sea, she told herself as she slid one way and then another. She must have slept because when she opened her eyes, the rolling had slowed. She heard men's voices and footsteps banging steel. When he reached for her, she was too weak to resist.

The sailor carried her on deck and sat her on an upturned bucket beside a coil of rope. "¿Donde está *mi papa?*" she asked. Gordon was not her father, but they didn't know. "*¿Gordon?*" They did not speak Sephardic, and they did not speak Serbo-Croatian, only a strange language that did not sound like Gordon's speech but had many of the same words: yes, no, up, here, look, crap, dammit, and my name is.

Men crossed the crowded deck, busy with tasks, and one lifted her off the bucket and pointed at land. They were approaching a busy harbor rimmed by many large buildings and a castle. A boat the size of Vjosa's motored straight for them, and men onboard called out to it, yelling out in their language.

When she realized they had reached Alexandria, she thought of Gordon and let the men hand her down to the smaller boat that rocked alongside, splashing and leaning. She gagged, but salt air blew in her face, and sunshine sparkled across the water. Soon she would find him.

The woman did not understand her either. There was barely room for them in the car, which was filled with bags of grain, baskets of soap, packages of food in brown paper, and piles of unbleached white cloth. The woman chattered in her language, and they bounced along the dusty road. The woman pointed at long-legged, long-necked animals. "Camel," she said.

"Kam-el," Bella repeated.

The woman wore a short white head kerchief and a white smock and apron and had a dimple and rosy cheeks. She patted her chest. "Nurse."

Bella patted her own. "Bella."

People were trudging alongside the road. Nurse walked her fingers along the steering wheel and pointed. "Red Sea," she said and made her fingers swim through the air.

"Tolumbat," Nurse said when they were greeted at the entrance to a camp.

"*¿Donde está Gordon?*"

"Oh, he speaks Spanish," another woman said. "What is your name, wee lad?"

CHAPTER FIFTY-SIX

Lucy
Tolumbat, Egypt, 1944

Meer kicked along a ball as the three of them passed nurses and a tent of schoolchildren reciting numbers in English. "I have to do something useful," Lucy told Margie. "I don't think I can bear seeing wounded men today, though. Not when we're already so tired."

"I feel the same way," Margie said. "Whatever the worst injury, I imagine it happening to Hart."

"Then let's skip Camp Huckstep," Lucy said. "I've been thinking about King Farouk's childhood. His behavior at Jill's party had me mentally reciting that it's harder for a rich man to enter the kingdom of God than for a camel to pass through the eye of a needle."

"It's seeing all these camels."

"All that wealth and power."

King Zog and King Peter, also friends of Jill's, had asked for a rain check, leaving King Farouk as the guest of honor at her party. She had posted a large whiteboard and asked guests to sign in when they arrived. The King arrived very late without Queen Farida and carried in a silver platter with a large cooked fish that he handed off to Jill. He scrawled "Bull Shit" instead of his name on the whiteboard. Later he picked Jill's husband's pocket. Yes, he returned Jim's wallet, but King Farouk's late arrival delayed dinner until 11 PM, and, as he was the reigning monarch, protocol required that all the guests stay until he left. At two in the morning, he was going strong, and Jill's father-in-law announced that it was time for breakfast, a broad hint that King Farouk chose to ignore.

Jill's cook had worked on the party all day and had been given the night and the next day off. Like most of the Americans and Europeans in Cairo, Jill was not one for cooking, but she'd brewed a pot of tea, opened jars of peaches, and announced breakfast, though her guests mostly went through a charade of eating. They sipped from quarter-full teacups and nibbled at leftover crackers or bits of preserved peaches. King Farouk, who had imbibed in the spiked punch, lingered until 3 AM. The houseboat where Lucy, Margie, and friends lived was within safe walking distance of the Bensons' new flat, but by the time Lucy fell into bed, there was little hope of sleep.

"Jill doesn't know what she should do with the silver tray," Margie said as they walked toward the children's tents. "Should she return it or keep it? I think she feels she deserves it."

The answer was clear as day to Lucy. Return it. But as she opened her mouth to comment, she heard a gasp and spun toward the sound. A small child in a white dress stood in the doorway of a tent, her mouth and eyes wide with astonishment.

"Mi mamá! Mamika!" the child called and ran into her arms and held tight to her neck.

Lucy hugged back, letting the child hang on—the little body shaking with sobs, straining for breath. "Mamá!" she got out between sobs. A nurse rushed out of the tent, her scrubbed face wrinkled with concern. Lucy rocked from side-to-side whispering and holding on. As the child quieted, she found herself humming Brahms' "Lullaby," the way she had when her younger brother and her cousin were babies.

"*Te necessito,*" the child whispered, and for no more reason than Lucy recognized it as Spanish, she found herself whispering back, "*Está bien. Está bien.*"

"Her name is Bella Mehita," the nurse said. "She arrived dressed as a boy."

Lucy sat on the ground and rocked forward and back, hugging the child. "Bella Mehita," she crooned, and the girl hugged tighter.

"*Ma-má*."

Tears streamed down Lucy's face. Why, she didn't know, but she couldn't help it. When the girl was quiet, Lucy sniffed and wiped her face on the back of her arm.

"Do you know her?" the nurse asked.

Lucy shook her head. No, she didn't. Though there was something so familiar about the little face, the big brown eyes looking up through clumped lashes and those small fingers rubbing the fabric of Lucy's dress. "How old is she?"

The nurse shook her head. "We aren't sure. These children are so malnourished. I would guess five, but she could be as old as eight or nine."

"I don't suppose I could take her home with me, could I?"

"No." The nurse made her voice stern. "We'll have to make a search for her relatives. She's Jewish. We know that much."

"Where did she come from?" Margie asked.

"They picked her up in the Adriatic Sea. Likely someone in Albania was hiding her. We've received a lot of unaccompanied Jewish children from there."

"Could she have come from Yugoslavia?" Margie asked and squatted by Lucy.

"We have no way of knowing," the nurse said.

"We can come back and visit her, can't we?" Lucy asked though she did not mean it as a question. Whatever the nurse answered, Lucy would return.

Except for interruptions from newer girls when they were stumped, Lucy had been glued to her desk, working with the strip board on a series of messages that no one else in the Cairo office could figure out. They'd come from one of their own in Kabul through the US State Department diplomatic pouch. Though others had failed before her, Lucy chalked up her own lack of success to her preoccupation with Bella. Tolumbat was at a significant distance, too far for workday travel and back, but she'd sent little notes every day. Between stabs at the Kabul agent's message, she'd concluded that it was unlikely that Bella's last name was Mehita. This was a child who believed her parents were named Mama and Papa and didn't know their surnames. Bella's mother could have called her, "Bella, *mi hijita*." Beautiful, my little daughter; Bella Mehita.

There was probably a similar, logical explanation for the difficulty with their man in Afghanistan's messages. Eventually, he had been recalled and would be flying into Camp Huckstep. He could arrive at any moment, and she or anyone in the communications department could ask him to demonstrate how he came up with his codes. Still, she should try to figure it out on her own before he arrived. But, no, there was a tap at her door. She stood up, ready to greet him. If he was like most men, he would prefer showing her to her showing him.

The door cracked open, and Lt. Jim Raymond stuck in his head. "Lucy," he said. "I have news. We've made contact with Gordon."

Jim beckoned her to follow and walked her into the sun outside. Bad news? Of course, walking outside meant bad news. No one would want to hear her cry out. Stiff upper lip, she told herself. Jim patted the steps, and she sat beside him on the warm stone.

"He's been shot," he said. "But he radioed out. He's on a ship in port in Alexandria. An ambulance will meet him and carry him to Camp Huckstep. If you leave now, you can meet him there.

Sometimes the moments before knowing were the hardest, Lucy reminded herself. This could be the worst or the best moment of her life. She was ashamed that she'd loved him more deeply during his absence than in his presence. He'd already lost his foot, and a gunshot wound might mean anything. The fact that he'd coded his own message was a positive sign. He was conscious and able to use his brain.

The motor pool had moved to the old OSS Headquarters, and a car and driver arrived for her within moments of Jim summoning her. This was a situation when quick service did not portend good news. The agent from Kabul arrived as she was leaving. In other circumstances, she might have stopped to meet him, but instead, she climbed into the back seat of the sedan that had arrived for her. Ordinarily, she was not someone who would show her distress, but she folded her arms against her chest and imagined hugging Gordon, simultaneously filling with the sensations of holding little Bella and of wrapping her arms around her mother that last time. She thought of her father on his deathbed and wished she had remained by his side. She recited the "Lord's Prayer" to herself and refrained from doing the same with the twenty-third Psalm. There was a limit.

From her seat in the back, she glimpsed feluccas sailing the low, mud-brown Nile. The water level was almost three feet lower than when she'd arrived. A houseboat near Jill and Jim Benson's had tilted against the bank. She passed palm trees and desert and a train heading north. The sky was uncharacteristically cloudy. Almost the rainy season, she supposed, though it was not raining, and the usual dust blew up behind cars.

When they reached Camp Huckstep, the driver stepped out to talk to the sentry. She didn't care that he pointed at her, except that she had to unfold her arms, sit straight, and look ahead. The hospital tents, when they reached them, were identical to the tents at Tolumbat. Poor little Bella.

She took a deep breath, blinked hard to summon a brave face, and stepped out. She thanked the driver, expecting him to leave, but he said he would wait. Chin up, her mother would have said and given her hand a squeeze. A soldier consulted a list and directed her to the tent where she should expect to find Gordon.

"Knock, knock," she called before she entered. After all, these were tents of wounded men, who could be in any stage of dress or undress, the importance of that being their dignity more than her preference.

"Who is it?" a woman's voice called. A nurse, probably.

Lucy identified herself and was invited in. Though the interior lacked the brilliance of the desert, daylight glowed through the white canvas, making the space inside seem otherworldly, like a watercolor or illustration in a book, someplace imagined more than known. "I'm here to see Gordon Aldrich," she said, scanning the cots without recognizing him. Her eyes rested on a man sitting on his bed silhouetted near the far end of the tent. One arm was in a sling, but as she watched, he raised the other and began waving vigorously.

"Lucy," he called in a hoarse voice she might not have recognized.

She rushed to him, calling his name. "What happened?" she said. "I was told you'd been shot."

His left leg dangled, ending in a rounded bandage; his right arm was hidden in a sling. "If I hadn't been interrupted, I'd have reassured you that the gunshot was nothing. Just a flesh wound."

"Deep through the muscle," a man said behind him.

"May I present Lucy Moore," Gordon said and, in turn, introduced Hank, the medic who'd assisted in removing the bullet from his deltoid shoulder muscle.

"Did your intended tell you he lost his leg?" Hank asked.

She caught Gordon signaling no with a back and forth of his eyes at Hank. Dear Gordon was trying to spare her embarrassment that the medic had misread their relationship. If only she really were his intended. Gordon covered his face with his hand.

"Hank means I lost my artificial leg during my escape."

Not the best timing. The medic wanted to look at Gordon's wound; Lucy wanted to know how he'd been shot; her ride was pressing for her to leave, but she didn't want to go without telling Gordon about the little girl at Tolumbat. "May I sit beside you for a moment?" she asked, glancing for permission at the medic, who answered with a wink and walked a few paces away to chat with her driver.

Gordon patted the cot with his good hand. She took the place he offered, careful not to bump the leg with the bandaged stump. When he put his arm around her and squeezed, she laid her head on his shoulder and closed her eyes. "Oh, dearest Gordon," she said and kissed his cheek.

"I don't want pity," he said.

She drew back. "What are you talking about? I don't pity you, you fool. I love you." She hadn't meant for that to slip out, and her cheeks burned. Maybe he didn't love her. She turned her face to him and kissed him on the lips. There was no sense in being timid with someone so brave.

His mouth was pliant and moist, his tongue probing, his cheeks fine sandpaper; their kissing came with faint swigs of coffee and peppermint and of salt and olive oil.

"I decided if I made it back alive, I'd ask you to marry me," he said when they came up for air. "But I have something to ask you. Do you want children?"

"Of course," she said. "Do you remember our houseboy, Meer?" She wasn't going to hesitate. Meer. Bella. But if Gordon didn't want children, what would she do? What she really wanted was to love children *and* to love him. She fumbled for words and told him that she'd thought of adopting Meer after the war and staying in Egypt. It would be hard to manage with him in Virginia. If she returned to live in the States, it would have to be in the North. Gordon said not a word but approved with his eyes until she mentioned the child in Tolumbat. The girl who'd thought Lucy was her mother. That was the moment at which tears flowed from beneath Gordon's creased eyelids.

CHAPTER FIFTY-SEVEN

Lucy
Egypt, 1944

As the water level in the Nile dropped, their houseboat settled onto a shoal, tilting their cabin, and it was as if Lucy had fallen overboard into muck through which she couldn't see. She forced her face into a cheerful expression while chiding herself soundlessly. *Be calm. Handle yourself. What is it you haven't considered?* They were dressing, getting ready for a day off, and Lucy would have to manage good spirits for her visits to Bella and to Gordon.

She'd assumed Margie would approve and even be happy for her and Gordon, but though Margie did approve of their marrying, she opposed their adopting either Bella or Meer and vehemently objected to their adopting both. "I don't see what the problem is," Lucy said. "We both want children, and we're both willing to adopt."

"You're missing the point," Margie answered. "Bella is Jewish. She should be with other survivors. And with Meer, the problems are obvious."

"What problems are those?" Margie meant race, of course. Meer would experience discrimination in Virginia, but he was a brave boy. Lucy felt she and Gordon could protect him or prepare him.

"Lucy, you're the one so disapproving of colonialism. You

can't just take children away from their people because you want them with you. I'm happy for you and Gordon. I insist on lending you my bridal gown. I'll go with you to Tolumbat and see if I can help find some relatives for Bella. But, no, taking these children for yourself is wrong."

Lucy found she could barely speak. "But she loves Gordon," she managed. "She thinks I'm her mother." Even as she said it, Lucy knew that Margie would object again and insist that Bella could transfer her mother-longing to anyone. But Margie had lost her own parents. How could she be so cruel to Bella? Or to Gordon, after all he'd been through?

It was to be expected that the English nurses at Tolumbat objected, but that was because Lucy was unmarried and the authorities hadn't yet finished a search for Bella's relatives. She and Gordon hadn't yet revealed their concern that Bella had made the same error as their friend from the ship, Wally Benzimra, who'd thought Lucy was his sister-in-law. It would have been an absurd coincidence for Bella to be his niece, but he was being sent away and thus wouldn't be able to go meet her and—anyway—would likely have no objections to their adopting.

Perhaps, Lucy thought, a common factor in the misidentifications was the way she, herself, responded to the faces of people who thought she was someone else. Maybe when their faces lit up, so did hers, and instead of realizing they'd found the wrong person, they clung to her. Maybe Bella's real mother was alive, and what Bella had seen in Lucy's face was the wish to take a child in her arms.

Gordon had been fitted with a new leg, but his arm injury had not healed enough for two crutches, so he limped along with just one. Lucy was determined to show respect rather than sympathy, which was easy because Gordon was all smiles. They'd set a tentative date for their wedding and were about to leave for the DP camp to see Bella. Gordon hadn't yet been directly subjected to Margie's objections to their adopting either Bella or Meer. It was only in the deepest recesses of her mind that Lucy felt anything like her old insecurity. Would he want to ditch their marriage plans if they couldn't keep Bella? She didn't think so.

Margie had set out ahead of them with a group of her Jewish Palestinian friends. Possibly they had already arrived at Tolumbat and were checking camp bulletin board posts, reviewing logs, and interviewing families who might know something about Bella. Margie would probably visit Bella, though Lucy selfishly hoped their visits wouldn't overlap.

She and Gordon would take the vehicle provided by the motor pool. After they married, they would get a car of their own, Gordon had said, though he'd not yet mastered driving with a prosthesis. "All things in time," he added as their ride approached.

Neither of them had brought sunglasses. The glare off the windshield forced their eyes to the ground and to Gordon's feet. The shoe on his artificial leg had been shined, while the other, on which he hopped on crutches, was dusty. With each step, the shined shoe grew more like its mate, and, in due course, they reached the waiting car. The driver opened the back door first for her, second for Gordon, which seemed to her wrong, though, of course, men had their pride.

Gordon was fixed on the idea that the little Bella who'd nursed him past his amputation and the Bella who had run into Lucy's arms at Tolumbat were the same person. Lucy, beside him in the back seat, loved his certainty, though it seemed to her more likely that his belief was driven by longing for what he'd lost. Both he and she were determined to keep Margie's opposition from interfering with their plans. What a rare and precious circumstance: two people attracted to one another despite adverse circumstances and both in love with a child or children and with each other and set on adopting. Whether

Bella was the child from Yugoslavia or not, their welcoming her as their child seemed meant to be.

"The people from the camp at Moses Wells walk to the Red Sea every day to bathe," Lucy said, making conversation as they drove. Gordon had not wanted to talk about his winter except to speak of Bella and their discovery that he and she both spoke Spanish. Every once in a while, he would come up with some bit of wisdom or history about the people who'd rescued him, but only if the people who'd aided him had survived. The man who'd pulled him out of the sea after he'd ditched his leg had not. Gordon's own gunshot wound came a moment later. That was all Lucy knew.

Every time it came up, Gordon changed the subject. "From what my friend Matija told me," he said when Lucy steered the conversation back his way, "I think the Albanians are less divided by religion. They have Islam from the Turks, Eastern Orthodox Christianity, Roman Catholicism, and Judaism, but they seem to tolerate their differences a bit more than their neighbors to the north."

"Yugoslavia?" Lucy asked.

"Yes," Gordon said and launched into a discussion about the bravery of the Chetniks, the mistrust between Partisans and Chetniks, and the difficulty faced by those who kept a foot in all camps.

"Did I tell you that Margie and I had a long chat with King Peter?" Lucy said. "He's under the impression that the war is going very well in Yugoslavia. He suggested it would be a good place to live."

"I think he may be in for some disappointment," Gordon said. Lucy laid her head on his good shoulder, and they rode in silence for a while. Lucy hoped they all wouldn't be in for disappointment.

Lucy and Gordon planned to walk to the tent where Bella usually stayed. Of course, the children had classes and activities.

In her previous visits, Lucy had been allowed to play catch and hopscotch with Bella. She could be anywhere but had been told Gordon might be able to visit. Unless Bella was predicting some disaster, she would be watching for them.

It was very hot under the desert sun, and the doors of tents were open. Sheets and other laundry hung on clotheslines casting shadows in the sand. It was Gordon who spotted small feet behind an adult-sized garment of the sort nurses wore. "Bella?" he called, and there she was.

Lucy expected her to run to him, but she came cautiously, respectful of his crutches.

"She used to think my name meant fat," he whispered to Lucy. His eyes were still locked on Bella's and hers on his.

"*Mi papá*," Bella said. "Gordon." She held out her arms, apparently sensing it would be hard for him to stoop, and hugged him gently around the waist.

"*Tu pelo*," he said and equally gently patted her short hair. It was dark brown, almost black, and cropped unevenly.

"Did she call you *Papá* when you were in Yugoslavia?" Lucy asked.

"No," he said. "Did you tell her what we hope?"

Lucy had mentioned nothing of the sort. That was the kind of error that she knew might botch an adoption and leave a child feeling betrayed. "No," she said out of the side of her mouth. "But be careful. I've been teaching her English."

Gordon and Bella were still frozen, looking so solemn that Lucy could barely breathe. Bella pointed to Gordon's arm, and he removed it from the sling, undid the buttons of his shirt, and showed her his wound, an angry red scar, which Bella inspected without wincing. She nodded gravely and carefully placed her arms around his neck.

CHAPTER FIFTY-EIGHT

Hart
Virginia, 2002

"You're Lucy's daughter, aren't you?" Hart heard Bella say as he approached the front desk at Alspy House. They hadn't visited in almost a month.

Nancy looked up in surprise from the sign-in log. "Bella? It's been so long."

"I think you were a second-grader that summer when I visited. I was a high school senior."

"I thought you were magic like the bedtime stories mother told. 'Once, there was a little girl who lived in a wall. She had large brown eyes and long brown hair and a magic chicken named Sheena.'"

"Her name was Tišina. It means silence."

Nancy looked worried. "I think I missed so much. Have you visited Mother here before? For a while, she was a little more willing to talk about the War, but she won't mention my father or any of their secrets."

Hart had noticed that too: Lucy's avoidance of speaking about Gordon as if she didn't want to acknowledge his death, though sometimes she asked for "the man."

Nancy glanced at Hart and back at Bella. "It would mean a lot to me and my brother, Rob, if you could tell us what you remember about Mother."

They took the elevator together, Nancy and Bella inquiring about one another and Hart at a control panel that required a code to exit at Lucy's floor. Fortunately, Nancy supplied that, and they found Lucy, in her wheelchair, at a table with Lettie Nash.

"Momma," Nancy said. "It's me, your daughter, Nancy. Look who's with me. Your old friend Bella Golden and your friend Hart McCann."

Lucy beamed her young smile from her old face. She looked at Hart. "Where is Meer? I saw Muhammadu."

Hart pulled up a chair from an adjacent table to join the ladies, who were already seated. "He couldn't come today." Since 9/11, everyone working in intelligence was busy. Hart was out of the loop and didn't know the name of the department where Meer worked, but his security clearance was intact. He knew Meer's son was on the mend, using a different last name, and had been given maintenance work at Alspy House.

"Your mother wants all of you to be together," Lettie said. "Nancy and Rob, Bella, and Meer."

"Did she say that?" Nancy asked.

"In a way. She whispers your names when she says grace." Lettie turned to Nancy. "I was at your parents' wedding in Cairo. Did you know that?"

"I didn't realize."

Hart saw Lucy shut her eyes as if she were praying again. "I wasn't there," he said. "I was still in Yugoslavia, but I know the dress."

CHAPTER FIFTY-NINE

Lucy
Cairo, 1944

From her office at *Rustum Pasha*, Lucy heard the rhythm of Gordon's footsteps and plunking cane and then his voice, lightening her heart as he told yet another coworker, "This place must be named after *Damat Rüstem Pasha*. He was a Bosniak, born in Croatia." She heard a soft reply from the coworker and then Gordon going on:

"He was grand vizier of Sultan Sulieman the Magnificent of the Ottoman Empire." During his recuperation at Camp Huckstep, Gordon had studied history to distract himself from pain. Back at OSS headquarters, he was like an eager boy reciting what he'd learned. Or perhaps he was preparing to hold his own with Ambassador Kirk, who'd asked to attend the wedding.

What touched Lucy's heart most was Gordon's fondness for children, which matched hers. When she spoke of her wish to adopt Meer, he'd suggested adopting both Bella and Meer, and suggested the idea of Bella as flower girl and Meer as usher.

The only thing that could have made it better would have been for Gordon's foot to grow back. Or so it seemed for a few precious days. The first sign of resistance, aside from Margie, who still opposed the idea of their adopting, came from an administrator at Tolumbat. General policy forbidding taking children away from the camp had been instituted after some sort of problem with a Cairo woman seeking servants, and Lucy found herself irrationally blaming Margie.

After several go-rounds with the administration at Tolumbat, Lucy and Gordon were informed that they could apply as adoptive parents as soon as they were married. In the meantime, they would be allowed to see Bella at the camp. She had refused to eat when their visits to her were restricted, but in Lucy's backup daydream, they worked it out. Bella and Meer would participate in a reenactment of the wedding at some later date. In the meantime, she did her best to hide her concerns from Bella and reluctantly suggested an elopement, which her thoughtful Gordon feared would be like a double disappointment for Bella. As he pointed out, approval for them to live together after their elopement would take as long as plans for a small wedding. Meer could still be an usher.

Lucy hid her concerns from Bella and refrained from arguing with Margie or her Jewish Palestinian friends. Still, a layer of strain fell over what might otherwise have been undiluted joy. Margie's dress fit Lucy perfectly without alterations. That seemed to please Margie. In her place, Lucy might have felt jealous, but perhaps lending the dress eased Margie's conscience about opposing the adoption. After a pleasant meeting, the dean of the Anglican Cathedral in Cairo agreed to marry Gordon and Lucy, and the new OSS Colonel, who was no relation to Gordon but had the same last name, Aldrich, offered to host a wedding reception for them at his villa.

Most importantly, Gordon contacted Wally Benzimra and set up a meeting at Camp Huckstep. After applying for a flat where they might be able to live, Gordon and Lucy set out in a motor pool car with high hopes. Whether Wally was or was not Bella's uncle, he would be a strong ally in their push for adoption. After all, his reaction to Lucy had been similar to Bella's.

"I wonder if he still has the picture of his sister-in-law?" Lucy said.

Gordon sighed. "It nearly did me in when Bella destroyed your photo by washing my bloody clothes."

"I'm sure she didn't mean to."

"I know. And now I have you in the flesh. Let's just hope Wally gives us his blessings. I'm going to try and do without my cane, so he won't worry this will happen to him." Gordon rapped on his artificial leg. "Did you hear our silly Bella say I should call my new foot Cluck after a hen she once knew?"

Wally sat alone at a table facing away from the door through which Lucy and Gordon entered the mess hall. A chessboard was set up with a game in progress. Either he was playing against himself, as he was prone to do, or his opponent was temporarily absent. Gordon, without his cane and holding Lucy's hand, walked so quietly she could hear him breathe.

When they were halfway across the wooden floor, Wally spun around as if both startled and sure of himself. If they'd been enemies, he could have shot them, but they weren't. He rose politely and offered coffee. A stainless-steel urn sat on a table next to a dishpan of clean cups, a sugar bowl, and a small, insulated pitcher of milk.

"Would you like some too, Wally?" Lucy always took hers black; Gordon liked milk and sugar.

"Had my quota already." He slid his chessboard to one side so Lucy and Gordon could sit opposite him. "You wanted to talk to me about a child helping the Chetniks?"

"She nursed me through my injuries."

"Remember on the ship?" Lucy asked. "You thought I looked like your sister-in-law? Could it have been more the look on my face than the resemblance? I mean both."

"You resemble her," Wally said firmly.

"The same thing happened at Tolumbat," Lucy said.

Wally sat up straighter, his face lit for an instant with hope which receded so quickly it might not even have been there.

"I think my face lights up in response when someone seems to recognize me. A child came running up to me, calling '*Mamá*!'"

"Oh," Wally said in a disappointed tone.

Gordon laid his hand on the table. "It turns out she was the child who nursed me through my injuries. We evacuated on separate vessels, but Lucy had already found her by the time I got here. Or they found each other."

"Tell me her name."

"They had her down as Bella Mehita, but she speaks Spanish. We think her mother might have called her 'my little daughter.' She knows she's Jewish, but she doesn't know her last name."

Wally's face clouded, and he struggled for words: "I only saw my niece when she was infant, but I want to visit her."

"That's why we came to see you. We'd like to adopt her, and we're hoping for your support."

Bella

She unfolded her latest letter to the page with a drawing of a cat beside the word C-A-T and of a tree with the word T-R-E-E. She studied the pasted picture of a car from a newspaper. C-A-R. Each letter from Lucy ended with the word L-O-V-E which meant *Te amo*. The plump British nurse with freckles read aloud the parts Bella could not sound out on her own.

"Off with you, Bella," the nurse said. Her name was Miss Williams. Miss was the same as *mademoiselle* or *señorita* or *göspodica*. "Time for lessons." She held Bella by the shoulders and aimed her at the mother with the white dress and scarf, who was writing English letters in the dust. T-O-L-U-M-B-A-T. The name of the camp. There were ten children studying with Bella, two from Albania, one from Romania, and the rest from the Kingdom of Yugoslavia.

Bella's mother and father were Americans and not allowed to live in the camp. She knew that they were not her first parents. She was not stupid, though Miss Williams might have thought so. But Lucy had the spirit and face of Bella's first mother, and Gordon carried the spirit of her father. Her past had vanished into mist rising from a lake. It had disappeared like ice cracking off trees, melting into rivulets, and bleeding out from under a ledge of snow.

She concentrated on the lessons and on the pronouncing of the words. *Hello. My name is Bella. This is a stick. This is sand.* They recited *Jack Sprat could eat no fat. His wife could eat no lean. London Bridge is falling down, falling down, my fair lady. How are you? I am fine. Please give me some water.* The sand was made of tiny grains that swirled when she took her turn writing with a stick. *Please. Please.* Shadows crossed the words as she wrote. A small head, trapezoidal body, and legs stretched to meet dusty shoes. Another shadow covered the *l-e-a* of her *Please*, and she looked up to see who was standing between her and the sun.

The sight of Lucy and Gordon made her heart stop. They stood one on each side of a man who cleared his throat and spoke in a way that seemed familiar. Bella didn't know why. His voice sounded like long, long ago. Like Papá and Mamika. The man squatted near her and began to talk. He asked her about where she lived before Tolumbat. *In a wall.* Where she lived in her village. *In a store below the synagogue.* What her uncle was named. She did not know. What her Mamá was named. *Mamá.* She wanted to sit in Lucy's lap, but the man kept asking her questions. He showed her a picture of Lucy and asked if it was her Mamá. *Yes.*

Bella backed away to stand against Lucy, but the man followed her. Changing into a mouse would help nothing. If he were a fox, he could have snapped her up. He smelled like bitter smoke and danger.

"It's okay, Bella," Lucy said. "Corporal Benzimra may be your uncle, the brother of your father. We're trying to find out."

CHAPTER SIXTY

Hart
Virginia, 2002

Hart sat at a table with Lucy and Lettie and the youngsters, Bella and Meer, waiting for Bernie to join them.

"He's an odd duck, Bernie is," Bella said. "But he found me the first time I got away from Tolumbat."

"I wasn't there," Hart said, meaning in Cairo when Bella ran away. D-Day had been barely a month off, though as an agent in the field subject to capture and interrogation, he wasn't in on attack plans. He supposed Bernie and the others back in Cairo at headquarters had known.

Meer smiled at Lucy as if seeing the beautiful woman from his youth. "I was an usher at their wedding. It was held in the Anglican Cathedral."

Lucy patted Meer's hand.

"They wanted to adopt you both," Lettie said to Meer and Bella. "They wanted to bring you to their flat in Cairo for trial visits."

The look on Bella's face was sad and, for an instant, close to tears. "They did have me there once," she said.

Hart felt his own eyes water in response. That was something old age had given him: a kind of sentimentality that made him cry in movies. When he was younger, he'd barely have noticed.

"After their application to adopt me was turned down, I wasn't allowed to see them. I didn't speak for months."

"Was that a tactic?" Meer asked.

Bella looked up as if startled by the thought. "I suppose it was deliberate, as things can be for a child. I was torn. I knew I would need to learn English to find her."

"Her?" Hart asked.

"Lucy." Bella's resemblance to middle-aged Lucy was striking.

"I used to wonder if you were her biological child," Nancy said. "I mean, she wrote to you every week, and you look like her. I know the ages don't work. She didn't go to Cairo until 1943, and no one would have sent a child to Yugoslavia, but you look so much like my mother."

Lucy was shaking her head, but Nancy didn't notice.

"She looked exactly like my first mother," Bella said. "Even my Uncle Wally said so."

"Why didn't my parents adopt you? I don't think Dad opposed it."

"Uncle Wally found a cousin in the DP camp."

"What's a DP camp?"

"Displaced Persons. Survivors." Bella lowered her voice, making Hart think of the Czech-American agents he'd trained for OSS, all tortured by the Nazis. They hadn't survived. "It was important to my people to be with one another. I don't hold it against my uncle. My cousin tried to be good to me. We lived in Israel. I suppose I would be a different person if I'd grown up in the States with your parents."

"And you, Meer? Do you know what stopped them from adopting you?" Nancy asked with the faintest hesitation, as if realizing mid-sentence that she'd crossed a line.

Over the years, Meer had acquired the air of a distinguished statesman. Grizzled hair, upright manner. "It was my choice," he said. "The war ended. My only regret is what my son went through." He remained composed, though Hart knew how tortured Meer had been when Muhammadu was kidnapped. "Ah,"

Meer said. "Here comes Bernie."

Hart rose to greet his old friend. At least both of them were walking. Hard not to think of 9/11 seeing Bernie with that familiar upturned nose. Stiff, gaunt, and bowlegged, but there he came, though something had caught his attention, and he stopped to look behind him.

Bernie had managed to turn up at all the significant times. He'd driven Margie to meet Hart when he arrived back at Camp Huckstep as the war ended. He'd been with Hart and Margie when they received the news President Truman had dissolved the OSS. No need for spying during peacetime, except peace wasn't peaceful, and with the rise of the cold war, Eisenhower pulled them back together as the CIA.

After Gordon finished law school, he stayed stateside to start his own practice, but Hart and Bernie drew him back in. Gordon formed dummy corporations, rented safe houses, and occasionally he and Lucy used tradecraft to deliver messages overseas. Perhaps more. And Bernie had found Muhammadu a job at Alspy House, a job that had started a week before 9/11, was interrupted when he was assaulted, and resumed several weeks after he was discharged from the hospital.

Hart pulled out a chair.

"See what I mean?" Bernie said. Hart wondered if he meant that Alspy House was the retirement home for old spies.

"About?" Nancy asked. As far as Hart knew, she was just a doctor and—unlike him, Lettie, Lucy, Meer, Bella, and Bernie—had never signed on for intel work. With her there, Bernie might not say a thing. But it was worth asking.

"This place," Bernie said. "I told Hart it was old spies. OSS and whatnot. But I could be putting you on."

Nancy looked at Lettie. "You?" she asked.

"Just OSS and an advice column," Lettie said.

"And you're just visitors," Nancy indicated Meer and Bella. Hart recalled that Margie, he, and a handful of OSS friends had been at her parents' fiftieth wedding anniversary party.

Nancy and her brother would've heard them swapping stories, but she wouldn't have known secrets about Meer, Bella, or Meer's son.

Bella and Meer looked at one another. Both had moved to the States, and Meer had become an American citizen. Both had worked with the CIA. "Yes, we're visitors," they said almost in unison, making Nancy laugh. Across the room, at the nursing station, Fatima, the beautiful nurse, looked up and caught Hart's eye, for a moment resembling a young Margie, though maybe it was just his own old eyes, Hart thought.

CHAPTER SIXTY-ONE

Lucy
Egypt, 1945

A living area, kitchen, two small bedrooms, and a balcony overlooking the Nile: the flat Lucy and Gordon rented in Aguza would have been perfect if it had included a bedroom for each child. Lucy didn't know what would happen next, but on the day of her wedding, she kept thinking everything in her life was too good to be true. She wished someone could make a newsreel of the ceremony in All Souls Cathedral for her mother, but she made do by remembering details and indulging in imagination: her father's ghost watching from somewhere and storing up an account to give to her mother when they were together again in an afterlife. She felt childish but didn't believe such a fantasy could cause harm. When they were outside, Bernie took several pictures with a Brownie camera.

Lucy was able to change into a going-away dress without perspiring on Margie's lovely white gown. The reception at Colonel Aldrich's flat in Garden City was marred only by the fact that everyone there was on pins and needles about something or another. Margie about Hart, who was still with the Partisans in Yugoslavia. Colonel Aldrich about the uncertainty that he would get back home to the States in time to participate in his daughter's wedding. Meer about being both wedding guest and servant. He took her aside and told her that he felt uncomfortable with how he was treated at the reception and would like to leave early. She managed to slip outdoors, kiss him on the cheek, and give her blessings to his departure, but it was as if a tally of disappointment had begun. Meer would not be happy in Virginia. She knew it.

Back inside, almost all of them, even her dear, new, handsome husband in his dress uniform, were preoccupied with the winding up of the war. How could they not be? The disinformation campaign about the Allied invasion plan for France had succeeded, yet so many had died, and they knew very little about what would happen next. The same for her and Gordon's adoption plans. Children's hearts could be broken by false hopes.

She saw Gordon start toward her, but King Peter of Yugoslavia, who was barely twenty-one and looked like a teenager, intercepted him. King Peter had pinned a medal on Gordon's pajamas at Camp Huckstep hospital, so they'd invited him to the wedding, and to their surprise, he had accepted. As usual, the young king was bursting with praise for his valiant Chetniks. He was sure they would win the war. "My country is beautiful," he was saying when Lucy reached Gordon. "We have mountains and seashore and orchards and rivers. After the war, you should come and live in Yugoslavia. General Mihailović is running a brilliant campaign."

King Peter's optimism didn't correspond at all to what Lucy had heard at the message center: Chetniks were evacuating wounded soldiers but otherwise not fighting, and the Partisans were cozying up to Stalin. But loose lips sank ships, and she kept hers buttoned while Gordon answered with praise for the brave Chetniks who'd saved him and little Bella. Perhaps King Peter would have some influence in the British-run camp where she was staying? They wanted to adopt her, Gordon said, though little Bella hadn't yet been told.

"Yes, no sense getting false hope," King Peter said.

Lucy and Gordon took the train from *Bab El Hadid* station for a weekend honeymoon in Alexandria at the Carleton Hotel, a block from the beach. They were told their room would include a private bathroom, though, to Lucy's surprise, that meant facilities plus a deep tub partitioned from the rest of the room with frosted glass, through which they saw blurred images of one another. Her of him on crutches, removing his leg and changing to clean boxer shorts and nothing else. She slipped into her silk nightgown, knowing his eyes were on her. This was their time. She wanted nothing more than to be in his arms, but had no wish to receive visits from ghost witnesses.

The next morning, they remained in bed late, snuggling, and enjoyed an elegant room service breakfast and a day on the white sand beach from which they could see a British destroyer and, in the distance, the hulk of a British battleship that had been sunk by Italian frogmen. They visited Pompey's Pillar and the catacombs of *Kom ash-Shuqqafa* but agreed that what they really wanted was to visit Bella.

Bella

Bella was getting better at speaking English, though sometimes she held her lips together, refrained from saying a word, and sorted through a pile of picture postcards sent by Lucy, whom she was not allowed to call *Mamá*. The Sphinx, the Great Pyramid, various animals at the Cairo Zoo, the harbor in Alexandria with the castle she'd seen when she arrived, and a suspension bridge built by a man named Eiffel who had also built a tower in France. She'd learned English names for the animals: Elephant, antelope, lion, giraffe, and zebra. Lucy had said she wanted to take Bella to the zoo but would not be allowed until she and Gordon were married. *I would like to go to the zoo, please*, Bella would ask when she saw them after their wedding. *May I please have a trip to the zoo? Will you please be my mother? Will you please be my father?* But she had learned not to say these things where the nurses or the strangers from other parts of the camp could hear.

Bella dreamed that night about searching for Lucy and Gordon at the Cairo Zoo and seeing Gordon riding a camel with yellow teeth. It spat at her when she came close, because it had swallowed a spirit.

"May I please write a letter to Lucy and Gordon?" she asked a nurse the next day but was told she could practice her writing in the sand; there was not enough paper to waste. Another girl of her size had lived in her tent for several weeks but had been found by an aunt and taken to the part of the camp where families lived. Mothers, fathers, aunts, and uncles. On the Shabbos, they lit candles and said the blessing together, but the children in her tent said English prayers except when adults from the other part of the camp visited.

She did not want to be an English child, but she wanted Lucy for her mother and Gordon for her father. Thus, she wanted to be an American. There was no sense in writing a letter in dirt, but she drew the American flag with her finger. Lines for stripes and dots for stars, hunching over her picture, hoping not to be disturbed by an older boy who liked to kick away the drawings or lessons by girls.

"There's our girl!" someone called out, the voice enough like Lucy's for Bella to look up and see both of them, Gordon and Lucy without Meer. They waved as they approached, smiling and holding hands.

CHAPTER SIXTY-TWO

Hart
Virginia, 2002

When Hart asked Bella how she escaped from Tolumbat, Meer's face lit up as if he wanted to speak, though he remained silent with his eyes on Bella.

"You're making me uncomfortable," she said.

"Ah," Hart said. That was that. He'd asked too much. Most of them had something that made them shut down. For him, it was the small boy he'd seen machine-gunned by Nazis in Slovenia.

A nursing assistant carried a plate of oatmeal cookies to the dining room, where they sat together at Lucy's and Lettie's table: Hart, Bernie, Meer, and Bella.

"This hurts." Lettie jiggled her leg and worked her slipper off the offending foot, revealing toes black as tar.

"Your toes," Bella said with alarm. "Does the doctor know?"

"They hurt," Lettie said. The rest of her foot was pale, and all her toes, including the black ones, were crammed together, giving her foot the same point as her gold slippers.

Bella rose from her chair. "I'm going to speak to a nurse," she said.

For a moment, they all were silent. Lucy hadn't seen Lettie's foot but seemed to understand something was wrong, and Bella was attending to it. "The other one isn't here," she said.

"Who?" Hart asked.

"The doctor."

"Lettie's doctor?" he said, but then wondered if Lucy meant her own daughter, Nancy, who was a doctor. Bella was conversing with someone at the nursing desk and returned shaking her head:

"They know about her toes. They said Lettie's daughter won't give permission for the surgery. They'll bring pain medicine."

"Take them off," Lettie said.

Hart cringed, Meer shook his head, and Bella frowned.

Bella

Bella knew the nurses at Alspy House couldn't hear the high-pitched whine. It came from inside her, a sustained background scream, like what she'd heard when she served in the Israeli Army. For an entire year afterward, when she was twenty-five, Bella had lain on a psychoanalyst's couch three times a week and re-experienced the washing of Abdullah's body and Gordon's cries the day he lost his foot. At the end of a year of treatment, Dr. Rolnik had shocked her by saying she'd barely spoken during her treatment. It had seemed to her that he was the one who'd barely spoken, though she'd felt a supportive presence from him as she plunged an hour at a time into a vivid past, where she found nuggets of treasure amidst terrible, terrible fear.

Though Bella supposed analysis had helped her, all she could recall of it were one or two questions from Dr. Rolnik and her decision to live in America. Waiting for the head nurse, she was unable to remember whether she had ever processed the day she ran away. Such jargon. Process. As if she were cured meat. But not cured. At the moment of 9/11, she had called out *Mamá*. She had been alone in a hotel and had called silently first, and then aloud, *Mamá*, then *Gordon*, and then *Lucy*.

The day she ran away, the children of Tolumbat had ridden the train to the Cairo Zoo for an outing sponsored by King Peter of Yugoslavia. Something had happened the week before, and Bella had never mentioned it to Dr. Rolnik because it had seemed impossible. It was that deafness and blindness descended over the camp. She saw nothing. She heard nothing. Instead, there was a terrible absence, as if all of her being vibrated like a cramped foot going to sleep. Later in her life, she'd seen a movie about voodoo and thought, yes, that's what it was, some witch doctor torturing a doll with pins. She'd felt prick after prick, along with an unbearable absence.

She felt the same way when the head nurse at Alspy House unbeckoned her into a small room and sat behind a desk. "I understand you're worried about Lettie."

"She has gangrene," Bella said. She wasn't a doctor, but Lettie's toes were tar black. Either they would wither and drop off or make her sick, and she would die from the toxins. They wouldn't fall off, though, because there was a bone inside. The bone would become sick. Dr. Rolnik had explained something like that to her. She couldn't have saved Gordon's foot.

CHAPTER SIXTY-THREE

Bella
Egypt, 1945

Bella knew they were talking about her, but she couldn't hear. She didn't want to, and she couldn't. If she had heard, she would have screamed and squeezed herself into a hiding place. She felt the postcards in her hands, but the tent was both too bright and too dim for her to see them. The giant tortoise card had been on top. A tortoise could be very old and large.

If she had worn a shell, she would have drawn her neck and head inside. Her cheeks would have pressed against a wall. If she had not remembered that *Mamá* wanted her to live, the embers of life within her would have grown cold. Do not give up, Lucy had said. If I can be your *Mamá*, I will. But Bella was not allowed to go with Lucy or Gordon.

She shut her eyes tight. I will stay inside a wall, she said to herself. "Look at those eyes; nobody there," a nurse said. But that was false. Bella was listening from inside the shell of a tortoise.

When she heard there would be a trip to the Cairo Zoo in Giza, her old tortoise eyes opened enough for her to see through her lashes.

It's understandable. Her uncle wants her to live with family.

Shhh. She'll hear you.

The war will be over soon. These children will go to Palestine.

If her uncle doesn't get killed, he could take her to America.

Lucy

"It will be best if you leave without seeing her." The eyes in Mrs. Hempson's otherwise pleasant Irish face—ruddy cheeks, freckles, nose like a nine-year-old's—hardened as she faced Lucy and Gordon. "There can be no histrionics. Drawing it out would be cruel."

"How does one make an appeal?" Lucy asked, and getting no response, asked to whom did Mrs. Hempson report. Surely there could be some formal process. In the States, she would have consulted an attorney and filed an appeal. Histrionics would be of no help, though the pressure in her chest had grown enough to make her wish to shout.

"There will be no appeal. Bella's uncle has located a cousin who wants her."

Lucy forced calm into her voice. Tried to, though it didn't come out as intended. She sounded too argumentative, and though she tried not to repeat the word *but*, the rest of the conversation proceeded along similar lines. Wally wanted Bella with his scant surviving family, a cousin who could raise her in a new Jewish state in Palestine. But Bella had chosen Gordon and Lucy as her parents. The image of Bella crying *Mamá* and the feeling of her little body clinging was something Lucy couldn't have forgotten if she'd tried.

An international adoption would certainly carry red tape. Even her and Gordon's unopposed marriage had required permission from both Colonel Aldrich and General Giles. There was no way the Army would approve the adoption if Bella had living relatives who disapproved. Margie had foretold the whole thing. Too many Jews had died. They would not be willing to give up any of their children. Still, it was difficult to believe that Wally had betrayed them.

Bella

Bella squeezed into her hiding wall with Tišina, but her ghost walked with the other children under a sun that bleached every sight they passed and shone over the desert where her ancestors were slaves to pharaohs. The limping girl, Anna from her tent, winced away from the freckled hand of the matron who herded them one by one through the heat onto the hot bus.

The girls were dressed in white frocks and the boys in bleached shirts and short pants. On their last trip, they had been driven to the Red Sea and allowed to splash in the water, but that was before. The matron's voice made the sound of words, but Bella laid her head against the window glass and allowed the bus to replace the words with a buzzing like the sound of a boat engine. Anna took hold of her shoulder. "Bella, wake up. Let me see your cards."

She opened her eyes and shut them. She had not brought her postcards, because she was inside her hiding wall, ready to change into a ghost. Tišina had become as hard as a pot for cooking, her feathers blown away by the propeller of an airplane. Because Bella was still inside the wall, the cards meant nothing, but they were not in her hands or her pocket.

Anna shook her again. "Bella, look at the pyramids!" Next, Anna would say that their ancestors were slaves, and the matron would hush them. Egypt was their host country, and they must be polite. But Anna was outside the wall, and Bella was inside, so she said nothing, and Anna smacked her arm and said nothing more until they arrived at the zoo and they lined up like good children.

Before the trip to the zoo, Bella had not thought of animals as slaves or as prisoners, but a man outside the gate was switching the rump of an overloaded donkey. The sight made her own bottom ache, but she stayed in line and came out of the wall to see long-legged birds like storks on a small island surrounded by a moat. The birds were of different sizes, all extremely lean, except for the tallest, which she recognized as an ostrich. Anna had stopped trying to make her talk, and Bella followed along with her group, half listening to the voices of the others. They walked down a path shaded with palm trees to an ornate pavilion from which they could see a large suspension bridge over a waterway. This was one of her cards, the bridge built by the man who built a tower in France. Lucy and Gordon had been at this zoo. On the far side, giraffes stood in an enclosure with trees and a high iron fence. The children were to hold hands, but she clasped the empty space where she wanted to hold Tišina and crossed her arms over her chest. Anna clutched the fabric of Bella's dress, and the girl ahead simply shrugged.

The elephant stood in a yard surrounded by an iron fence and a moat. When they approached, it lowered its trunk into a tub of water and sprayed its own back. The adults and all the children let go of their neighbors' hands to watch. When Anna released Bella's skirt, she slipped out of her hiding wall and squatted as if to tie her shoe. The elephant reached with its trunk back into the tub, and a squirt of hot urine wet Bella's underpants. She spread the dribble with the sole of her leather shoe, so no one would see. *Mamá*, she called silently, *Papá*. She wanted Lucy and Gordon. Anna grabbed her skirt again, and they walked in line beside a large building to see more animals: jackals pacing in a cage, a large bear that looked out from behind iron bars. Feed me, it was asking with its kind face. The matron reached into her handbag, pulled out a small loaf of bread, and tore off a piece. "Children, find me a stick," she said, and Anna let go of Bella's frock to search under nearby trees for a stick. The bear was looking at the matron, who rolled and pressed the bread between her fingers until she had made a ball the size of a marble. One of the bigger girls handed the matron a stick, and the matron pressed the marble of dough onto the end and poked the stick through the outer fence and through the inner bars into the open mouth of the bear. He closed his lips around the stick and shut his eyes as he tasted. Soon the children had gathered around and were making their own marbles of dough to feed to the bear, but Bella's wet underpants were chafing her bottom, and Gordon and Lucy had not answered her silent call.

The man wore a uniform like Gordon's. The woman beside him was dressed in a skirt and blouse and had brown hair curled like Lucy's. Tišina awoke fluttering against Bella's chest, but Bella could only see the woman and soldier from the back and would be punished for running after them. The matron handed the stick with bread to Anna while the other children lined up for their turn with the bear. All Bella needed to do was run past the woman and soldier to glimpse their faces. She didn't decide; her legs just giant-stepped and began pumping. The man and woman stood beside ornate cages for a lion and tiger, the same cages pictured on postcards from Gordon and Lucy. Bella ran with all her might and had almost reached the woman and solder when she tripped, fell smack almost on her face, and gasped in pain. The heels of her hands and her knees stung and were bleeding.

The woman who bent over Bella was not Lucy, but she spoke English. "Oh, let me help," she murmured. The man, who was not Gordon and had no cane, picked her up and gave the woman his handkerchief.

"Where are your parents?" he asked as the woman dabbed at Bella's knees.

"*14 Sharia Ibn Zanki,*" Bella answered because that was an address she remembered. The woman and the man asked her more questions, but all she could think to say was that she wanted her mother, who was named Lucy Moore Aldrich.

CHAPTER SIXTY-FOUR

Hart
Virginia, 2002

"What happened then?" Hart asked. His Margie had always seemed uncomfortable talking about Bella. Twice they'd taken in foster children for a month or so, and he'd thought, oh good, she's forgiven herself for warning Wally that Lucy wanted Bella. She and Lucy never had an open rift; they'd remained friends. Once, before his niece Rita and her husband moved to Paris, Hart overheard Margie telling Rita about Bella. She'd been using what happened to Bella, Lucy, and Gordon as an illustration of situations with no optimal solution.

"I didn't actually run away. I thought I saw Lucy and Gordon."

Lucy, who sometimes seemed as if she were unable to understand anything, looked up with intense concentration.

Margie had often accused Hart of lacking the ability to read people, but since her death, it was as if he could see straight into them.

Lucy wore on her face the look a mother might have in the instant before she ran to an endangered child. Bella emitted palpable angst. Meer, across from them, seemed confident yet oblivious. It was only near his son's bedside that he'd leaked emotion. Bernie, who was walking toward them with his sagging chin in the air, looked as if he owned the place yet was unaware of the ghost inhabitants.

Bella greeted Bernie. "We were talking about the day you found me."

"Ah, yes. At the Cairo Zoo," Bernie said. "The Bensons and I were escorting King Peter. The guards at the zoo alerted us that one of the children from Tolumbat was missing. Their escort told us that the missing child was Wally Benzimra's niece." He cleared his throat with the dominance of a retired professor about to expound on some matter in which he considered himself an expert. "Which brings us to our task."

Hart noticed the gleam fade from Lucy's face. Bella emitted a nanosecond of mild irritation. How odd that all this was so visible. Margie's parting gift to him, he supposed. Was that how it worked? Someone would pass away, and some characteristic of theirs would grow inside survivors? When his mother died, he'd learned to make bread according to her recipe. Now he felt spirits.

"Task?" Bella asked.

"I couldn't tell you when Lucy's daughter was here. She doesn't have a security clearance. Listen up. Before Meer's son, Muhammadu, was attacked, he made contact with one of his old friends, a boy kidnapped with him." Bernie looked down his pug nose at Hart. "I tried to tell you when you came in for your knee."

Meer sat straighter. Hart thought, here we are again, Bernie and his over-the-top ideas, some of which were true, so they had better listen.

"Muhammadu was one of the men we pulled from Somalia," Bernie said.

"Why?" Hart asked. "Did he provide intel about Nine-Eleven?"

Bernie frowned. "His friends thought so."

"Did we have advance warning?" Hart asked, afraid the answer would be *yes*, but they'd discounted it. Or that there had been too much data to sort through. In a way, it was as if they had an Enigma machine to decrypt two-thirds of Mid East message traffic. The sheer volume would have been a haystack, and a message about airplanes attacking America, a tiny needle.

"We knew Bin Laden was determined to strike in the US," Bernie answered. "Not the location. We pulled Muhammadu back from Somalia when it looked as if his cover was blown."

"But he'd already made the report?" Hart asked.

"We had multiple sources," Bernie said. "We suspect there's a connection between Muhammadu's old friend, who may have al-Qaeda contacts, and one of the people who assaulted him. That's problem number one."

"And problem number two?" Hart asked.

"It's minor. The maintenance supervisor is in a snit about a Medicare audit. If there's as much as a footprint on stairs, he's on Muhammadu's case."

Meer and Hart exchanged glances. Problem number two was plausible and would be hard on Muhammadu. But if al-Qaeda wanted Muhammadu dead, they could have killed him. More likely, it was Americans venting. As Margie used to say, venting thwarts goals and unfocused vengeance could cost a war. Bush the younger would have to be careful what he did next. But Bin Laden had already made his fatal mistake, and possibly Muhammadu knew something.

"Your boy is here," Lucy was looking at Meer, her face full of concern.

"Yes, he's back at work," Bernie said. "Look out for him, will you?"

Bella

All Bella recalled about King Peter was that he spoke her language and had worn a uniform. "I want Lucy and Gordon," she'd told him. She suspected that Bernie, in those days, had not been such a know-it-all. Her own memory was spotty. There'd been a car ride. Then a goat with a bell.

"Where did they take me?" she asked Bernie.

CHAPTER SIXTY-FIVE

Bella
Egypt, 1945

Bella was trying not to cry while King Peter spoke to the matron, whose stern look disappeared as she answered him and curtsied. The soldier with wide nostrils held Bella's shoulder while the matron lined up the other children so the girls could curtsy and the boys bow. Then, to Bella's surprise, the soldier marched her to a shiny car and opened the door for her to get in, which she did. The soldier, the driver, and King Peter all wore uniforms. "I want Gordon," Bella said. "I want Lucy."

The soldier did not speak to her, and she wondered if he spoke English. Her voice was not easy to find—ghosts had hidden it in a cellar—but when they gave it back, she asked to go to Lucy's old address at *14 Ibn Zanki*. The driver laughed, and the soldier beside her said, "No. Take her to *Rustum Pasha*, and we'll get a driver to take her to the DP Camp." Then he laughed too. The matron had warned all the girls in her tent that men could hurt them and that they should never go with soldiers, but the car started without King Peter and began to drive away from the zoo. *What will I do?* she thought. She did not want to go back to Tolumbat. She wanted to find Lucy and Gordon, but the ghosts buried her voice again.

She watched out the window so she would be able to find her way back to the zoo. That was a place that Lucy and Gordon would visit. They would look for her there. But the soldier kept his hand on her shoulder and joked with the driver. Palm trees and buildings sped past her window. They drove over a bridge, and she looked down on a wide river with brown ripples and boats lined up near the shore. The car kept going. They passed cars and gharries and houses with walled gardens. Each time they slowed, she moved a bit closer to the door. After a while, the soldier with wide nostrils let go of her shoulder. He joked some more with the driver, but soon so many horns honked that they could not hear one another. A man on a camel crossed the road in front of the car.

Bella did not know what bad things the men would do to her. It was more that they would not take her to *14 Ibn Zanki*. The car stopped completely, and the driver honked his horn. It hurt her ears so much that she moved up against the door and pulled the handle. To her surprise, the door swung open, and she tumbled to the sand. As fast as she could, she scrambled to her feet and began to run. She scooted down an alley and crouched behind a pile of stinky baskets. When she heard shouting, she made herself smaller and held her breath.

A very old man led a donkey past her. The honking and shouting had stopped, and the sky had dimmed enough for her to see the large moon and one star. She did not know the language around her, but a child shouted, *Ana kamman*, and a woman laughed and said many other words. Several men in red hats and white robes walked past together, their faces a beautiful shining darkness. A boy led a goat in the direction of the moon. Lights shone from windows, giving the alley a magical feeling that reminded her of a mountainside covered in snow.

If she had brought her postcards, she might have found the name of the street where Lucy and Gordon lived. All she remembered was the address she had told King Peter, but she did not know where that was, and she did not think it would be safe to ask a grown person. The goat had a bell on its collar, and she followed the clanging as long as she could. She heard traffic again and sometimes voices and sometimes the screams of fighting cats.

The smells of spices and meat wafting from houses made her hungry. She snuck past a wiry man rummaging through garbage that stank. If she walked far enough, she should come to the end of the city, but the streets went on and on. She saw more houses than she had seen in her entire life. As the air grew colder and colder, she began to shiver. Perhaps if she headed for the sound of traffic, she would find Gordon and Lucy.

Lucy

Because husbands and wives were not permitted to work in the same office, after the wedding, Lucy had been reassigned upstairs to SI, the secret intelligence branch, which meant she missed a great deal of news about her friends. "You can't mean they lost her," she heard Gordon say as she headed outside to meet him. Her ears perked up. He was standing beside a driver from the motor pool, who had arrived to pick them up in an Army truck, their usual ride to and from their new flat on *Sharia al Gameh*. It took a moment for her to understand that Bella was lost and had been missing for hours after running away at the Cairo Zoo, turning up, and running again after throwing herself out of a car.

"A moving car?" she asked.

"No, stopped in traffic," the driver said. "But she was too fast for them."

"They must still be looking."

"No," he said. "I believe they've given up for the night."

She and Gordon exchanged looks. "Could you drop us where she went missing?" The answer was *no* since the driver hadn't been informed even of the general location. He let them off at their flat, where Meer was waiting to tell them Bernie had stopped by earlier to ask if Bella had made her way to *Sharia al Gameh*. The answer was *no*. Lucy telephoned Tolumbat, and a nurse—not the unhelpful Miss Hempson—said that they'd had no word of Bella, but kidnapping charges would be filed if she had taken Bella.

Someplace in the back of Lucy's head, she imagined shouting in anger, but instead, she told the nurse that Americans obeyed the law and did not steal children. She was tempted to argue her case, but Gordon laid his hand on her forearm to caution her, and after she hung up, she stomped and took the Lord's name in vain. The next call was to the motor pool on *Sharia ibn Zanki*, and they found out the name of the street where Bella had run away from Bernie.

She and Meer packed food for Bella, and Gordon hailed a gharry pulled by a brown horse wearing a harness with blinders. By this time, the moon was directly overhead, and many houses were dark. The three of them kept their eyes peeled and stopped to call Bella's name when they saw street children, but the only response other than general scattering was from a boy who wanted candy.

When they reached the intersection mentioned by the phone operator at the motor pool, they set out walking down a narrow street. Meer translated questions for the people they passed. Had anyone spotted a little girl in a white dress? A boy with a goat might have seen her, but that was hours earlier. So as not to bother people in houses, they called out Bella's name once on each block. They tried side streets and guessed which would have appealed to Bella.

Lucy would have continued all night without stopping, but Gordon was limping badly, and Meer's eyelids kept closing, so they made their way to a wider street and found another gharry from which they could call out and peer down alleys on their way home. It was almost 5 AM when they arrived at the flat, where they searched around the building and looked out from the balcony before they fell into bed and jangled dreams. Lucy's were of Bella sleeping on the back of a donkey led by a bearded man dressed like Jesus.

CHAPTER SIXTY-SIX

Lucy
Virginia, 2002

He pulled his chair beside Lucy's bed, bending close to look into her eyes.

"Lucy," he said. "Does Muhammadu talk to you?"

She liked his brown hands. "Meer," she said when his name came to her.

"Fatima told me that the supervisor has been berating my son."

What he said seemed true; she remembered only his son's worry. When she shut her eyes, Muhammadu stood in her memory near her bed with a knife. She was telling him not to kill anyone, but her life had become a series of apparitions, and she could no longer tell what she remembered from what she hoped she had done or said.

"Fatima said his supervisor shouted at him for bringing water to Lettie before he mopped up a spill."

"You're my son, aren't you?" she asked. "Is Muhammadu my grandson?"

"In a way, I am your son."

His saying this made her happy, but something was not right. She wanted to tell Meer, but all she could say was that something was wrong. After Meer left, she napped and could not tell how much time had passed until she heard the push of a broom. She opened her eyes. Meer's son leaned on his broom handle:

"I see you are awake, Grandmother."

When Muhammadu stood by her bed, she felt she was back in Egypt with Gordon. Though Muhammadu spoke English, he whispered in Arabic as if he were talking to someone else.

"I will not kill you," he said. "When it happens, you stay back."

She did not know what he meant, but she answered that he must not kill anyone.

"I must try," he said. "I will die, and it will be over."

"Do not kill anyone," she repeated.

Muhammadu

It was almost time to report for work at Alspy House, but the floor under him shifted like dunes blown by *khamseen*. This was what had happened after his captors fed them poison. All the boys had felt it. Faces changed to monsters. None of the boys had wanted to kill, but a spell had been cast over them, and they were required to shoot at targets that held their own souls. When they were freed, they were still boys, but with bits of their souls shot away. His father, Mahmoud Meer, a distinguished man, a friend of Americans and Muslims, a man who knew President Gamal Abdel Nasser of Egypt when he was a rebel and who had met King Farouk, did not believe in such spells. But Muhammadu had lived through them twice. Once when he was but a boy. And again, in America after 9/11, when he was beaten. He did not know if the men who held him to the ground and kicked and hit him had been sent by the men he betrayed by telling his American friend about what they had bragged, but their faces made him see the evil spirits had taken them over.

He liked the people at Alspy House, the old Americans who lived there, and liked most of the staff except the supervisor, Fred, who told him, *do dis, do dat*, and ordered him as if he were a servant, shaming him in the presence of the old Americans. His father had taught him jihad was the struggle against the evil inside himself, but the whispers droned on and on, arguing about whether the struggle was against enemies of Islam or the enemies of America.

Bella

She tried to get to Alspy House once a week, but the drive took nearly an hour, which led to streams of thought, often about her time in psychoanalysis, which had been like a journey in a dream version of the truth. While she was parking, she noticed an old man shuffling along with a walker and wearing a backpack that must've contained oxygen. He resembled Abdullah, which made her think of Adem, whom she had failed to find. A clear plastic tube led from his narrow shoulders and across his cheek to prongs in his nostrils. Someday, if she were lucky, she would shuffle ahead like the old man taking step after step into the future.

She took the stairs to Lucy's floor. Her plan was to visit Lucy and then Lettie, whose daughter she had called the week before in hopes of persuading her to relent and allow amputation of Lettie's foot instead of the advance directive endorsed by Lettie herself before the pain of dead toes: pain medicine and an unobstructed journey to death. Not exactly an L-pill, but the equivalent.

"Pick that up now," Lucy heard a man yell at Muhammadu, who'd leaned his mop against the wall and helped her clean a spill off the tabletop. Lucy sat alone at her table. She didn't like shouting; she did not like the voice of the man who ordered Muhammadu to report to his office.

For a while, she sat alone. Her eyes were not good, but she

could see the tops of trees and sky out the window. A nurse pushed a wheelchair with an old woman to her table. She knew the woman and soon would remember her name. Her foot was bandaged, and her eyes were half-closed. Neither Lucy nor the other woman spoke. Let me, the nurse said, and Lucy remembered her old friend's name, Lettie.

Sounds came from behind them. Shouting and running feet. "He attacked Fred," a woman screamed. "He's killing people." Lucy tried to shove away from the table and turn toward the sound, but her chair tilted backward as if it might fall. Do not kill anyone, she thought, though she didn't know what was happening. Help, she thought.

She caught movement out of the corner of her eye and tried again to push back her chair so she could see. A man thudded by, and crimson bloomed across a woman's neck and dripped onto her dress. People were shouting. Lucy put all her weight on the table and stood, but she was weak. When she took one step, the floor rose and smacked her face. She pulled herself toward the bleeding woman and the legs of the man.

"No," he wept. "Stay back."

She gripped the table, trying to rise, but slumped near Lettie and reached for the man's leg to make him stop.

Bella charged through the door from the stairwell into the jangle of emergency. Alarm bells. Shouting. A nurse pushing a woman in a wheelchair by at a run. Here, quick, another nurse shouted. Get them in here.

Drill? Bomb? Bella grabbed the arms of an old man's wheelchair and ran, pushing him after the nurse. Now, the nurse called, and double doors opened to a room jammed with old people. Transfer, someone yelled. Two staff members helped the woman and then the man out of wheelchairs into folding chairs and went back for more. Go, go, go! Someone shouted. Wheelchair out. The door slammed.

"What is it?" Bella asked. Over the indoor alarm, sirens screamed from the highway.

"Staff with a knife," the RN called, back in at a run, closing doors. All in.

Where? Three West. Lucy's wing.

Bella barged out the door and took the hall at a full sprint. Empty. Damn. Shoulder bag slapping her side. She skidded up to the corner. A man in a maintenance staff uniform stood with his back to her. The knife in his hand dripped crimson. A blood trail snaked across the floor. He waved his knife at Lucy on the floor and jabbed toward three other people: Fatima in a bloody tunic standing, an old woman in a wheelchair. Lucy's arm was bloody. The man raised the knife at the woman in the wheelchair.

"*La, la,*" Fatima called. "No, Muhammadu, no, no!"

Sweep her foot across his shin and grab his wrist. That's what Bella thought. Hammerlock on the arm with the knife. Bring him down. But her shoulder bag slid to the crook of her elbow. Muhammadu spun toward her. Bella banged him with her bag. Someone ran behind her. "Police," a male voice shouted from far down the hall. Muhammadu raised the knife, but Fatima jumped onto his back. Bella swung her bag at his face while Fatima bit his neck. The rest was confusing. Running footsteps. Lucy on the floor bleeding. Police. Fatima sank to the floor and gathered Muhammadu in a hug while they all wept.

Bella heard snatches and static from a walkie-talkie: "ambulance ... downstairs." Fatima rose from a crouch. Someone named Fred, the maintenance supervisor, had the worst wounds, Fatima explained to police. He's in the maintenance closet with the door locked.

Bella imagined him lying dead. Her own hands were shaking. "I'm taking Lucy to her room." Perhaps Fatima heard.

Perhaps not. The blood on Fatima was from Fred, the maintenance boss. Muhammadu slowly pulled himself upright, and Lucy clenched her bloody left forearm with her other hand. "Hell's bells," she said aloud, which made Bella want to laugh.

"Keep pressure," Bella said, and took clean towels from the bathroom. She wet a corner of one under the shower and used it to slide a crumpled flap of Lucy's skin back over her raw forearm. This was something she'd seen, though not from knifings: old tissue-paper skin that ripped and peeled back. Just the pressure from the straps on a heavy bag could leave deep purple, almost black bruises on the forearm of the cousin who raised her. "Let me get you cleaned up, darling." Bella had never before called Lucy darling.

CHAPTER SIXTY-SEVEN

Lucy
Cairo, Egypt, 1945

Every evening Lucy, Gordon, and Meer searched. Margie asked her Jewish women friends to help, and they, too, lured street children with sweets and asked if they had seen a lost girl who spoke Spanish and some English and was Jewish. Though some children reported seeing such a child, their descriptions did not match. They offered one false lead after another. Lucy began to think that Bella had been kidnapped or killed, but she kept her fears to herself. Worst of times, she began thinking, though dear Gordon soldiered on.

The war was going well, people said, and there was talk that Hart might soon come home. "It isn't as if finding Bella will make up for the horrors," Gordon said the fifth night, and they got into a horrible shouting match that lasted until Gordon grabbed her face and yelled that she hadn't heard the rest of what he was going to say: that it felt like finding her would make up for something. He explained after she composed herself enough to hear: he knew it was irrational, but if they found Bella, then their role in the war would have been for something.

"It is for something," she said, though she knew what he meant.

Two weeks after Bella went missing—after she and Gordon

had given up for the night and lay suffering side-by-side but alone—someone rapped on their door. Lucy bolted upright and threw it open while Gordon was strapping on his leg. Bernie, eyebrows furrowed in distress, stood holding a filthy child with skinny legs, dusty snarled hair, and dangling bare feet. "I hope this is the right one. Either that, or they'll have to lock me up for kidnapping."

The child was sleeping or feigning sleep, but when Bernie handed her over, her eyelids fluttered, and Lucy sank to a floor cushion with the child in her lap. She wanted it to be Bella. What a terrible thing it would be to mistake some other child for the child she loved. She was in two places at once. On the floor with a beautiful, miserable, dirty child, and thinking in some far rational part of her mind, *This is what happened to Bella. She saw me and thought I was her mother.* In the first place, Lucy knew with complete certainty that she was holding Bella. And in the other place, she was Bella realizing her error. No, Lucy is not Mamá.

She asked Gordon to draw a bath. While the water filled the tub, she kissed the dirty face. "Are you asleep?" If Bernie was a kidnapper, so was she.

The girl was both there and not there. She didn't speak but obeyed commands in English. Lift your arm. Bend forward. She allowed Lucy to peel off her rags, set her on her feet, and walk her to the bathroom.

"Let me get you cleaned up, darling." Lucy wet the corner of a towel and wiped Bella's face. She tested the bath with her elbow. "I'm going to wash you in the tub. Would you like bubbles? *¿Te gusta burbujas*?"

Bella's eyes opened, and she looked Lucy in the face with some mix of joy and grief.

CHAPTER SIXTY-EIGHT

Hart
Virginia, 2002

The first call about Lucy came from Bella. There had been an incident, a stabbing at Alspy House involving Muhammadu. Nothing surprised Hart. At least this time, the traffic was tolerable. Lucy's son had called too, and her daughter was also on her way. When he got close enough, he tuned into a Washington news station but heard nothing. Perhaps the stabbing had been covered up. Bella was stingy with details on the phone, but Lucy had been injured, as had three other residents and the maintenance supervisor who shouted at Muhammadu in front of witnesses. Muhammadu was making no sense.

Hart had forgotten the code to exit the elevator on Lucy's floor, but knew to ask the receptionist. The hall where he arrived was entirely empty. He was used to residents in wheelchairs and at tables in the large dining room where he'd been on 9/11, but there wasn't a soul in sight, not even at the nurses' station. He peered around a corner and saw a man in a guard uniform, not someone he recognized.

Lucy's room was empty. There'd been a picture of Gordon on her bedside table. Her daughter had told Hart that Lucy slept with his leg after he died.

"Excuse me, sir? Are you looking for someone?" The guard was exceedingly polite.

Hart explained and was told that the residents of that hall had been transferred. Odd. He wondered why the receptionist hadn't told him. Perhaps he'd shown too much confidence when he arrived. But he followed instructions and walked down a long, empty corridor, and a nurse directed him to Lucy's new room. She was lying in bed, beaming, facing Bella at her bedside, their faces saying more about love than words could have. Bella was stroking Lucy's hair.

Soon Bernie would arrive and tell the story of finding Bella when she was lost in Cairo. Perhaps Meer would turn up and explain about the stabbing. Was it entirely related to the trauma his son had experienced? Or was it related to 9/11? Muhammadu had been taken to jail but transferred to a mental health unit because he made no sense. Fred had berated him in the presence of visitors. Muhammadu had assaulted Fred and rushed down the halls weeping, slashing residents, claiming to have been poisoned.

Hart stood next to Bella as she explained. Though Lucy's arm was bandaged, and she clearly understood Bella's loving expression, she seemed to entirely miss the account of the stabbing.

"Lettie's new roommate had her face slashed," Bella said. "They stitched her up with tiny, tiny stitches. When I stopped by their room, she was touching her wound. She asked me if I thought she was growing a mustache."

Hart chuckled. Bella's laughter was close to tears.

"Any more information?" he asked. He meant about the assault and what would happen next.

"The maintenance supervisor had the worst lacerations. But it was a kitchen knife and pretty dull by the time Muhammadu got to the residents. They're mostly fine. I don't think Lucy remembers."

"Do you remember when we met?" Hart asked Bella, a non-sequitur, but he didn't care. It had come into his head. Bella as a child showing him and Margie solemnly around the kibbutz.

They'd brought her a picture book. *Raggedy Ann.*

She looked up over her shoulder. No, she didn't, but she remembered meeting Margie at the DP camp in North Africa.

Hart told her he'd wondered at the time if he'd been to any of the places she'd lived in Yugoslavia but hadn't wanted to upset her by asking. Not then.

"I don't remember much," she said. "I had a pet chicken. I think she couldn't make a sound, but I've never heard of another hen like that. Sometimes I wonder if I killed her when the Nazis came." She wiped a tear off her cheek. "My analyst thought I felt guilty because Abdullah was killed. I arranged for him and Nura to be declared righteous gentiles," she said. "They died protecting me. Him first. She got an infection. Their son was in the resistance, but I don't know if he survived."

Lucy's bandaged arm was resting on a pillow. She looked up at Bella and at Hart as if she were a devoted child.

"Margie regretted you didn't get to live with Lucy and Gordon," he said.

"My cousin was good enough as a guardian."

Hart heard sounds behind him, something wheeling down the hall. A cart with medicine. Fatima appeared at the door to Lucy's room and produced a paper cup of pills and a mortar and pestle. She did resemble Lucy. So did Bella, Hart thought. While Fatima ground the largest of Lucy's pills, Bella asked Fatima about Meer and Muhammadu and learned that Muhammadu had a good lawyer and had been transferred to Central State Hospital, where he would stay until he was competent to stand trial. Most of the staff liked him, even Fred, who told police Muhammadu had always been friendly and cooperative.

"Meer is dating her," Bella said after Fatima had left.

"What about Meer's wife?" Hart asked, and Bella shrugged. She didn't know. He supposed they would never know most of it, though while he watched Bella so tenderly caring for Lucy, he felt Margie watching from inside him. It was as if all he'd seen—the bereft families in Yugoslavia, his years of trying to predict where the next dangers would arise—were at that moment running through him, and all the importance he and Margie's ghost could sift out of his life was this moment: little Bella returning the love Lucy had offered her.

ACKNOWLEDGMENTS

This work of fiction was inspired by my parents, Nancy Montague McCandlish Prichard and Edgar Allen Prichard, who met and married in Egypt during their World War II service in the OSS, forerunner to the CIA. My father's autobiography offered details unavailable elsewhere, though both he and my mother took many secrets to their graves. One of the few OSS stories shared by my mother was of her clandestine trip from Washington in the back of an Army truck to her hometown of Fairfax, from whence she'd set out the same morning on the trolley. I have taken liberties with the timing of events and many facts. Station S at Kim Roosevelt's Fairfax home, for instance, was not acquired by the OSS until January of 1944, and my mother's arrival in Cairo was via Brazil in June 1944 rather than late in 1943, when Lucy arrived.

My thanks to fellow novel group members, including Lenore Gay, Jean Huets, Maja Bality, Julia Hebner, Ron Andrea, Chip Jones, John Maxwell, and Laura Jones. Thanks also to members of the Writers Group at First Unitarian-Universalist, including Joe Ball, Kenneth Brown, Ellen Dugan, Denise Dolan, Drew Fridley, Joel Gottlieb, Buddy Hensley, Emily Kimball, George Knight, Larry Landon, Mitch Lee, Rebecca Lightle, Meg Lindholm, George Love, Lynn McMartin, Duke Pearson, John (Bari) Ramsey, Mary Lou Sheridan, Tammy Reed, Sallie Lupton Jennings Rugg, Maggie Waugh, and Ann Woodlief. Many thanks to other helpful readers, including Claudia Balderston, Henry Bowen, Becky Burckmyer, Kristin Dittmann, Betty Livingston, Robin Mathews, Mary Olinger, Mary Petersen, Gwen Taylor, and Bob Weekley. Special thanks to beta readers Ron Andrea and Henry Rosycki, to my Godmother, Jane Smiley Hart, to my brothers, the Rev. Canon Thomas M. Prichard and the Rev. Dr. Robert W. Prichard, to the other members of our childhood secret society (the Seven Xers) and to my children, Becky Brown and Peter Foster and my supportive husband, Thomas C. Foster. Much appreciation is owed to Gene Hayworth of Owl Canyon Press for his encouragement when I was close to putting this project aside. Thanks also to Megan Turner for her inspiring editorial suggestions, to Ronaldo Alvez for cover design as well as to many helpful others at Atmosphere Press.

Books I've found helpful in patching together this novel include: *Undercover Girl* by Elizabeth P. MacDonald and *Sisterhood of Spies* by the same author under her later name of Elizabeth P. McIntosh; *Fairfax, Virginia: A City Traveling Through Time* by Nan Netherton, Ruth Preston Rose, David L. Meyer, Peggy Talbot Wagner, and Mary Elizabeth Cawley DiVincenzo; *Rommel's Spy* by John Eppler; *Code Girls* by Liza Mundy; *Sephardic Jews and the Spanish Language* by Angel Pulido (trans. by Steven Capsuto), *Ghost Wars* and *Directorate S* by Steve Coll *OSS; The Secret History of America's First Central Intelligence Agency* by Richard Harris Smith; *America's Great Game, the CIA's Secret Arabists and the Shaping of the Modern Middle East* by Hugh Wilford; *Shadows on the Mountain, the Allies, the Resistance, and the Rivalries that Doomed WWII Yugoslavia* by Marcia Christoff Kurapovna; *A Man Called Intrepid* by William Stevenson, *Arabian Knights, Colonel Bill Eddy USMC and the Rise of American Power in the Middle East* by Thomas W. Lippman, *The Overseas Targets, War Report of the OSS*, Volume II By Kermit Roosevelt, *OSS and the Yugoslav Resistance 1943-1945* by Kirk Ford, Jr., *A Man Called Intrepid* by William Stevenson, *Saudi Arabia and the United States* by Parker T. Hart, and *Beacons in the Night* by Franklin Lindsay. In addition, I was helped by numerous online resources about the Holocaust, including yadvashem.org, The World Holocaust Remembrance Center.

ABOUT ATMOSPHERE PRESS

Atmosphere Press is an independent, full-service publisher for excellent books in all genres and for all audiences. Learn more about what we do at atmospherepress.com.

We encourage you to check out some of Atmosphere's latest releases, which are available at Amazon.com and via order from your local bookstore:

Icarus Never Flew 'Round Here, by Matt Edwards
COMFREY, WYOMING: Maiden Voyage, by Daphne Birkmeyer
The Chimera Wolf, by P.A. Power
Umbilical, by Jane Kay
The Two-Blood Lion, by Nick Westfield
Shogun of the Heavens: The Fall of Immortals, by I.D.G. Curry
Hot Air Rising, by Matthew Taylor
30 Summers, by A.S. Randall
Delilah Recovered, by Amelia Estelle Dellos
A Prophecy in Ash, by Julie Zantopoulos
The Killer Half, by JB Blake
Ocean Lessons, by Karen Lethlean
Unrealized Fantasies, by Marilyn Whitehorse
The Mayari Chronicles: Initium, by Karen McClain
Squeeze Plays, by Jeffrey Marshall
JADA: Just Another Dead Animal, by James Morris
Hart Street and Main: Metamorphosis, by Tabitha Sprunger
Karma One, by Colleen Hollis
Ndalla's World, by Beth Franz
Adonai, by Arman Isayan

ABOUT THE AUTHOR

HELEN MONTAGUE FOSTER is a poet and retired physician. For thirty years she worked in private practice, specializing in the psychotherapy of adults, and for much of that time enjoyed a clinical faculty role at her medical school alma mater, Virginia Commonwealth University in the Department of Psychiatry. She and her husband Thomas C. Foster live in Virginia and spend much of their time canoeing, hiking, and vicariously enjoying the adventures of their children and grandchildren.

Printed in the USA
CPSIA information can be obtained
at www.ICGtesting.com
BVHW040713140823
668539BV00003B/3/J